THEY DON'T
MAKE THEM LIKE THAT
ANY MORE

THEY DON'T
MAKE THEM LIKE THAT
ANY MORE

JAMES LEASOR

PAN BOOKS LTD : LONDON

First published 1969 by William Heinemann Ltd.
This edition published 1971 by Pan Books Ltd,
33 Tothill Street, London, S.W.1

ISBN 0 330 02736 0

*This edition is set from the American edition published
by Doubleday and Company Inc, New York*

*Printed and bound in England by
Hazell Watson & Viney Ltd,
Aylesbury, Bucks*

For Joan,
who has helped to buy, sell,
start, stop and even drive more
of my old cars than she can remember.
With love.

CHAPTER ONE

I got back to London late that first evening when Sara rang. I had been down in the outer wilderness of the south-east suburbs, and it had been raining all afternoon, which meant that the morons in the old A30s and Ford Anglias, with woolly gloves on the steering wheels and dollies dangling in the rear windows, drove as though they were delivering eggs on ice, while the pinheaded nutters in the Minis with their go-faster chequer tape over the roof and big-bore exhaust pipes roared about as though they were overtaking each other in the Mille Miglia. Also, I had eaten nothing but a piece of congealed pink pie that looked (and tasted) like a dead embryo, in a vile pub in Blackheath, and so by the time I turned into my mews in Belgravia, I was in no mood to horse about.

I had wasted most of the day on a wild-goose chase, for one thing; my shoes were leaking, for another, and I had that raw feeling in my throat, as though someone had been sandpapering it, which, in my mind, meant either great pox or small pox or flu.

I run Aristo Autos, which is a better-sounding title than it is a business. Cut down to size, it means there are four cars in a mews garage, within, as my ads say, 'easy walking distance' (so long as you've got legs) of the Connaught, the Hilton, the Dorchester, and the Ritz.

This is useful, for often I make an unexpected sale to some bored American, marooned in London over a wet weekend, who strolls round to my place just to pass the time. The sale may be unexpected to him, but not to me.

I have a hutchlike cubicle in one corner, which I dignify with the name of my office, where the groom used to clean tack with saddle soap fifty years ago, or rub down his master's horses, hissing like a hose as he did so. And years before even he was born, the local noblemen would keep their hunting hawks here when they were changing their feathers, or mewed; hence the name. Sometimes, when I see the little London sparrows dart around, I wonder what the ghosts of these great, grave birds must think. Perhaps it's as well I don't know.

I have a couple of rooms up the back stairs, a tiny bathroom, and what the estate agents euphemistically call 'all the usual offices'.

These, in fact – and why shouldn't we have fact? – mean a lavatory that does not always flush, and a bath with plumbing that was probably around when the Romans were shouting for hot water after a trek up Watling Street from Verulamium to Londinium Town. Otherwise, the place is adequate for my particular business, which is trying to find aristocratic cars – cars of quality, with pedigrees and individuality, as I say in some of my classier ads. I transform them, with new chrome, paint, hoods, tyres, even new bodies, if need be, and then sell them for as much as I can.

Nowadays, many cars are basically the same behind their badges, and they were to some extent even thirty years ago. Then, the makers of dynamos and lamps and so on pointed out to motor manufacturers that if they altered a few screw slots here, or a mounting there, they could fit the same accessories as some other make, and so save money. In the Thirties, there really wasn't all that difference between a Morris or a Wolseley, say, or a Rolls and a Bentley. Now, there's even less, so cars that were built before such economies began have a character and an individuality all their own – plus a price to match.

Old cars are becoming as rare as other antiques and, like other antiques, because relatively few were made, their prices climb higher every year. Of course, as in most branches of the antique business, there's a good deal of faking, but unlike other simulated antiques, it is usual for even a phony old car to have at least a genuinely old chassis under its new body, and these aren't all that easy to find.

You can always ask (and usually receive) a good price for an old Rolls Phantom I or II hearse if you replace the old coffin carrier with a boat-tailed open body, sporting wood decking, a V-shaped windscreen, nickel plate instead of chromium, to keep it in period, and then what may have originally cost you £500 should sell for £2,500. If is doesn't, you're in the wrong business altogether, and should be back on an office stool or wherever, writing letters like those I receive from the tax man: in re the matter of your communication of the 17th inst to hand, and all that crappo.

I had a boat-deck, boat-back job built on a 1932 hearse only a few months ago and sold it to a Texan – one of those oilmen with a derrick in his back garden, and every time the arm goes up and down it's made him several hundred more dollars. I asked why he wanted the car so badly (he was paying me $15,000, so he must have done) and he explained his reasoning: 'It'll make a mighty fine conversation piece in the back yard when folks come around. I can talk to them, and they can say, "Look at that quaint old English car".'

So that's the kind of client I'm after, preferably with a wish for that kind of conversation, and certainly with that kind of money. Sometimes I find them, sometimes I don't. I place my ads in the glossy magazines, in hotel lounges, even inside taxis, and then I sit and wait for trade to come. Some days, I only sit and wait.

Anyhow, on this particular day, I'd prised my jack off my bed and went down beyond Bexleyheath, for a fellow had written in to say he had an Auburn Cabin Speedster he wanted to unload. Now an Auburn Cabin is a very rare car indeed; no faking about that. It was made in America for a very short time, around 1930, with a fast-back, pointed tail, and, according to the original brochure I have in what I laughingly call my office, it was described as 'a veritable road plane, with wheels instead of wings'.

It was a curious two-seater with an interior deliberately made like an aeroplane cockpit. There was a vogue for such oddities around that time; the 1936 Cord actually had aircraft-type controls on the dashboard and retractable headlamps, adapted from landing lights in the wings of Stinson aircraft, which was a subsidiary company. The Crane-Simplex sprouted boat ventilators on its bonnet and secured its spare wheel by a copper-plated boat propeller.

In the Auburn Cabin, you sat on wicker seats, looked out of a very deep windscreen, so you could see as much sky as road, and had a rear view through a periscope window in the back. It even had an aeroplane domelight in the roof. Altogether, not the sort of chariot you want to drive down to collect the fish and chips in, but a quaint period piece and, as such, worth a bomb.

I believe in looking the part of the man who drives what he sells, for this helps trade, so I drove down in an SS100. That's not a bad car, either, but damn cold without any side screens, and a bit hard on the base of the spine; rather like travelling on a board with square wooden wheels, but dependable as the Chase Manhattan, and as temperamental as an undertaker's mute.

Of course, it was dusk by the time I found the street, which didn't appear to be marked in the A–Z guide. It turned out to be a little back road off another little back road, off a third little back road; rows of terraced houses with shacks and tin huts and allotments behind them, everything wet, dark, dank.

I rang the doorbell, and a fellow came out wearing carpet slippers, no collar, smoking one cigarette and rolling another. I said who I was, in case he thought I'd called about the rent.

He said, 'Oh, you've come about the car. You want Bert.'

Why should I want Bert? I thought, I'm not that way, or maybe I look as though I am after this ride around.

'Where's Bert?' I asked. 'Who's he?'

'He's not here yet,' he said. 'He's late.'

To hell with that, I thought. I was on the nose for the lousy appointment, so couldn't Bert be as well? I hate unpunctuality, just as I hate women with shrill voices and thick legs, and I could use a wait in this place like I could use an early burial.

I hung about in the alleyway waiting for Bert, in lieu of Godot, and he finally turned up with no apology, no explanation; a greasy-looking fellow in a flat cap, the sort of character you see walking a greyhound that's favourite to win, and then slipping the beast a heavy meal just before the race, so that it's sure to lose, and Bert, who's backed the outsider at a hundred to one and slipped a little pepper up its jack, just to encourage it on its way, wins a packet.

We went out to a corrugated-iron hut that was padlocked, and smelled as though cats liked it a lot. There was no light inside, but I'd brought a torch. The battery was down, though – it had switched itself on in my pocket – so there we were, striking matches, looking at this car.

It was an Auburn, but that was all, and it wasn't quite enough. It was one of the early straight-eight saloons with a motor the size of a ship's engine. Damned great thing; high enough for you to walk around inside with a top hat on and still have room to stretch, if that's the sort of thing you have a mind to do when you take a drive.

I said, 'This is no more a Cabin Speedster than I'm Shirley Temple's mother-in-law'. My disappointment must have sounded in my voice.

'No need to be insulting,' said Bert, very aggrieved.

'I'm not,' I said. 'I'm just stating a fact. This is a wasted journey.'

'What's it worth?' he asked.

'Probably fifty quid. No more.'

'Fifty quid?' he repeated, as though I'd made a dirty suggestion, but not quite dirty enough. 'Why at Sotheby's auction last year a car went for ten thousand.'

'Sure, but that was a Silver Ghost Rolls. This thing's a heap of old rubbish.'

'Well, I'm not parting with this for less than five hundred.'

I said, 'Good luck. At that price you're stuck with it for life. Like marriage.'

'Up yours, mate,' he said, and on that note, we parted.

It was cold coming back, especially over Shooters Hill,

where the highwaymen had been replaced by yobbos having a quick fumble in parked Anglias, then round the new Elephant and Castle, over the river and, as Pepys might say, so to bed. Or at least, so to Belgravia, which, for me, is much the same thing.

After all that, I was late, and when I got in, George had gone. He's the character who helps me. He's very good on anything – from tarting up some ash-framed coachwork that's as thick with worms as gorgonzola, to putting in a replacement rear end on a low-chassis Invicta, which is by no means a task to attempt lightheartedly. He used to be a sergeant in the Tank Corps, a regular, and did twenty-seven years, including five out East during the war.

He talks most of the time in rhyming slang, which I'm beginning to pick up now. There's an old lie about people being worth their weight in gold. No one is, but George is about worth his weight in paper money. I calculate that if I pay him £25 a week and in three weeks – £75, plus a few spares, say £150 – he can make me £500 worth of profit on a car, then he's valuable.

Of course, you may say, if he can make me that kind of profit, why doesn't he make it for himself? That's a good question, so it deserves a good answer, which is this: most people like to work for someone else in this world, and maybe in the next, too, for all I know. George is no different. The ghost walks every Friday if you're on someone else's payroll, while if you employ yourself, as I do, it may not walk at all.

I let myself in, undid the padlock, then the dead-man's lock, because you can't trust anyone alive these days, and switched on the light. For a moment, the fluorescent tubes flickered, and then they came on so brightly that, after the dimness of the mews outside, they hurt my eyes.

I shut the door, and turned up the hot-air blower to thaw myself out. I had been deep-frozen through and through; frozen fingers, frozen everything else. You name it, I'd frozen it, even though I might want to use it again.

I lit a cigarette and looked around the stock. It wasn't all that brilliant, I must admit. I'd a sleeve-valve Voisin I was trying to sell for someone on commission, but the owner wanted too much money, so anyone who looked at it just looked at it and then at me, and then went away. This was a pity, for the car bristled with odd ideas like a porcupine with quills: six gear ratios – a three-speed box and a two-speed back axle – two twelve-volt batteries (one to use for starting); twin oil pumps for the engine, plus a third for the gear box, and a fourth for the universal joints; an air-driven fan in front of the radiator to cool the oil, a vacuum motor to open the sliding roof, and so on. But then, the price was wrong, although so much else was right. And, unless the price is right, everything else is labour in vain.

I'd also got a 1932 Ford V8 coupé – one of the early ones where the only thing to show it was a V8 was the badge on the tie bar – and a rear-engined Burney. This had been designed by Sir Dennistoun Burney, a figure of some note when it came to designing airships, but here he had anticipated the rear-engined Volkswagen, the Chevrolet Monza, and the Hillman Imp by too many years – and none of those cars had a straight-eight Beverley Barnes engine sticking way out over the rear wheels, or nearly twenty feet of car *behind* the driver. It would take two meters to park a Burney now.

About the only thing that could be said in its favour, which I said often enough, was that the Prince of Wales had owned one in the nineteen thirties, but although I hinted in my advertisements that this car might even be his, the suggestion didn't bring any customers pattering in with money in their hands.

I rolled back the main doors, drove the SS inside, and was shutting the door when the telephone rang. I picked it up without enthusiasm. You get a lot of nutters in this business who ring up in the evening, apparently interested in a car, but really all they want is a long chat about old cars, which they can enjoy, turn over in their minds, and imagine they own one. They're sort of conversational voyeurs.

Not infrequently, these characters want me to take some

unlikely vehicle for their inspection to some impossible address in the outer suburbs or the West Country, or seventy odd miles up the M1, but having done that once or twice in my early days, I've never done it again. If I want to waste money, I know more rewarding ways, and people who are genuinely interested usually come in person.

This time, a girl was on the phone. I tried to imagine what she would be like, what she would be wearing. Her voice sounded interesting, cool, and in command of things. I wondered what it would be like to be in command of her, and who was.

'I see from your advertisement in *Motor Sport* that you buy old cars,' she began, as though she was telling me something new.

I agreed that this was so. She'd probably got some beat-up ruin, some bowlegged monstrosity or diabolical mechanical abortion that could hardly drag itself down a slope with a following wind, for which she wanted several thousand. But I just thought this; I didn't say it, although I might later; after all, I was buying, not selling.

'I know where there's a rather unusual Mercedes,' she went on, and stopped.

'How unusual?' I asked her, just for something to say. It was probably one of the gull-wing 300SLs. They were rather unusual, but not all that valuable yet. In ten years, it could be a different story, but we were here and now.

'Five point four litres. 540K supercharged,' she said. 'Roadster body. Apparently been stored for a number of years.'

This was so unusual that I almost added, 'in a heated garage, engine run once a week, tyres rotated, body waxed monthly by loving old-English craftsman' – which is the usual way these cars are advertised, although, in this cold country, you're lucky to have a heated house, never mind a heated garage, and if you've got a loving old English craftsman he's probably as queer as a four-pound note, and so are you, loving him.

'Where is it?' I asked, enthusiasm no higher; it still

seemed a con to me. So far as I knew, the last of these cars had gone to the States five or six years ago. To find one left now would be like finding a virgin in Lisle Street, and, frankly, I would rather find the Mercedes. There's too much, do you really love me or is it just because of this, with virgins.

'In Kent,' the girl said. 'I'd like you to buy it for me. I can give you the address where it is.'

'A car like that comes pricey.'

'I know,' she agreed. 'They don't make them like that any more. First of all, I'd like you to see the car, and then let me know what they want for it. I don't wish to appear in this myself. Cars aren't my thing.'

I wondered what her thing was; maybe I'd find out if I stayed around. 'Who owns it?' I asked, to bring my mind back to business.

'An old woman. It belonged to her son. He was killed.'

'Why don't you buy it through a friend?' I asked her. 'You'd save my commission.' I still didn't believe the car existed; I thought it was some kind of joke.

'It's better to use an expert for these things,' she explained. 'You know what you're looking for, and you know how much you should pay.'

'As you like it,' I said, quoting Shakespeare. And why not? There's no charge; he's out of copyright.

'And another thing,' she said, and paused. There seemed to be an awful lot of things in this dialogue. 'I'm really not interested in the car for myself, but for a family friend who collects old cars.'

'Who is he?' I asked. I know the whereabouts of most of the collectors here and in the States. Some are even my friends – especially if they've never bought a car from me.

'He's in Europe,' she said. 'I don't think you'd know him. Anyhow, he's got an agent over here looking for old cars. A Mr Diaz. I don't think he's found anything yet, but he's a pleasant little man who could use a good turn. If the car *is* any good, let me know first, and then ring Mr Diaz. He'll be round to you like a shot.'

'What's his number?' I asked.

She gave me a Euston number.

'It's a small hotel near King's Cross.'

This didn't sound very encouraging to me. People who could afford to spend the money I would have to pay for a Mercedes, plus my own cut, usually preferred better lodgings than a doss house near King's Cross.

'And don't mention my name, or Mr Diaz might be offended.'

'I don't even know your name.'

'Sara Greatheart,' she said.

'Sounds like something out of *Pilgrim's Progress*,' I told her.

She didn't reply. Looking back, I don't think I really expected her to.

'And where can I contact you?' I asked.

She gave me another number.

'I'll be waiting for your call,' she said. 'In the meantime, here's the address: Mrs Meredith, Grange House, Grange Lane, near Barming, Kent.'

The phone went dead in my hand. At once I flicked the rest and dialled the second number she had given me. It rang a couple of times and then a voice, very grave, very dignified, like a butler's butler at a rich man's funeral, spoke in my ear.

'This is Claridge's Hotel, sir,' this voice informed me.

'I'm sorry,' I said. 'I thought it was the public baths,' and put down the phone.

This didn't seem like a hoax, or she wouldn't have given me Claridge's number. Anyway, we might make a deal. And, like the man said, to travel hopefully is better than to arrive, although if you ever do arrive you can grow kind of weary on the journey.

I closed the little door of the office and came back into the garage with the old AA signs on the wall, the tin advertisements for Palmer Cord tyres, for Heldite Jointing Compound, and other ads of that nature, which I rather like to collect. They give an air of authenticity to an antique-car salesroom, just as the fellows flogging antique furniture like to cram their showrooms full of waxed leather chairs, each with dozens of brass, dome-headed nails, and Louis XIV desks and so on. Also, they will all find a buyer one day. Everything does. It's just a matter of waiting, as the old whore told the young whore.

I picked up the telephone and rang the Euston number. A woman's voice answered, in some indefinable provincial accent. Her voice sounded as though the roof of her mouth had fallen in on someone else's false teeth, and maybe it had, at that.

'Highland Brae Private Hotel,' she told me.

I could imagine it. The brown wallpaper, the smell of cabbage cooking, marked sauce bottles on round tables, dirty windows where flies had died trying to escape, the discreet and ambiguous notice in the downstairs cloakroom: 'Articles should not be flushed down the lavatory'. England, our England.

Scots wha hae, I thought, but I said, 'Good evening. I would like to speak to Mr Diaz.' Nothing like trying to cross-check before I wasted any more time.

'I will see if he is in.'

There was a whirring in my ear as some ancient crank was turned. A soft voice, rather the voice of a vole, if a vole had a voice, said: 'Yes? Mr Diaz here.'

I gave him my name.

'I run Aristo Autos,' I explained. 'I believe you're on the lookout for old cars?'

'I am. But who told you?' he asked.

'These things get around in this business,' I assured him. 'What are you looking for especially?'

'I'm buying for a client,' he said. 'I know a little about cars, but more about antique garden furniture. My client is interested specifically in Mercedes.'

'If I told you I could get my hands on a 1937 540K two-seater, would he be interested?'

'Very.'

His voice tightened like a wire. So the girl was right,

but then girls were not always wrong – only the ones I knew.

'Where are you speaking from?' he went on.

'My garage,' I told him.

'Aristo Autos,' he repeated. 'I'm looking it up now in the phone book as we speak. I'll be there in ten minutes.'

He was, too, before I could tell him I hadn't got the car. Foreigners!

It had started to rain again and all the cobbles glittered. I had the funny feeling that they were like a lot of eyes watching, seeing what? Nothing, but the underside of an old Beardmore taxi. Been a bit different if it had been a girl in a mini – and I don't mean the car, but the skirt.

The taxi door opened and the inside light came on. A little man in the back in a gabardine coat peered about, looked above me and read the sign. Then he paid off the taxi.

'I am Rodrigues Diaz,' he said, as though this was important, and maybe it was to him. 'Good evening.'

'It's a bad evening,' I said. 'But not to worry. Good evening, too.'

'You are Aristo Autos?'

'None other. So long as you're not a creditor, in which case you want my brother.'

'You will have your little joke, yes?' he said.

'I have very little else,' I told him. 'Come inside. It's wet out here.'

'That Mercedes,' he said. 'Where is it?'

'It's not here,' I said. 'You rang off before I could tell you.'

His eyes flickered around the room.

'I've got a very fine Ford, this magnificent old Burney, and this matchless Voisin,' I said. 'All late property of a district nurse. Never had a spanner on them.'

I rather liked that phrase. Years ago, when I was just starting, I couldn't afford much stock and hadn't even a shack to keep a car in, so I worked from a public telephone box, because my one room in Battersea wasn't on the phone.

I would put a cod ad in the evening paper, offering a Fiat 500 – remember the little Topolino? – at a fair price, late property of a district nurse. This gave it a very safe and sober sound. I'd always have at least half a dozen calls, but I'd have to admit that the car had gone. (In fact, of course, it had never been there.) However, I told all the callers that, by chance, I knew of another similar car, even better, if they would only let me have their telephone numbers.

I copied these down, then looked up every other Fiat advertised in the same paper and took £1 options on the best two or three. I found I could usually do a deal, if I offered cash, at around two-thirds of the advertised asking price. When I bought one, I stripped off any accessories to sell them separately, poured Gunk all over the engine to freshen it up – would-be experts think a car has been well looked after if the engine looks clean – and flogged it to the first inquirer. Then I went out and bought the second and flogged that, and so on, through the list.

But, to return.

'I'm interested only in the Mercedes,' said Diaz. 'Where is it?'

'At a friend's house,' I replied, hoping it was.

'Can we go there?'

'Not tonight,' I said.

'How much will it be?' he asked.

'It's not even touched yet. It may have to be redone completely.'

I wanted to cover myself in case the car was a wreck.

'How much when it's redone?'

'A lot of money.'

His face was very dark, like a sort of walnut, and not much bigger, either, but polished shiny. His sad little brown eyes looked like beads that had crept into it and forgotten the way out. His teeth were tipped with gold. Maybe he liked to gnaw bones or maybe he was a strong kisser. I didn't like him much, but then, why should I? I hadn't got to go to bed with him.

'I am buying some cars on behalf of a rich collector,' he went on.

'You told me,' I said. 'He'll have to be very rich to buy this.'

He smiled, as though everything was relative and, of course, it is; only the hungry talk of food, only the poor count the cost.

'You must have *some* idea of the price?' he persisted. 'What do you *think*?'

'I don't know. I don't want to break your arm, but there may be three months' work on it – or there may not. I may have to get things specially made. It may need rechroming. I may have to pull off all the old beading on the body. It may be rusty underneath, and the beading is almost bound to break. There are so many "mays" about it, it shouldn't be a Merc but a Maybach. I'm sorry, but I just can't give you a price yet.'

'Quite so, quite so,' he said. 'When will you know?'

'Tomorrow,' I told him. 'I'll know tomorrow. And it would have to be in notes,' I added.

When I can, I like to be paid in notes; many people do in our business, for then you make a profit both ways. You put the money you've paid for the car against income tax, but obviously you don't declare the money you've received for it. So you've made a loss on that deal. Actually, you've made a profit, tax free, *and* you've made a tax loss, which you set against some deal when you've had to accept a cheque. It's a double-headed deal; you're making money both sides of the street.

'That's no problem,' said Diaz. 'But how much do you think? Two thousand?'

He was guessing: I frowned as though I didn't like his guess.

'A lot more,' I told him. 'Nearer four, I'd say.'

He screwed up his face.

'That's a lot of money.'

'It's a lot of car,' I said. 'They don't make them like that any more.'

'No. That is true.'

I was piling it on a bit, of course. You can always come down when you're doing a deal, when you're selling something, but you can never go up once you've made your number. Therefore, pitch it high. Being a cheap skate never made anyone rich.

'It's the sort of car my principal likes, but it's still a lot of money.'

'Everything's a lot of money,' I said. 'Don't give me all that again. It's a lot of motor-car. That's where we came in. Please, I've got a headache, I've got the flu. I must go to bed. After all, I didn't ask you here.'

Also, I wanted to have a pee. I had been bursting all the way home from Shooters Hill, but I didn't want to say this to the fellow.

'Of course,' said Mr Diaz, all contrite. 'I am keeping you. Forgive me.'

'Now I know you are interested, I'll be in touch as soon as the car is here,' I promised him, but I didn't make it sound too eager, for if this character Diaz didn't buy the car, then I knew someone else who would. An advertisement appeared in *Motor Sport* with a box number for a Mercedes of this type several times a year. I'd guessed the number was simply a cover for a trader, so I answered it once under my own name, but giving a club address which wouldn't link me with the motor trade.

A week later I received a reply from Tobler Autos, a firm in Hanover, who said they had a waiting list for interesting European cars, and if I could provide the chassis and engine numbers of the Mercedes I said I owned, they would be pleased to send a representative over to inspect it. Of course, I hadn't a car at all, so I did nothing, except file away their letter in case it could ever come in useful. Now, it seemed as though it might.

Maybe I could lever Diaz against these other people. I'd done it before often enough, sometimes even inventing buyers to force up the price. No doubt I'd do it again, too.

Diaz held out his hand. I took it. I would rather have taken his money, but he wasn't offering me any. His skin felt dry, like a lizard, and cold. I didn't altogether take to the guy, but, as I said, I didn't have to.

I watched him walk away through the mews. He must have been wearing high heels; there was a click from every step he took on the cobbles. Then I shut the door and went upstairs, had my pee and went to bed.

I had one hell of a dream, not about girls with big bristols and tight white pants, climbing in and out of old cars with the doors hung at the back, but about cars. I was in that breaker's yard in the South of France on the right of the road between Nice and Antibes. It has to be on the right, because on the left lies the sea.

You'll find almost every kind of imaginable and unim-aginable vehicle there: Delahaye, Hotchkiss, Delage, His-pano, Isotta; a fantastic selection, a graveyard of grand old cars. And I was walking from one to the other, looking at the bonnet straps and the three-note Stentor horns and the Marchal lights with the amber lenses, and the man was saying: 'But, monsieur, we do not want to sell these cars. They are yours, for a *gift*.'

'A gift,' I said, 'I'll be damned,' and banged one of the bonnets, and the bonnet went on ringing after I took away my hand.

I swam back to wakefulness.

The telephone was ringing by the bed. I picked it up. Seven o'clock in the morning. Who the hell could this be but a creditor to see if I was in, or a wrong number, or some nutter who was just going to breathe and say nothing, or a bad word? I could forestall him there.

I scooped up the receiver, shovelled myself out of the blankets and said, 'Hello.' There wasn't much else to say.

Diaz was on the other end of the line. He made no apology for this ungodly hour, no small talk.

'I've been on the phone to my principal,' he said. 'He'll buy the car up to three thousand five hundred pounds. You can have the money when you want it.'

'Thank you very much,' I said. I like everything when I want it. Preferably a pretty girl, I thought, but money was not a bad substitute. With the second you can sometimes obtain the first; but with the first you can't buy the second. Moral: if you must marry, then marry for money. Love is another thing altogether that doesn't last so long.

'I'll be in touch,' I said, and the telephone died. I put it back in its cradle until the next time, and groped for a cigarette. I couldn't find one, so I burrowed my way back into the bed, and looked at the ceiling. It needed decorating; a cobweb trembled in one corner. I'd noticed this before often enough, but now so many dead flies were hanging there that even the spider must be feeling this was a rough old place.

The theory is that when you're single you've lots of girls to come in and out. What with one thing and another, you'll get your washing done, you'll be cooked fabulous meals and your house will be cleaned. But, in practice, it mostly boils down to one thing, and then they go and others come.

You need a wife to do the slavery, and I've never had a wife (though I've had other people's, if you get me) and marriage seems a high price to pay, when you can still find a char at five bob an hour in London. So I lay and watched the cobweb, and a new fly flew right into the web.

The old spider, who was sitting there brooding on the meaning of it all, started to uncoil his legs and he looked at the fly, and then he squeezed the fly and I knew how the fly felt, like I feel when I've seen the bank manager.

I didn't want to see any more, for I feared there might be a moral in it, like Robert the Bruce, so I climbed out of bed and went into the bathroom and ran the shower, and stood under it. Then I dried myself, found a cigarette, smoked it, and threw the stub down the lavatory pan. Then I put some coffee on the stove, broke two eggs in a bowl, mixed them with a squeezed lemon and a squeezed orange, and drank the result.

I don't know why, but I read an article once that said this carried all the nourishment you needed, without any fat; it tastes like hell, so maybe it must do you good. Nothing that tastes so bad could possibly do you any harm.

I was down in the garage by eight. George was already

there, pulling on his dungarees. He is a short man with broad shoulders and thinning black hair.

'Where's all the action, then?' he asked, as though I knew.

I told him about the Mercedes.

'Want a German?' he asked.

'German?' I thought he referred to the car. Now I realized he was talking in his rhyming way.

'German band. A hand?'

'No, I'll manage on my own,' I said. 'I'll ring you if anything happens.'

'How are you paying for it? With a Charlie? Charlie Beck, cheque.'

'I'll take the mad money,' I told him. 'If I take a cheque, I might be tempted to spend more.'

He nodded, and bent over the innards of the old Ford V8, a rat's nest of pipes and wires. The mad money is a phrase I picked up from a girlfriend who always kept a ten-shilling note in the lining of her purse, in case she got mad with whoever was taking her out, and then she could pay for her own way home. So far as I recall, she never had to.

Anyway, I always keep twenty-five £10 notes in a brown envelope under the passenger seat of the SS, where the designers thoughtfully built a cubby hole for tools.

You never know your luck in my business, and to help your luck you need money. Not cheques, but cash. Once, I saw two young fellows pushing an Austin Chummy, one of the originals, with big brass lights and a soda-siphon top on the radiator cap, over Blackfriars Bridge. I asked them what was wrong, and they said they didn't know.

'And the way I feel about the bloody thing, anyone can have it for a tenner,' said the elder.

'I've got a tenner here,' I said flashing it at him, the note, I mean.

He was a bit taken aback, but he sold me the car. There was £3 10s to collect on the licence, so I collected it, and then the car had only set me back £6 10s. I stuck a bit of paper in the windscreen with 'Tax applied for' on it, while I advertised the car for £250: 'Late property of invalid surgeon on South Coast', although, looking back, it seems odd that an invalid surgeon should have been driving about in such an unsuitable vehicle.

The medical touch is always good, though; something reassuring about it, all black jackets and black bags. Solid. Sound. No messing. But if you want a tip, avoid a doctor's car if you're offered one, for if he's a GP it's done nothing but stop and start all day as he makes his rounds, and the cylinder bores will be worn oval. Anyhow, I sold the Chummy to the third inquirer at £235, so you can see how useful it is to have a bit of the ready with you – but never too much in case you get carried away by your own enthusiasm.

In the back of the SS, behind the seats, I threw a can of petrol, a nylon towrope, my blue metal box of tools, a couple of cylinders of compressed air to blow up the tyres – using ordinary hand pumps can take years off your lifespan – and then I zipped up my flying jacket, pulled on my gloves and cap and took off.

I retraced my trip of the evening before, down the Old Kent Road through New Cross, and then branched right. At traffic signals, drivers would lean out of their cars, or look down from the high cabs of lorries, to tell me they didn't make them like that any more. As though I didn't know.

I reached Sevenoaks by ten, had a slash in the station lavatory, wiped my face and hands with a damp sponge I carry in a polythene bag, because you collect a lot of dirt in an old open car, or a new one, too, for that matter, and then asked about for Grange Lane.

I had been stationed near Sevenoaks in the Army, outside Barming, only a few miles away, and the lane was vaguely familiar. When I found it, it didn't look as though it had changed much since Edward VII was having it off with Lily Langtry, and probably it hadn't. I half expected to meet a 50-hp Napier with a chauffeur and footman 'on the box', and if I had done so, I'd have made them an offer – for the car, of course, not themselves.

The banks on either side of the lane were high and the grass looked fresh and green, not festooned with litter and brown with diesel fumes as it is around London. I wondered whether children still called the blossom on the hedges, bread-and-cheese, as we used to do? I had the strange feeling that somehow I was driving out of time, going back to my boyhood; maybe it was because I had been born and brought up in Kent that made me feel like this. When I turned off the engine, so that I could hear myself ask the local parson, who came cycling by, where Grange House was, I could also hear the bees working non-union hours, and enjoying every one of them.

Grange Lane grew narrower, and was made narrower still nearer the house by the fact that half a dozen workmen were digging a trench for some reason or other. A traffic light had been set up for one way only, but this wasn't working, and a policeman waved me on. The thunder of the pneumatic drills drowned the beat of the SS exhaust as I passed him.

Grange House stood at the bend in the lane. Two old stone gateposts supported metal gates, once no doubt black and tipped with gold, but now raw with rust and propped open by stones. The gates opened into a drive almost indistinguishable from the lawn because of weeds.

I stopped outside the house, climbed a flight of stone steps, cracked and split and green with lichen. An ancient metal handle, on a chain, like a refugee from a lavatory, bore one word: PULL. I pulled. Nothing happened. I heard no bell ringing anywhere, so I beat on the door with my fist and when that produced no result, I used a small spanner I keep in my jacket pocket.

Beyond the drive there had been a tennis court; the metal frame for the fence was still standing, although the wire netting had almost all rotted away. Huge weeds sprouted through splits in the asphalt. I wondered who had played there, and where they all were now. Behind the tennis court stood a broken gazebo. I wondered who had watched the games from its shade, who had kissed and been kissed there for the first time. I smelled again the sweet smells of summers long gone; that warm July excitement of being shut in a summer-house or a tent, close together, with a girl, when no one else knew you were there and after a few minutes, you were damn glad they didn't.

I could almost hear the twang of racket strings, the ripple of polite applause, the tinkle of ice in the glasses that the maid, in the black uniform with a little white apron and crimped cap, would carry across on a tray.

It must have been good to live in this house then, I thought, but not so good now. Within months, possibly less, the speculative builders would be here in their Mark Tens and S2s, wearing camel-hair coats, sharp little eyes set too close together, unrolling dreary characterless plans for maisonettes for young executives, of sculptured landscapes which, in fact, meant leaving one tree out of a hundred.

I beat on the door again and it opened suddenly, so that I was left in mid-blow with the spanner in my hand. An old woman stood framed in the doorway, and behind her the hall stretched into what seemed an infinity of gloom, for the light was filtered by leaded glass in high windows. The floor was tiled beige and white, like a drab chequerboard on which we were both pawns.

'Excuse me banging on the door like this,' I said, for this was no way to make a good impression, 'but I couldn't get the bell to work.'

'The bell doesn't work,' the woman said reproachfully, as though I should have known this. She could have been any age between ninety and a hundred, and looked no stronger than a sickly child. She wore a black silk shawl around her shoulders, and her hands, all blue veins, and wrinkled like the branches of a tree that has grown up against the wind, were folded together in front of her. That was how they would be folded in death, I thought for no reason at all.

'I don't buy at the door,' she said.

'Nor do I, madam. And I don't want to sell you anything.' I spoke quickly for she might think I was flogging insurance, and this was another image I did not want. 'You are Mrs Meredith?'

'Yes.'

'I understand you have an old car here. I wondered whether you would sell it to me? I collect old cars.'

This, I've found, is always a better and more promising opening than to say bluntly that I deal in old cars. Half the advertisements you see from people who want rare cars are couched in such careful terms as: 'Collector seeks early Rolls-Royce or similar; sedanca or open body preferred. Bentley or Delage not objected to if coachwork unusual,' or 'Connoisseur adding to stable wishes to buy Hispano or early Isotta. Good home assured. Definitely not for export.' They emanate from back-street dealers working out of a station coalyard, or from a couple of sheds piled together near some cruddy allotment. It's a tough business, ours; sometimes I feel that if I could find something honest, like working the shady side of Jermyn Street, I would quit. This was almost one of these times.

'I have such a car,' Mrs Meredith admitted, surprised. 'How did you hear about it?'

'Some local woman rang me,' I said, which was nearly true; after all, Sara Greatheart might have been local, and she certainly sounded like a woman unless she was a transvestite stoker in the *Ark Royal*, and just spoke like that.

I could imagine her playing on that tennis court if she had been twenty years older, but if she had been, her partners would probably all be dead, lost in the Battle of Britain, or sunk on some forgotten Atlantic convoy, defending an Empire due within years to disintegrate and be given away.

'Come in, then,' she said. 'What's your name?'

I told her.

Inside the hall, a Negro slave of polished ebony, wearing a red loincloth over what must have been noble secrets, held out a wooden platter for visiting cards; the heads of stags looked down on the wall from under dusty antlers; one had a cobweb stretched between the tips. The air felt cold and somehow stale, as though no windows were ever opened, and in the background, muted by doors and walls, I heard a continual shrill chatter which I couldn't place at first.

'Well, young man?' the woman said, paying me a compliment with the adjective.

'Well, could I see the car?' I countered.

She took down an old Burberry from a wooden hook on a stand beside the door. I helped her pull it over her shoulders; they were thin and bony, and I guessed the bones would be brittle as old china or dry twigs. I didn't like the idea of growing old. What did the man say? Every man would live long, but no man would be old.

Mrs Meredith picked a key off a peg.

'Follow me,' she said.

We went out one of the half-dozen doors on the side of the hall, and into a glass-roofed conservatory. Now I discovered the cause of the chatter. Birds. With feathers.

They were everywhere, spreading grey wings like huge parentheses, sweeping, diving, or just perched along broom handles that had been wedged against the walls. The floor was white with their droppings; the air smelled like a lime kiln.

The only birds I like wear skirts. Of all others, I have a horror. I thought of where their claws had been, lacerating the putrefying guts of dead animals, their feathers crawling with lice, their beaks hooked like sharp scimitars into the rotting flesh of furry vermin.

In a cage separating him from all this frenetic fluttering sat an old parrot, head on one side, fluffing out green and yellow plumage, chuntering to himself. He sharpened his beak against a piece of cuttlefish and watched me.

'Be sure to shut the door,' Mrs Meredith said, opening a side door. 'They could fly out.'

'Not me,' said the parrot. 'Not me. Not Joey boy.'

I shut the door behind me, but not before half a dozen birds had flown away. They didn't fly far; only to the branches of the elms behind the house, and there they sat preening themselves and watching us. I supposed they

29

would fly back when the door opened again. Like office workers who complain about their dull suburban lives, they really liked captivity. As captives they knew they would never starve. Joey was the wise one; he admitted he had it best where he was.

The door opened on to a small courtyard behind the conservatory. Facing this was an old stable block, the sort with haylofts and beams and tackle, where once grooms swung up bales of hay. The courtyard was cobbled, and above it a clock held its hands, like the one in Grantchester, at ten to three; a weathervane swept and turned, a coach and horses riding on its arrow.

Mrs Meredith stopped outside a set of double-sliding stable doors, blue once, now faded and powdered to a dull green. She turned the key, leaned against the far door. The rusty rollers turned and squealed as we disturbed the sleep of years. I peered inside at whitewashed walls; wooden hay-racks still straddled the far corners, and someone had nailed up a horseshoe behind the door. Most of the nails had rusted away, and the ends of the shoe pointed downwards. That was unlucky, I thought; all the luck would run out. Maybe it already had.

The floor was cobbled. The window at the far end was opaque with grime, behind a curtain of cobwebs, splattered with dead flies that trembled in the breeze from the open door. I saw all this, but most of all I saw the car that almost filled the building.

It was red, the colour of wine, with a film of oxide over the enormous glass-reflectored Zeiss headlamps and the Grebel searchlights on either side of the raked windscreen. Droppings from birds that had flown in through crevices stained the long, sweeping tail.

I walked round to the front. On the radiator stood the famous three-pointed star, chosen to symbolize Mercedes' supremacy in the three worlds of land, water and air. I thought how the car came to be called Mercedes.

In 1901, Wilhelm Maybach had designed a new car for the Daimler company in Cannstatt, which, with throttle control of the engine, mechanical inlet valves, instead of valves opening by the 'suction' of each piston, gate-change positive gear lever, and a lot of other ideas besides, made an instant appeal to rich enthusiasts.

One of the best sales areas for the car was clearly the French Riviera, where moneyed people escaped from cold North European elements, and where old man Daimler's agent was Emil Jellinek, who doubled as Austro-Hungarian consul in Nice – a post that enabled him to keep on social terms with potential customers. So, to help matters along, Daimler decided to call the car Mercedes, after Jellinek's daughter.

Of course, many cars, probably most, have been named after people, usually their makers. There really was a Mr Humber, a Mr Ford, a Mr Morris, a Mr Chrysler, a Mr Bentley and a Mr Buick, who made galvanized-iron bars in Flint, Michigan.

Other cars were called after people for other reasons. Henry M. Leland had an historical turn of mind and named his car after his hero – Lincoln. Studebaker's cheap car of 1927 was called the Erskine, after their president at that time. The Marmon concern aimed a bit higher with their light car two years later. They called it the Roosevelt, and every radiator bore a fine likeness of President Theodore Roosevelt, who was said to have been the first American president ever to travel publicly by car (in Lansing, Michigan, in 1907, with one R. E. Olds driving). Olds, by the way, perpetuated his name in the Oldsmobile.

Sometimes, people couldn't call their car after themselves for one reason or another. Dr August Horch, of the Horch concern, for example, fell out with his fellow directors way back in 1909, and moved off to make cars on his own.

Lawyers forbade him to call his new car a Horch, so he confounded them by creating a bad pun and translating his name into Latin; he called his new car the Audi. Years later, in 1932, Horch and Audi were united into the Auto Union concern. Today, the Horch is only a huge if hazy memory – but the Audi is a great success.

Ettore Bugatti called a daughter 'L'Ebe', which was an assonant pun on his initials as they appeared on the Bugatti emblem. And much more recently, so it is said, the Swallow sports car was called the Swallow Doretti, after the daughter of their American concessionaire.

Incidentally, Jellinek had another daughter, Maja, as well as Mercedes, and he gave her name to a car which was made in the Austrian Daimler works at Wiener-Neustadt. But who remembers that now?

This beast before me, the 540K (K stood for Kompressor, the supercharger in this model; Kurz, for short chassis, in earlier cars), was a beautifully made creature, but a bit too heavy for my own taste. And it had vices, just like its country at the time when it was made. The 540K could spin as quickly as a Catherine wheel in the rain, and, if you were careless with your right foot on a wet and slippery road, you might find yourself with both feet flat out, in somebody else's ambulance.

Nevertheless, at rest, the 540K looked as impressive as a Nazi demonstration. From the bonnet sprouted great chrome-steel exhaust pipes, glittering like huge metal serpents. The wheels still wore their balance weights, but now cobwebs crisscrossed the door handles to the edges of the wings.

To my mind it was one of the most beautiful cars ever to come out of Germany, and as with all great cars, peculiarly symbolic of its country and its era. This had been born at the height of Nazi Germany's power, which showed in its Teutonic arrogance of line, the enormous bonnet, the slightly bulbous wings with their chrome flashes, the complete absence of any compromise in cost, either to buy or to run. If you couldn't afford this, then you did without; and if you had to consider what this cost, then you should do without. Sara Greatheart, whoever she was, had been right; this must be the last of the line.

Mrs Meredith's voice scattered my thoughts.

'It belonged to my son,' she explained. 'He was killed.'

'I'm sorry,' I said, because I had to say something.

'At Suez,' she went on. 'It's been in here ever since. I've often thought of getting rid of it, but somehow . . .' Her voice ebbed away.

'Can I look inside?' I asked her.

'Please do,' she said. 'I can tell you like rare cars.'

'I love them,' I admitted, and pulled down the driver's door handle.

The leather inside was cracked but otherwise sound. There was the familiar smell of old oil, wood rot and carpets with moth, the scent of a car that has been stored for too long. I shut the door. It closed like a Fabergé box; there was no rattle here, no drop in the hinges, no concessions to lightness.

'How much?' I asked her.

'What is it worth to you?' she asked.

I walked round the car, thinking. I hate it when people throw the ball back in my court over price. You either insult them by offering too little or screw yourself by offering too much.

'It wants a lot doing to it,' I began hesitantly.

'I know all that,' she said. 'But it is a very rare motor-car. And, since you won't make an offer, I'll tell you what I want for it. A thousand pounds.'

I didn't feel inclined to bargain with her. If she had been a man half her age, I would have walked back to the door, shaking my head, and repeating in shocked amazement, 'A thousand pounds? I don't want to buy the stable, too, you know. Just the car.' But, really, it was a steal at the price. It was worth three or four times that, maybe more, if I gave it the full treatment: rechroming all the bright parts, putting on a new hood, fitting new tyres. Then I remembered Mr Diaz: he had first claim. Somehow, he was such a negative little person that I'd forgotten all about him.

'I haven't got a thousand pounds on me,' I said.

'I don't expect you have,' she retorted, smiling for the first time. 'Only dealers and people like that would carry that amount of cash.'

I swallowed. I was a person like that.

'I didn't quite know what to expect,' I told her. 'I didn't even know if there was a car here, or if I was just having my leg pulled. But I did bring two-fifty pounds in notes because, after all, I couldn't expect anyone to take a cheque from a stranger. Can I give you that as a deposit?'

She nodded and moved towards the door.

So, the deal was concluded. You get deals like that sometimes, but not very often, because there aren't so many people left who take your word, and with the number of times they're let down when they do, why should there be?

We closed the door.

'I can bring you the balance whenever you want it,' I told her. 'And, in the meantime, I wonder if a friend of mine, who is also an enthusiast, could come down and clean it up a bit? Then he will probably drive it away.'

'Of course,' she said. 'You'll want the registration book as well?'

'If you have it,' I told her. 'Or I'll collect it when I come back.'

'I'll look it out for you,' she promised.

We went back through the room of birds. They weren't so excited this time; maybe they recognized me. The parrot appeared to be sleeping, with its head under one wing, but as we went into the house I saw its eyes watching me with a glitter like glass.

'Not me,' he said. 'Not Joey.' I didn't argue. He wasn't bidding against me.

I went through the lounge to the SS, lifted up the front seat, took out my brown envelope, brought it back and handed it to Mrs Meredith. She didn't even count the money; she trusted me. I had given my word and, for her generation, that was good enough. I felt somehow that I couldn't ask for a receipt from her; if she trusted me to this extent, then surely I could trust her.

'Has anyone else tried to buy it?' I asked out of genuine curiosity, and to shake off this unusual feeling. Usually, I like my fellow men so little that I wouldn't cross the road to pee

34

on them if they were on fire, but Mrs Meredith seemed different.

'My son had several friends who were interested,' she replied, 'but I didn't want to sell it. Then he was posted missing. I thought he might come back one day. But he never did. Gradually his friends married, and had children, and I suppose it was really too expensive for them.'

I could see that. It wasn't the sort of car that would fit into the garage of a new semi-detached, with a baby's pram blocking the entrance. In fact, it wasn't the sort of car for crowded roads. Like so many great cars and great houses, it belonged to another world altogether, an age of space and leisure and privilege and time. I wish I'd belonged to that age: maybe I did, in spirit.

'But I did have a phone call a couple of days ago from someone who said they had heard there was a car here years ago,' she went on.

'Did they leave a name?' I asked her.

'I wrote it down somewhere,' she said. 'But I can't remember now who it was.'

'How would they know?' I asked.

She shrugged. She was too old to bother with such questions.

'Perhaps they knew my son,' she suggested.

'They?'

'She. It was a girl.'

'What did you tell her?' I asked.

'Just that I did have such a car and that I might sell it.'

'How did you fix on the price?'

'My own process of mental arithmetic,' she said brightly. 'I knew that my son paid two hundred and fifty pounds for it in 1953. I calculated that the pound had dropped at least four times since then, so I came up with a thousand. Is it too much?'

I couldn't look her in the eyes and say it was, but it was no part of my job to tell her it was too little. I hadn't beaten her down, but I still didn't feel very proud of myself. She was a lady, if you know what I mean, and I felt if she knew what I hoped to make out of the car, I would fall far short of her ideal of a gentleman.

'You're not losing, are you?' I said, turning the question. 'Remember the Rothschild family motto: you never go broke taking a profit.' Even if it wasn't their motto, then it still made sense. I tried to make it mine.

'I'll remember,' Mrs Meredith assured me, and we shook hands.

On the way out of the gates, I turned and looked back at her. She was standing on the top step, the doorway dark behind her, waving with one hand, shielding her eyes against the sunshine with the other. I wondered whether she had stood like that, waving goodbye to her son. That's how I remember her, anyway, for I never saw her again.

Alive, that is.

CHAPTER TWO

I was back in Belgravia by late afternoon, after a stop in Sevenoaks to buy a local paper just in case anything interesting was for sale. It wasn't, so I pressed on and arrived to find George brewing up tea by holding a blowlamp against a kettle of water. He explained that there was some trouble with the gas ring. Maybe I'd not paid the gas bill.

'Anything?' I asked him.

'Man called Diaz been on the phone three times,' he said. 'People will say you're in love. He keeps asking about this Merc. What was it like? Any good?'

I nodded.

'You go down tomorrow morning with all the gear and get it running,' I told him. 'I'll deal with Diaz.'

He was very easy to deal with. He was in his bedroom, apparently waiting for my call. I rang him before I rang Sara; I didn't really know why. Perhaps because he had telephoned three times. Perhaps because I was a bit disappointed she hadn't even rung once. Women. Not a different sex, a different race.

'How much will the car be?' Diaz asked me.

'Three thousand five hundred pounds,' I told him. 'Like you said.'

'A lot of money,' he said. He was obviously regretting he'd told me his ceiling figure. He wouldn't have lasted long in my business. But then he was supposed to be a buyer – or so Sara had said. He should have known better.

'Lot of car,' I said. 'They don't make them like that any more.'

He breathed into the phone and clicked his gold teeth together, as though trying them for size.

'Well, do you want it, or don't you?' I asked him. I was

thinking of the Tobler people; their money was as good as his, and there might be more of it.

'Certainly, yes,' said Diaz quickly. 'When will it be ready?'

'Today's Tuesday. It depends when you want it, and where it's got to go.'

I had to know this because some countries insist that old cars being imported are steam-cleaned underneath to kill Colorado beetle larvae. This is a simple enough job, but it needs arranging in advance with the one or two firms that do it near the docks.

'We would like it for Friday.'

I noted the royal or editorial plural.

'Where will you collect it?' I asked him in the motor trader's singular.

'I'll come to your garage at ten Friday morning. If it is as you say, you will have the money at once. In cash, as you ask. Then perhaps you could drive it to the docks?'

'See you here then,' I told him, and put down the telephone.

I didn't ask for a deposit because it wouldn't hurt me at all if he didn't buy; it was a seller's market so far as I was concerned.

At that moment, it seemed that I'd made myself a profit of £2,500, or at least on paper, or in theory. I still hadn't heard from Sara, though. Maybe she wouldn't be pleased. So what? I asked myself. I'd done all she asked me, and the Bible lays down that the labourer is worthy of his hire. My hire here was £2,500.

I sat down in my cubicle, opened a handful of letters, for I'd left before the post arrived. One was a complaint from a man in Penzance to whom I had sold a pretty well original 1930 M-type MG, one of the little fabric-covered, boat-tailed jobs. Odd how many great cars have grown boat-tails, I thought. Phantoms, the Auburn Speedster, Delages, Hispanos, the lot; must be some close association between boats and sports cars. And while I'm on this psychological jag, let me point out that every successful car has a masculine, often phallic, attraction. The greatest failure I know was the Ford Edsel, which had a feminine appearance. Its radiator, front on, was just like a girl's you-know-what. In chrome, of course. Maybe some psychologist will do a study on all this one day, and I can quote it in my ads.

Anyhow, this nutter, this Penzance pirate, had assured me he was an expert on M types, but now he proved himself a liar, for he wrote to say how annoyed he was to find oil seeping down through the dynamo from the overhead camshaft.

I could have told him it would. Oil had run down even when the cars were new, so why should he worry nearly forty years later? So much for the Herbert from Penzance. I tore up his letter, and opened some others.

There were the usual demands for rates, telephone bills, and one marked 'Private' from my bank. Someone signing himself as per and pro the manager begged to have my advice in re the matter of my outstanding and unsecured overdraft of £1,250 14s 7d. I had assured the writer that certain monies were due, but they had not yet been paid in. He remained mine faithfully.

Damn, I thought, tearing up that letter, too. I had bought the old Ford because a clergyman in Norwich had assured me he wanted it at a mark-up of £200 over my buying price, but now I couldn't contact him. Someone at his number when I rang said he was in retreat. I hoped it wasn't because of his creditors.

I'd find a buyer in a few days, though, but time was something I hadn't too much of. Money, of course, was another, although after this Merc deal I should be all right.

I lit a cigarette. The bank obviously wouldn't want to lend me another £750 to pay for the Mercedes, even though I knew I would get it back within days. Once bitten, and so on.

I rang the manager just to find out. He was with a client, and I hoped he was a richer client than me. Some husk at the other end of the phone listened, without notable enthusiasm, to my assurances about the profit on the Mercedes.

'You told us that before,' he pointed out.

'But this time it's definite,' I said. 'A foreign buyer. Currency coming into the country. The export drive.'

It meant nothing to him and very little to me, really, but I had to find £750 in three days. Then I remembered my promise to ring Sara first. So I rang her.

There was the usual business of, 'Is she registered here?' I was passed from telephone operator to receptionist, to hall porter, back to Inquiries.

'Miss Greatheart is not registered here, sir,' said a sombre voice. 'We have no address for her.'

I put down the receiver. This just wasn't my day, but then what day was? I rang a couple of dealers asking what they would give me for the Ford and the Voisin and even offered them the Burney. Their replies were predictable. Trade was bad; the bottom had dropped out of the old-car market; Americans weren't buying. I hung up. Why add to my telephone bill?

The next couple of days passed as days do pass, simply because there is no way of stopping time, and seemingly for no other reason. They were just two days nearer the grave, so far as I was concerned. I didn't like to ring Diaz and say I was short of money, and I'd no address for Sara. I decided to wait until Diaz arrived, and then explain there had been a hitch – some mechanical defect which had taken rather longer than I thought to repair.

I'd ask him for £1,000 as his deposit, and we'd go down together and bring back the car which, after George's work on it, would be in good shape, and driveable. I'd say that this would also give Diaz a chance to see the English countryside, or what's left of it after motorways, new towns, modern complexes and all the rest have devoured their acres, and he could see for himself how the car handled; a bit better than a blip in second gear around Berkeley Square. So out of necessity, we'd make a virtue, which is better than making nothing at all.

At ten o'clock on Friday morning I was tarted up in my suède shoes, cavalry-twill trousers, split-back jacket, silk handkerchief in my pocket, flat cap, string-back gloves. I looked the part of the car enthusiast, and looking the part is half the battle. If you don't believe that, just try for credit anywhere if you are dressed like a tramp. But if you appear in pepper-and-salt trousers, black coat, stiff collar, you can run up a bill at any good restaurant, because you look rich – or how hired hands imagine the rich look, which isn't always the same thing, and as is well known, the rich never carry money on them. The poor don't always have that much, either.

George had made the engine run by Wednesday afternoon. The oil in the sump was no thinner than Fowler's West Indian Treacle, so he'd changed it, greased all the nipples, checked the plugs and distributor points, blown up the tyres, washed the paintwork, done the upholstery over with Connolly's hide food, and the car, in his opinion, was ready to go anywhere.

Mrs Meredith had given him a cup of tea at eleven every morning, and shown him some photographs of her son in the car. They'd got on well together; she told him her son had been in the tanks at Suez.

Actually – I like that word, actually; it adds tone, as the man said when he stuffed a bugle up the bishop's backside – I wasn't unduly worried about my lack of money. The Lord would provide, or if He didn't someone else would. Someone always did; someone had to. And, anyway, although I never keep any money in the bank, I suppose I'm not really poor. I've been buying and selling cars for a long time, and for cash when I could.

I took most of it abroad before the currency restrictions began and bought a few bits and pieces of land in France and Portugal and Italy. Some I've sold since, and some I've kept and built on. I suppose I could give up work now if I wanted to, but what would I do then? You have to have some interest, apart from sex and food.

I always recall my entry into the used-car business when I feel short of cash: it gives me a shot of confidence. I was living in one room in Belsize Park then, just out of the

Army, and I'd borrowed an American book, one of those that tells you how to be a success, even though it didn't define what success meant, apart from wealth, and that's a better definition than some. The best lesson this book contained was this: if you're down and out, don't mix with down and outs because they can't do anything to help themselves, never mind you. Get where the money is: some may brush off on you.

I was wondering how I could make any brush off on me as I walked past a taxi rank. The second taxi had a card in the windscreen: 'For sale, £50. Apply driver.' The driver was sitting there reading the *Morning Advertiser*. It was no strain at all to apply to him.

'Why is your cab for sale?' I asked him.

'Because the police won't pass it,' he explained. 'We have to get these things tested every year. This is just too old.'

'It may be too old to use as a taxi, but not for me,' I said. The tyres seemed sound. The driver lifted the bonnet; the old side-valve Austin engine looked quite content and cared for.

'If you can bring it to me at six tomorrow,' I told him, 'I'll give you thirty pounds. Cash.' It's a wonderful word, that. Like half a pound of Epsom salts, it nearly always starts things moving.

'You've got a deal,' he said, as though he believed I actually had £30 cash. By then, such is the power of positive thinking, as the American book would put it, I almost believed it myself.

I gave him the address of my rooming house, for I'd nothing else to give him, then walked into the nearest telephone box and rang the Small Ads of the *Evening Standard*. I offered the taxi, 'suitable for student, just overhauled, four new tyres, magnificent condition, £70', and added my address. They take adverts on credit, or they wouldn't have got mine.

By six next day, a queue of fifteen students, or long-haired characters in scarves and sports jackets who looked like students, were outside the house, and the landlady thought business must be looking up. So it was, but for me and not for her.

I had just time to whip the tools out of the taxi, to sell them separately, before I sold it to the second fellow in the queue for £60 cash. I'd proved I could make £30 in an evening for the cost of an advertisement. This restored my confidence in myself, and that's how it all began.

And so, after many years and innumerable car deals, I had very few worries about raising £750 somewhere, though I like to have a worry of some sort, otherwise, if everything's going absolutely perfectly, I feel something must be wrong, and I don't know what, so I worry all the more.

At ten o'clock I felt as full of confidence as a bottle with beer, but by a quarter past, I was a little less sure of the outcome, and by half past I began to feel downright uneasy, although I hope I didn't show my feelings.

Why should a girl I'd never met tip me off like this and then disappear? And surely Diaz had agreed to my price far too easily, without seeing the car? Was I being made a fool of, but if so why and by whom – and, indeed, how? After all, I had the car, or at least I'd put a deposit on it, which in my line of country is virtually the same thing. Questions looked for answers in my mind and didn't find them. At a quarter to eleven George coughed meaningly.

'If you want my opinion, and you don't, I think your Mr Diaz is a Joe.'

'Joe?'

'Joe Hook. Crook.'

'Maybe he's got difficulty in raising the money,' I said, which didn't give me any comfort to think about.

George spat on the floor.

'He's not the only one,' he said.

This added nothing to human knowledge, but I assured myself that Diaz could be late for all kinds of reasons. Unfortunately, none of them cheered me at all.

I stood in the sun, feeling its warmth through my jacket, thinking how nice it would be to spend my life in the sun, with a glass in one hand and the other up the sweater

43

of some lovely girl – or even, if not actually *up* the sweater, at least within working distance. There's my yacht riding at anchor; and aboard it someone else is mixing another drink for me, cold as the tip of an Eskimo's tool, and towards me a serf is padding across the sands holding a cleft stick in his hand because he has so many dollar bills for me he can't carry them all in his pockets. Well, I can dream. Don't you, ever?

At that moment in my dreams, a man came round the corner holding a clutch of evening papers under his arm and shouting the winners. Business was slow, even for him. He came down the mews, past the no-parking signs, and the Bentleys of the Harley Street abortionists being washed by men in rubber boots, past the dolled-up little cottages with carriage lamps and yellow front doors and gay window boxes, and stopped right in front of me.

I took a paper off him, not that I bet unless the race is rigged – because why make the bookmakers richer? – but I felt I might as well read as just stand there. He went on, flapping his papers like a broken white wing. I turned over all the stuff about runners and riders and the Kempton Park selection. The early edition of an evening newspaper is mostly set up the night before; it is more paper than news. But on page 14 there was some news I could have done without. I read it with a stone growing where my stomach had been.

MAN DEAD IN KING'S CROSS HOTEL

The body of Mr Rodrigues Diaz, aged 56, of Sao Paulo, Brazil, was found by a chambermaid in his room in a King's Cross hotel yesterday. He was fully clothed. Mr Diaz, who was on a visit to this country, buying antiques for various collectors, was due to leave tomorrow for Europe. An inquest will be held next week. The chambermaid, Mrs Rose O'Haglan, said: 'He was ever such a nice man'.

She could say that again. He had ever such nice money, too. Three thousand five hundred pounds of it.

I turned into the garage, showed the paper to George. He had nothing to say, either. We just stood looking at each other.

At that moment in our lives, a taxi slowed and stopped outside the door. A girl climbed out, paid off the driver with four half-crowns, and didn't wait for the change. The driver looked at the money and then at the girl, and then he winked at me. I'd have winked back if I hadn't been too busy looking at the girl; she was the type who gives your eyes a holiday.

I don't know what you personally first notice in a girl, for there are tit-men and tail-men and leg-men and bottom-men, and I've even met people who admit being nose-men and armpit-men, but while each should have his own, these are rarer than the rest. All these people notice *their* particular thing on any girl they meet. (So do the pants-men and thigh-men, when they get a chance, but their chances grow fewer, for after a brief boost with the mini-skirt, the girls grew wise to what they were giving away each time they crossed their legs in an easy chair, and the sales of tights zoomed.) Then there are the roll-on men – always interested, like the suspender-men, for the slight ridge or bump beneath the skirt. But I could go on and on and still not do more than skirt (pun) this matter of initial attraction, and the odd thing is that everybody else's interest seems ludicrous and absurd and foolish and maybe even downright disgusting, unless it happens to be yours, too, in which case it is completely natural and harmless and unperverted.

Well, I don't know what your thing is, but speaking personally, I'd say that I'm pretty much of an all-rounder: tit, tail, leg, thigh, pant, bra – anything is better than nothing, and, like the man said, you don't *have* to look at the mantelpiece when you're poking the fire.

What I'm coming round to, as another man said running round the lighthouse, is that this girl rated a high number in each class. Just the right swell of charley to let you know it wasn't all Maidenform or antiseptic sponge rubber 'B' cups; just the right length of leg to make you wonder at the hidden mysteries beneath the skirt. You describe the sort of girl you'd best like to come calling on a hot summer Sunday after a Bombay curry lunch and this was the girl I saw walking towards me.

I thought of seventeen different people she could be, and I didn't know any of them.

'You are Sara Greatheart?' I asked her.

She nodded. We shook hands. Her hand was warm and firm, with long silver fingernails, everything a girl's hand should be. There were rings on it. I looked at her left hand instinctively, for why head for trouble? But she wore no ring on the third finger, which is the important one if you want to avoid a whiff of grapeshot up your jack from an angry husband, or what hurts the single men even more, being dunned for costs in court.

'I tried to ring you,' I told her. 'They said you weren't there.'

'Yes.'

She didn't say why, and somehow I didn't ask her; if she'd wanted to tell me the reason, she'd have told me. There is no mileage in asking girls questions: if you have to ask, they won't tell the truth, anyhow, unless they want to, and if they want to, they'll tell you without asking.

I showed her the newspaper.

'He's dead,' I said, in case she couldn't read.

Sara nodded.

'I know. A heart attack.'

'Who told you?' I asked her. 'It doesn't say here how he died.'

'Someone in the hotel.'

'Well, there goes my dream, like the man said. Also my profit.'

She smiled.

'You might make more,' she said.

'We might make love,' I said, unlikely as this might seem, and looked at her to see how she took it.

She took it.

46

'How do you mean?' I asked, backpedalling. After all, I didn't want to offend her, at least until we had a deal, or until I saw what she wanted out of the deal.

'First, where's the car?' she asked, looking around the garage.

'Still down in Kent.'

'Why?'

I took a deep breath, sorting out several reasons, and then told her the real one.

'I can't raise the money. Simple as that. I've a lot tied up in these cars. And I owe the bank even more. I paid Mrs Meredith two-fifty deposit and promised her the rest. I was going to peel some specie off Diaz, and suggest we drive down together to pick up the car.'

'And you call yourself a businessman?'

'I don't call myself anything,' I told her. 'I leave that to my friends.'

'I've got some money with me,' she said. 'Let's get that car before someone else does.'

'You seem to know this business pretty well,' I said, meaning that so many dealers of antique cars are chasing so few cars. I've even known them to bribe printers and clerks in magazine advertisement departments to tip them off if any unusual car is being advertised, so that they can buy it before anyone else has a chance. There's nothing sacred here, I tell you, as the roué told the nun.

'How do we get there?' she asked. 'Your cars here don't look particularly comfortable.'

'I don't have to ride in these,' I said. 'I just sell them. We'll use an SS.'

'I don't like the initials,' she said. 'They have a traumatic effect.'

The fact is, I can't really say what the initials do stand for, and nor can most other people, although they like to say they stand for Standard Special or Standard Sports or Standard Swallow, because from the small Swallow Coach-building Company in Blackpool, which first made special side-cars and then car bodies on Standard chassis, grew the enormously successful SS Jaguar. The SS part of the name was dropped after the war. Maybe other people also thought it had trauma associations.

I held open the door for her, and she climbed in, keeping her knees together and giving nothing away. Pity, but my opinion of her rose; it's a great test of a girl's sophistication asking her to climb into a sports car with the old-fashioned, rear-hung doors. They don't hang them like that any more, either. And maybe for that reason, among others.

'Be back this evening,' I told George.

'I've put ten gallons into the Merc for you,' he said. 'You should be able to reach a pump on that.'

But with the consumption of that thirsty beast I guessed I wouldn't be able to do much more.

I pulled on my cap, jumped in behind the wheel, blipped the engine, ran an eyeball over the oil pressure and amps, and then we were away.

We didn't have much conversation on the journey. It's difficult to talk, and harder to hear, when you've got the wind rushing past you, the bellow of two three-inch exhausts only feet from your ears, and one hundred and twenty-five angry horses going mad beyond a piece of five-ply, which is all the floorboards are in my SS.

We stopped in Barming for a drink and a sandwich. I washed some of the dust out of my hair and eyes, and Sara spent a penny, and then we went on more slowly. It was two o'clock before we reached Grange House. Half a dozen cars and lorries were waiting in line on either side of the roadworks as a policeman waved us through. So the traffic lights still weren't working; things move slowly in the country. I braked for the sharp turn into the garden, dropped into third, and then accelerated up to the house.

Nothing had changed, and there was no reason why it should. I still felt the strange sensation of stepping backwards out of time. The sun still shone on the ruined tennis court, the paint on the door was as faded as it had been on Monday, as it had probably been for the past thirty years. I didn't even bother with the bell this time, just banged on the panel with the spanner.

On the third blow, the door opened, not because there was anyone behind it, but because it hadn't been closed properly. The hall stood empty, with the sun stained purple and green and amber by the Victorian windows at the far end. The birds still twittered behind their door. I looked at Sara; she looked at me. I hadn't told her about the birds.

I raised my voice, shoulder-high.

'Anyone in? Shop? Mrs Meredith!'

The birds stopped chirping for a moment, and then started again, one, two, half a dozen, and finally all of them in a jagged shrillness of unease.

I tried the next door. Perhaps Mrs Meredith hadn't heard us with all this other commotion? The door opened on to a room lined with dark brown books on dark brown book-shelves. A centre light hung from the ceiling inside a huge circular Tiffany shade that had been fashionable in the nineteen twenties, and was now fashionable again. It didn't look as though many people had used the room since the Twenties, either. I closed the door.

'Where do you think she is?' Sara asked in a whisper. It was that sort of hall. I felt as though I was in a church and shouldn't raise my voice in case people would look at me.

'Maybe she's asleep,' I suggested, with vague memories of a grandmother who used to doze for two hours every afternoon, in front of the fire with a cat on her lap, and then, at teatime, indignantly deny she'd been asleep at all.

There's something about being in someone else's home when they're not there, even if you're invited, and arrive before they'd expected you, perhaps when they've nipped out for a packet of cigarettes, that I don't like. I feel I'm taking some sort of personal liberty without them knowing, and now I felt a whole lot worse. I should have written to Mrs Meredith, or phoned her to say what time I was arriving; she could be anywhere, shopping, on a visit, even away from home altogether.

I stood and looked at Sara, and she looked at me, and behind the doors the imprisoned birds chirped away like a roomful of rusty ratchets.

A whirring suddenly began in the corner of the hall. Sara swallowed and I saw her face tighten; she looked nervous as a child bride, but why? I looked around as the grandfather clock cleared its throat and began to strike. It was a very old clock, with pictures of Asia, India and the Americas painted on the dial, and a huge second hand, all scrolls and curlicues of metal, that clicked on slowly, measuring away our lives.

I cleared my throat.

'Anyone in?' I asked again.

I opened another door and put my head round the post. It was a kitchen, or rather an ante-room to the kitchen, with an old-fashioned stone-glazed sink, an unpainted wooden rack for plates – the kind I vaguely remember being in fashion when I was a small boy. High up on one wall hung a polished wooden box with a glass front and little windows with red tabs behind them, each labelled 'Bedroom 1', 'Bedroom 2', 'Study', 'Living-Room', 'Lounge' and so on.

It must have been many years since any maid had watched those flicker, and then gone, in her neat black uniform, with her pinafore and crimped hat, to see whatever the person wanted; perhaps tea, or the curtains to be drawn, or another piece of coal put on the fire with tongs.

'Where do you think she is?' Sara asked again.

'Maybe she's in with the birds,' I said. 'We'll go and look.'

I opened the door and the birds fluttered their wings madly. The air seemed filled with flapping grey feathers, and the atmosphere was sour with the smell of lime. And soon it would be sour with the smell of something else, for, on the floor, face down, white droppings already dappling her dress, lay Mrs Meredith.

I knelt down by her side and felt her pulse, which was the sort of thing I had been trained to do years ago as a Boy Scout in first-aid classes, but which I'd never done on a real casualty. I could feel no beat.

I turned Mrs Meredith over on her back. She was about as

lively as a sack of stones, a very small sack. I felt her forehead. It was cool, but not yet cold. I held up one eyelid, and the eye looked out at me without accusation, without interest. Mrs Meredith had gone to her long home. Perhaps her spirit, I thought obliquely, was now with the spirit of her dead son. I wondered what they'd have to talk about, how they'd recognize each other. I wondered if any life existed beyond the grave, as the parsons and priests are so certain is the case. Whether there is or whether there isn't, Mrs Meredith would now know the answer, for she was dead.

I stood up.

'She's had a stroke or something,' I said to Sara.

'How do you know?' she asked.

'I don't. I'm guessing. But she's dead.'

I bent down again and lifted up the other eyelid, but the eye had no message. There is a belief among primitive Central African tribes that the image of the last face a person sees before dying is mirrored in the eyes. Like many other beliefs, it is just not true. Her eyes were blue and empty. Death had ironed out the wrinkles of old age so that the skin on her face seemed as firm as when she was young. Perhaps she'd been ready to die, but something inside me said, no. I don't think anyone ever is, unless they've been ill and in agony for years.

'We'd better get a doctor,' I said.

'There's no use if she's dead, is there?' asked Sara more practically.

'You're right. We'll ring 999. Call the police, I suppose.'

I took a step towards the door and paused. Outside, beyond the yard, I heard a click of a metal door, a heavy door. As I stood, straining my ears for more important sounds than the mad, empty squawkings of the birds and the fat feathery beating of their wings, I heard the growl of an exhaust, the beat of an eight-cylinder engine, and then tyres spinning on loose gravel. I jumped for the door.

The Mercedes was halfway out of the yard.

'Stop!' I shouted.

The man at the wheel heard me and turned, so that I saw his face full on. He was in his late thirties or early forties, with broad shoulders, tweed cap, sunglasses. He knew what he was about, for you need glasses or goggles in an open car, even on a dark day, because the wind has a painful way of poking its fingers in your eyes, round the edge of the windscreen.

But it was his face that struck me. He was the most extraordinarily handsome man I have ever seen: aquiline nose, tanned complexion, strong jaw, small dark moustache, the lot. But then he was gone and only the smell of exhaust hung in the air with the rich oily perfume of Castrol R. It took me back years to when I'd been a boy, standing on the edge of Brooklands track, watching the ERAs and the Delages and the little Rileys thunder round the rutted concrete, with the smell of hot paint and burnt oil and Castrol and Ethyl and Benzole that was too heavy to be lifted on the wind and so hung like incense on the warm afternoon air. It was always sunny then, or so it seemed looking back. What had happened to all our summers since?

'Who's that?' asked Sara.

'God knows,' I said. 'Some idiot's just stolen the car.'

'He can't have.'

'He has. Didn't you hear him?'

'I heard a car. Call the police,' said Sara practically. 'Maybe he was a thief and Mrs Meredith disturbed him. Maybe he killed her. He'll never get far in that car, anyway. It's too distinctive.'

'Let's stop him getting any place,' I said, and ran for the telephone.

It was one of those without any dial; you pick it up and wait for the operator to answer, probably in some exchange at the back of a little village post office or local shop.

I stood there, jigging the rest up and down impatiently. A woman's voice answered.

'The police,' I said. 'There's been an accident.'

'You want an alarm?' she asked.

'I want the police. For God's sake, quickly.'

'All right, all right,' she said testily. 'No need to lose your temper. Where are you speaking from?'

'A phone with no number on it,' I told her. 'Grange House, Grange Lane, near Barming.'

'I'll put you through.'

There was a click and a whirr and the line went dead. Damn the thing, I thought, she's pulled the wrong plug.

As I stood there, furiously jigging the telephone rest, I heard gravel crunch and splutter under other tyres. I dropped the phone and ran to the front door. Who the hell could this be?

A police Jaguar 'S' Type, with its blue light revolving on the roof, had stopped at the bottom of the steps. A man in uniform climbed out from behind the wheel. Another man, older, with a pale hard face, dressed like a cavalry officer in a light rubber raincoat and trilby hat, jumped out from the passenger side and ran around to me.

'Who are you?' he asked brusquely.

'Never mind the introduction,' I said. 'I've been trying to get you on the phone.'

'When?' he asked.

'Now.'

They exchanged glances, like some people exchange letters; maybe they meant something to each other. They meant nothing to me.

'We've just had a telephone call,' said the driver. 'It said two people were trespassing in this house.'

'There's no law against trespass,' I said. 'Unless you do damage.'

'Don't give me that chat,' warned the cavalry-officer type.

'I came down here to buy a car from Mrs Meredith. But she's dead. That's why I was trying to ring you.'

'Dead?'

They were both coming up the stairs now, walking easily, but purposefully, hands loose by their sides. I'd seen men walk like that before. I didn't like the sight very much, because I knew that if I moved quickly they could move much more quickly. I suddenly realized that I probably wasn't in a very happy situation; in somebody else's house, with that somebody dead on the floor.

I swallowed. My mouth felt dry as though I'd been breathing through my mouth instead of my nose, and maybe I had.

'Where is she?' asked the man in the raincoat.

I jerked my head towards the door where the birds were now thoroughly awake.

'In there.'

'You wait here,' he said. The uniformed man hooked his thumbs in his jacket pocket and stood, whistling out of tune through his teeth, watching me. I watched him for lack of having anything better to watch, then I turned back to Sara.

'You knew this lady?' asked the man in the raincoat, coming back and meaning Mrs Meredith.

'I met her,' I said cautiously. 'Once.'

The next thing he'd say was that I'd raped her, or been watching her bedroom window through bushes, dressed in a raincoat and claiming to be a bird-watcher.

'Who are you, anyway?' I asked him. If in doubt, fight back.

He flapped an identity card at me. Through the cellophane cover I saw a passport photograph that could have been of him, an indecipherable signature and the rank 'Inspector'. So he was a policeman. You can never be too careful, or too sure.

'And what is your name, sir?' he asked, calling me 'sir' for the first time, like a headwaiter who suddenly wonders uneasily whether the diner he has been insulting could actually own the freehold of the restaurant.

I told him.

I could have told him that I didn't like coppers overmuch either, but I didn't. I keep out of their way, and they don't bother me. About the only times I see them close to is when one turns up with a customs officer to examine a car I've imported, just to check it's not worth ten times what I'm putting it in at.

That's another sign of the times; nowadays, every old car

that is imported has to be registered through the Greater London Council. Up to a few years ago they could be registered anywhere, which was a great help, for ten to one the licensing officer in some remote border county or in the outer Welsh marches had never heard of an old foreign car needing a British registration number; the trick was to buy a £10 heap, then say you wished to transfer its number to an old car you'd been left by your dear old granddad and you couldn't find the log book.

Often enough, I'd driven a car in from France on trade plates with a £50 value on the bill of sale and there was no problem; and on the few occasions when my value was doubted, I produced a mass of estimates on notepaper of famous firms quoting exorbitant prices for reconditioning work. I got a sample of their notepaper by writing them a letter about something and then had it copied. It's wonderful what you could do a year or so ago in all fields of endeavour, but not any longer. There's that much less room to manoeuvre nowadays; we're all fenced in.

I had this feeling very strongly as the policeman kept looking at me; I wondered whether he thought he'd seen me somewhere before, or whether he wasn't quite sure how I'd look behind bars.

'How did you get in here?' he asked suddenly.

'Through the door,' I said.

'But the door was shut.'

I took a deep breath.

'It was open when we arrived,' explained Sara.

'It works on hinges,' I said. 'You can open and shut it, according to your wish.'

The inspector swallowed, and looked at me as though he would like to take me in for questioning. I looked at him as though I wouldn't like to go.

'While we are talking here, a car has been stolen outside,' I went on. 'I saw it being driven away.'

'A car?'

'Yes,' I said. 'A rare car. In fact, *my* car.'

'Isn't that green SS outside yours?'

55

'It is. But we came down here specifically to buy an old Mercedes, on which I paid two hundred and fifty pounds deposit earlier this week. I should have collected it before but I didn't have enough money. Miss Greatheart was to drive my car back, and I'd take the Merc.

'When we couldn't make anyone hear, we came into the hall, then into that room, looking for Mrs Meredith. Suddenly, I saw a man drive the Mercedes right past us from the garage.'

The inspector looked at the constable. The constable felt he should say something. He did.

He said, 'They won't get very far, sir, for this is the last house in the lane, and the road's up. Constable Scroggins is controlling the traffic.'

I think this was the constable's name, not that it matters much. It could have been Buggins or Shagworthy.

'He can't miss the car,' I said. 'It's probably the only one left in Britain. Maybe in Europe.'

'How would you describe the car?'

'Oh, heavens,' I said. 'It's about twenty feet long. Red. Two-seater. Great exhaust pipes sticking out of the bonnet. Can't you get on the radio to someone? Maybe this fellow who stole the car frightened the old lady to death.'

'What fellow are you referring to?'

'The driver of the car, for God's sake,' I said.

The inspector went out, opened the front door, stood for a moment on the steps, and then went out to the Jaguar, picked up a hand microphone and began to speak. We stood watching him as though we had never seen a man speak into a microphone; anyhow, we'd never seen him do it.

He came up the stairs rather more steadily, as you climb the stairs in a lighthouse and slowed down for the last few. Maybe he was feeling his age. I know I was.

'You definitely saw this car?' he asked, looking at me and then at Sara.

'Of course.'

'And there's no other way he could get out except past the road repairs?' he asked the constable.

56

'None whatever, sir. The lane goes up a few yards on the left, but it only leads to a field with a padlocked gate.'

'Well, I find this very odd,' said the inspector slowly, looking at me as though he found me very odd, too.

'Constable Scroggins is on duty there in the lane, and if what *you* say, sir, is correct, this car must have left only minutes ago. And yet no vehicle remotely resembling your description has passed him. He's a bit of an old-car enthusiast himself, too. Got a Vale Special he's doing up. So he wouldn't have missed it. What do you make of *that*?'

'No one could possibly miss that car,' I said. 'Here's what it looks like.'

I pulled out a photograph of a 540K that had gone through another dealer's hands some years before, the sort of photo some old-car dealers like to frame on their walls, just to impress customers with the class of cars they sell.

I had brought it down with me to check that the spotlights and the trumpet horns were original. I hadn't been quite sure whether the horns should be Bosch or Stentor, and now, maybe I would never know, and maybe it didn't matter either way. But my £250 did matter. This was my eating money; I'd grown used to three meals a day and a bed at night. Surely a car that conspicuous couldn't disappear as easily as my money?

'What brought you here?' I asked the inspector, to see if he gave the same reply as the constable. He did.

'Someone telephoned the station. They said that two suspicious characters, a man and a woman, were in this house with an old lady. Usually I wouldn't follow up such a call myself, but I used to know Mrs Meredith's son, so I came along.'

'The son who was killed at Suez?'

He looked at me sharply.

'She only had one son. He wasn't killed at Suez. He died six years ago in St George's Hospital. Meningitis.'

'Well, anyhow, he was the one who owned this car.'

'I don't know anything about that,' said the inspector.

'Come and look in the garage. You'll see where it's been standing.'

'You seem to know your way about,' he said accusingly.

Think, I thought: I'll have to be careful. This man doesn't like me, or maybe he's always like this. Maybe he doesn't even like himself.

'Mrs Meredith took me there when I came on Monday,' I said.

'I see. Don't touch the doorknob, please.'

He pulled out a silk handkerchief, threw it over the door-knob, turned it. We were out in the air, which felt fresh as peppermint frappé after the fug in the conservatory and the smell of the birds. We crossed the cobbled yard; the stable doors were shut. I pointed to them.

'What about touching those?'

He shook his head, pulled out a small screwdriver from inside his jacket, jabbed the blade into the wood at right angles and pushed it sideways. The door rolled open, and we stood looking into the empty garage.

There was no car, but then I didn't expect there would be. Instead, two old tables, thick with dust, took up the place where the Mercedes had been. On either side of them were stacked antique cabin trunks of brown varnished canvas with wood ribs; a washstand with a china bowl, a blue bird-cage; a bicycle, covered with rust, its tyres cracked and perished. Above the junk, a tennis net hung on hooks from the rafters; cobwebs joined the net to the top table, then to a rusty oil stove.

This was the stable I'd seen on Monday – or had I imagined the whole thing? Nothing here appeared to have been moved for months, possibly years. My amazement showed in my face; there was no other visible part of my body on which it could show. I just couldn't understand it, and said so.

'You're not the only one,' the inspector said briefly. 'What are your movements now?'

My movements. The words already had the smell of crime about them; the accused person, the alleged criminal, all the careful legal phrases you read in the papers ran through my mind, and didn't run out again. I felt about four hundred years old, and wondered whether I looked my age.

'I was buying this car for Miss Greatheart, here,' I explained. 'I deal in old cars. Here's my card.'

He looked at it, put it in his pocket carefully.

'I've paid two-fifty deposit on that car,' I told him.

'You have a receipt, of course, and the registration book?'

'I was collecting the log book with the car,' I said. 'I've no receipt, either.'

He said nothing, but just looked at me. We walked back to the house.

Another car was arriving outside. A doctor and two police photographers began taking out equipment. One was whistling to himself. He stopped when he saw the inspector.

'We'll need a statement,' said the inspector.

'Of course.'

'And what's Miss Greatheart's address?'

'It was Claridge's,' she said.

'And now?'

'I leave England today. I'm here on holiday.'

'Where from?'

'Canada,' she said. 'Toronto.'

'Have you any proof of identity?'

He looked at her as though he was sure she hadn't.

She pulled out a Canadian passport. From it, reading over her shoulder, I saw that she was twenty-six. I'd have put her down as eighteen, but then you can often be wrong, and I nearly always am.

He made a note of the passport number on a small pad, then held out his hand towards me.

I produced a driving licence, my Diner's Club card, and an insurance form which allowed me to drive any vehicle. He copied down the numbers and the address in a curiously schoolboy hand. Maybe he'd lost the habit of taking notes. I suppose an inspector usually has someone else to do that sort of thing?

'You're going back to your garage now?' he asked.

'If you have no objection,' I said.

'We'll contact you there,' he assured me. It sounded more like a threat than a promise.

'What about that car?' I asked him. 'There's my two-fifty pounds I'm anxious about.'

'He looked at me.

'If you want my opinion,' he said. 'I don't believe there ever was a car. It's finding why Mrs Meredith died, that we're anxious about.'

His eyes bored bullet holes all through my back as I walked down the front steps.

CHAPTER THREE

One thing life has taught me, as the millionaires like to say in their ghosted life stories in the Sunday newspapers, is that if you want to stay afloat in my business, you must move fast.

I remember once, years ago, learning the truth of this basic fact when I went down to Beckenham to look at a 1930 Packard Speedster Runabout. I've always liked Packards, for their founder, James Ward P., was the sort of man I could have worked with, if not for.

Apparently, in August 1898, as a well-heeled young man, James bought a Winton car – actually the twelfth car that Alexander Winton had made. It wasn't much of a car, and Packard arrived home after his outing being pulled by a team of horses. He criticized this poor performance to Winton, who retorted that if he didn't like the car, then he should build one of his own. To which Packard replied: 'You know, Mr Winton, I think I will'. And, of course, he did.

Just to show how history repeats itself, an Italian tractor manufacturer thought that the differential on his Ferrari was giving him a hard life, a few years ago, so he went to see Enzo Ferrari in Modena, who, being a man of spirit, said that he'd be damned if he'd alter the Ferrari differential for a lousy tractor manufacturer. So the tractor manufacturer replied, 'OK, if that's the way things are, I'll build my own GT'.

This struck Ferrari as funny: who had ever heard of *Un trattore gran turismo*? Afterwards, he didn't think the idea quite so amusing, because the tractor manufacturer was Lamborghini, and the car he made was the Lamborghini Miura.

Anyhow, this Packard I was after was a Twin Six with chromium-wire wheels and side-mounted spares and a boat-back that looked as though someone had turned a rowing-boat prow upside down. I saw the car in a shed, striking matches with flu coming on, and the seller wanted £150.

I offered him £100, and he told me to ring back next day, for someone else was going to see it. I thought that this was just a lot of chat, but it wasn't, for when I rang him back that day he told me that this character had bought it for £150. The buyer, so I heard later, asked the owner if he could let the car remain there for a couple of weeks as he had no garage space. He immediately advertised the car and took down prospective buyers to see it at the first man's house, thus avoided having to pay any garage rent himself, or even the road tax, insurance or petrol needed to drive it away.

Within two days he'd sold the car for £250, making £100 but even then there was a lot more mileage in the deal, for the second buyer advertised it as 'believed originally owned by Vatican high official' – though he was wise enough not to specify just who believed this, which was as likely as a village midwife owning a Black Label 4½-litre Bentley. However, belief is catching, for he sold it within a week for £1,500 to some rich nut in Porto Santo Stefano who had more money than sense, and thought he might somehow buy a back way into the kingdom of heaven by seeking out the original Vatican owner, and presenting it to him. He'd have a job, because the original owner made French letters in a basement beneath a warehouse in Stepney, but, of course, the buyer didn't know that at the time.

Anyhow, as I was saying when I rudely interrupted myself, one thing that life has taught me is the need to move fast; if I'd moved faster then I could have turned £150 into £1,500 very smartly. I didn't hang about now, and as soon as I reached the other side of the roadworks, I pulled into the hedge, waited until all the traffic stopped – actually there wasn't much, only three or four cars and a milk van – and had a word with the policeman.

'I've just come from the Grange,' I told him. 'Someone has stolen a car.'

I didn't say any more; there was no need to confuse the issue.

He nodded.

'I know. A Mercedes. The inspector's been on the radio to me. Well, it didn't come past here.'

'Where else could it go?' I asked.

He shrugged. He didn't seem particularly interested and there was no reason why he should be. He hadn't lost two-fifty quid.

'Nowhere,' he said shortly. He obviously didn't think there had ever been a car; disbelief can also be contagious.

'When did you come on duty?' I asked him. Perhaps he'd missed it.

'Five minutes before you came along. I noticed your car. I've always liked those SSs.'

'Well, make me an offer. It was owned by a district nurse. Never had a spanner on her. The nurse or the car.'

He laughed, not knowing whether to take me seriously. I climbed back into the SS, not knowing whether to take my-self seriously. Then I had a thought. The thief could have driven the car into a packing case on a low-loader. Had any low-loader come along the road?

'No, sir. Nothing like that. Only cars, vans, buses. Sorry to disappoint you.'

Sara and I didn't say much until we reached the garage; there wasn't really an awful lot to say.

George had managed to start the V8, and the tired old engine was throbbing there asthmatically on its frame, like a refugee from a diesel truck. He switched it off when he saw me.

'Anything?' I asked him.

'Nothing but bottles.'

'Bottles?' repeated Sara.

'Bottles and stoppers. Coppers. Bad for trade, the number of policemen who've been round here asking after your health. What have you been up to?'

I told him. He pursed his lips together.

'They'll be back, then?' he asked.

'I'm sure,' I said. 'No other calls?'

'A couple of blokes want to flog you insurance, that's all.'

'To hell with that,' I said and turned to the stairs. Insurance is too much like marriage for my liking; you have to die to beat them both.

'You want to come up?' I asked Sara. I was going to get her up there whether she wanted to or not. I wasn't at all happy with this business of Diaz, or Mrs Meredith, and my part in this deal, and I hoped she'd provide some answers to my questions.

If you employ yourself, you have to paddle your own canoe, to coin a phrase, and I wasn't even going through the motions. I was just drifting, and I didn't altogether like the direction of the current. I'd already lost £250, and maybe my own good name, which, as the Good Book says, is more to be desired than great riches. That, in my view, depends just how great the riches are, but I felt sore about my £250, and even more about the loss of the potential profit, exactly ten times as much – maybe more, if I dealt with Toblers in Germany.

Upstairs, Sara took off her coat and sat down on the chair, with the stuffing coming out of it, where I'd covered the springs with a rug. I brewed up some tea, poured out two cups, stirred in the sugar and sat down myself.

'Now suppose you tell me just how you became involved,' I suggested. She looked down at the arm of the chair and picked at it, not meeting my eyes.

'There's nothing much to add,' she said.

'Add what there is, then.'

I sat looking at her. I wouldn't be the first antique dealer to be taken for a ride, but I might be the first antique-car dealer, and I didn't need the distinction.

'Who was this Mr Diaz?'

'I told you. He was commissioned to buy antiques, and especially old cars, for a friend of my family.'

'Who is your family?'

'You wouldn't know them.'

She wouldn't know mine either, I thought, remembering suddenly my boyhood where Kent meets South London; the red General buses with the open roofs and solid tyres, and the dynamo pulleys spinning round under their radiators. The ponds where we used to skate on our Christmas holidays – no winter-sports trips for schoolboys then. When I last saw those ponds they had been built over by factories and housing estates and car parks. I wondered what South London boys did now, where they skated, if there was anywhere left to skate: or maybe they were too sophisticated for such simple things?

The only South London boys I know these days are the South London gangs who deal in what we call snatchbacks. By these I mean cars that people have bought through hire-purchase companies, and when they can't keep up the payments, the companies snatch them back – usually when they are parked unattended somewhere.

Now the last thing the finance companies want is a mass of old cars on their hands, for they've nowhere to keep them, so they sell them off, very often for the amount still owing – so that sometimes you can buy a car that is worth £500 for £200, simply because that clears the hire-purchase debt. Other hire-purchase firms insist that they must be auctioned, for they feel that's the fairest way, and this is where the South London boys come in.

Say they have a 1966 Zephyr, which is worth several hundred of anybody's money at the auction. First, they whip off the wheel trims, put on very old tyres, loosen the back bumper, pull off the overriders, rip out the carpets and radio, disconnect the spotlights, even take an aerosol of the wrong shade of paint, and blow over a couple of doors so that it looks as though the car has been in an accident.

By then the car looks such a heap that it is knocked down for £200 less than it's worth—oddly enough to someone who is bidding for the boys. Back it goes to their garage, where it has all the pieces replaced, a couple of bob-a-job Boy

Scouts are given five shillings to sweat their nuts off waxing it and cleaning off the aerosol paint with thinners.

Up it goes for sale – 'one owner, supplied and serviced by us' – and the South London gang may have made £200 in an afternoon – in notes, too.

When that little transaction is put down as a bad debt, because with paying drivers, fitters, electricians and testers and so on, they have technically made a tax loss, maybe their total real gain is £300. Do that a dozen times a week from one little garage only, and you see why they don't bother to sit for their 'A' levels. Do it from several, and you can see how they can afford villas in Antibes.

Other South London boyos used to work a very lucrative racket with new trucks and vans. They'd put two of their team into a big garage as salesmen, and then pay various layabouts to order new vans on HP under other names. The down payment each time might be £80, and they'd lend them this.

The gang would then take over these vehicles, split them up into spares and ship them out to the Middle East or Africa. When the hire-purchase companies tried to collect their payments, they'd find that the names and addresses of the buyers were as false as the buyers themselves. This little lot made upwards of £250,000 between them before they went down. Who said crime doesn't pay? It pays a lot more dividends than the three per cent War Loan – when it pays at all.

I poured two more cups of tea.

'Now, look,' I said to Sara, 'we're going to have the police round here any minute for a statement. I'll tell them all I know, which is precisely nothing, except that I've lost two-fifty quid. But how did you know the car was there in the first place? Who told you? And why didn't you get on to this family friend of yours direct and to hell with Diaz?'

I don't mind someone turning back a speedometer 10,000 miles, or pouring Fuller's earth into a slipping clutch, or even giving new tread to a bald tyre with a soldering iron, doing something honestly dishonest, but this smelled to me.

'There's nothing more I can tell you,' Sara said, stirring her tea. This sounded finite, and I stood up and looked out of the window. I'd never make a cop; I ask the wrong questions, or perhaps the wrong people, or perhaps both.

It was dusk, and half a dozen men, carrying blue metal tool boxes, were climbing out of a Dormobile on the other side of the mews. They filed into a garage opposite mine. It always amused me to see them arrive, because, as a believer in private enterprise, I approved of the enterprise of my neighbour, who bought Rolls-Royces and Bentleys that had been written off after accidents, usually fatal accidents. The insurance company paid out the owner (or the owner's widow) and were glad to sell off the wreckage for a few hundred quid.

Week after week, I'd see all sorts of expensive cars, including Continentals, Daimlers, Mercedes and Silver Dawns, arriving on low-loaders or in the back of trucks, barely recognizable as cars. In their hand-tooled leather seats stockbrokers had died in head-on collisions; company chairmen, dozing after heavy lunches, had been unceremoniously precipitated into eternity, and sometimes lecherous old fellows, in the Indian summer of their ductless glands, had gone unexpectedly to meet their maker with one hand on a secretary's thigh.

Not infrequently, the upholstery was spattered with blood or vomit, and even flesh and hair. Once they found a foot still in a shoe, but my colleague had a strong stomach. With his cigar going, he would hose down the leather and carpets and then set about rebuilding the cars.

These workmen, who arrived regularly, had been collected from various Rolls and Bentley dealers around London after working hours. They'd finish there at five, have a meal at his expense, and then start work again in his garage at half past six, and work on until ten or even later. No union rubbish; no tea breaks, either, but six or seven quid a night each, in notes, so no income tax, either.

As a result, my neighbour could offer Bentleys and Rolls, and other rich exotica, for upwards of a thousand quid less than an uncrashed car of that year would fetch. He made a steady £10,000 a year profit, and, as a sideline, he ran another garage that dealt in written-off Astons and Jaguars, and maybe the odd Facel Vega or Jensen. Nothing cheap, you understand, because there's no profit in cheeseparing. I suppose he's the only man in my neck of the woods who deals exclusively in cars that have been the cause or effect of violent death. But why should he worry? It's not his death.

The buzzer hummed by my bed. Someone must be at the back door; maybe a customer. I turned to Sara.

'I'll have to go down to the shop,' I said. 'Stay here. There's some drink in the cupboard, and if you feel like cooking a meal, you'll find bangers and bacon and beans in the kitchen – I won't be five minutes.'

'I'd better be going,' she said, standing up.

'You have nowhere to go just yet,' I said. 'Also, I want you to help me get back my two-fifty quid.'

She sat down.

'I see what you mean.'

'I hope you do,' I said, and went down the stairs.

George had gone, so I opened the door myself. A man about my own height and age stood framed in the doorway. He wore a Burberry and a tweed cap, and he had cut himself shaving that day and dabbed a little piece of cottonwool on the cut. He was old-fashioned if he used a cut-throat razor, I thought, so maybe he liked old-fashioned cars.

'I heard you'd got a Voisin,' he said, without any preamble.

'That's true,' I admitted, because it was, and held the door open for him while I switched on the main lights.

He looked around the car, saying nothing, kicked the front near-side tyre reflectively in a way that made me think he might be in the trade, too, although he hadn't said he was.

'You do part exchange?' he asked.

'What have you got to offer?'

'A Delage. Straight eight. Chapron body. Drophead. Thirty-one. In good nick.'

It could have been worse, although a Delage isn't everyone's choice. It might have been an Armstrong Siddeley, and that's hardly anyone's.

'Where is it?' I asked him.

'Down the mews,' he said.

'Bring it up here, then.'

'More light there,' he said. 'Won't you come and see it?'

'Sure, I'll come. What are you asking for it?'

'How much is the Voisin?'

'Fifteen hundred as is. Needs a retrim and a coat of paint.'

'So I see. I'd like five for mine. How does that strike you?'

'It's a lot of money,' I said.

'It's a lot of car,' he said.

This is where I came in, I thought, so I followed him down the mews. A record-player blared out music by Herb Alpert from one of the twee little houses towards the end, the one with lilac window boxes and brass carriage lamps on either side of the door. We turned the corner, and sure enough, an old Delage with a tattered hood waited under a street light. Only thing was, the light was out, which was the first time I'd known it out since the council's workmen had repaired it a month earlier.

'You'll have to bring it down to the garage,' I told him. 'I can't see it properly here.'

I lifted up the bonnet, and shone a pencil torch over the engine. How many other fine cars, like the Delage, had gone out of business to the sound of eight cylinders firing one behind the other? The straight eight in the Twenties and early Thirties had seemed the acme of excellence to the makers of so many cars, but their performance and viability had not always lived up to the dream, as the backers of Arrol-Aster, the Belsize, the Hampton, the Beverley-Barnes, and half a dozen others, had painfully and expensively discovered.

'You can have it for two-fifty, if you're interested,' the

man said softly, almost as though he didn't want anyone else to hear.

'Why the drop?'

'I heard you lost two-fifty on another car today.'

I let the bonnet fall shut and faced him. The record-player had stopped. There was no sound at all but my heart beating; I didn't like that sound, either, over much.

'Who told you that?'

'A friend.'

His face was very close to mine. I could smell his breath, and I didn't like the smell. He was squinting. His left eye began to twitch. The lid fluttered as though it couldn't make up its mind whether to stay open or shut. I guessed he was hopped up with some drug or other.

'Two-fifty and you forget the other car,' he said. 'Take your profit on this. OK?'

I shook my head.

'Who are you?'

'Never mind that,' he said. 'Have I got a deal?'

'No,' I said. 'Not on those terms.'

'Why not?'

'Because I'd rather have the Merc. Also, I don't like to be frigged about. That's why.'

'Listen, buster,' he said, coming closer to me. 'I'll *give* you two-fifty and we'll forget about the Voisin. Two-fifty and forget the Merc, too. I'll throw the Delage in – you can make a couple of hundred out of it, easy. OK now?'

I shook my head.

'Who sent you here?'

'Never mind that. Are you on?'

'No.'

'Look, I haven't time to argue the case. That Merc is out of your reach. Lay off it. Someone else wants it. Someone who gets what they want. Do I make myself clear?'

'No.'

'So you want to learn the hard way?'

'I want to learn no way. I'm just not interested in a two-fifty-quid bribe. If we can't do any other business, then goodbye, and the best of luck.'

I half turned from him, and as I moved, he hit me. I had almost expected this, but to expect something is not necessarily to be ready for it, and I wasn't ready. The blow hurt, as he meant it to. I sagged against the door; the cobbles swam in front of my eyes, blue and green and purple. Music that Herb Alpert never plays exploded in my ears.

When you see someone hit on the box or in a film it never seems to hurt. They're rubber men, untouched by pain and feeling. But it hurts in real life, it hurts like hell. Also, I felt shocked and surprised and frightened. Why should a stranger offer me money one minute and hit me the next? Could it be that he also was afraid – because I hadn't taken the bribe?

I slid my hand down into my right jacket pocket where I kept a bent length of petrol pipe with one end pointing forward. It's not a knuckle duster, but in my business it is sometimes wise to have some power of persuasion, and the beauty of a bent petrol pipe is you can easily straighten it, and then what looks more innocent?

I slipped it on my hand, over the fingers, with the spike pointing forward.

'Don't be a bloody fool,' the man said, seeing my hunched shoulder, wondering if he'd hit me too hard. 'You're mad, turning this down. You just don't know who you're up against.'

'If it's only you, I'll live the night,' I said, and hit him in the face with my fist. Hard.

The jagged, sharpened end of the pipe scored through his cheek, piercing it to the teeth. I felt it jar on them, like the ridges on a scrubbing board. He screamed in pain and surprise, then brought up his right knee, and we threw aside all pretence of dealing, and fought. He was far tougher than I had imagined. The soles of his shoes were tipped with steel, and he flicked them like an axe at my shins, and as I stumbled, he struck me with his hands locked together on the back of my head.

71

I drove my left fist with its bloodied spike up into what the newspapers euphemistically call the lower part of the abdomen, but what I call the cobs. He screamed now like an animal, whining and gasping with pain. I struggled upright again, and a man I hadn't seen, who had been waiting all the time in the doorway, brought down a half-brick or a half-ton on my head.

I don't know how long I lay on the cobbles. My watch glass was smashed, my teeth were loose, blood from my nose and mouth had soaked the front of my shirt. The mews was empty and very cold, and I felt the sweat of fear and reaction and violence drying on my aching body.

I tried to stand up, but only managed it by leaning against the wall. The Delage had gone, the men had gone. Only the music remained, faint and thin and remote; the braying of trumpets, the brass of a recorded Tijuana band. To move made me feel sick, and I vomited, supporting myself against the wall. Then I began to walk unsteadily down the mews. Had I been unconscious for minutes or for hours? I neither knew nor cared. My garage door was still open and the light was on. I went inside, shut it, slid the bolt, and leaned against it thankfully. Then I started to go up the stairs and stumbled. Sara appeared at the door.

'What's the matter?'

I couldn't speak just then. I crawled up, went into the kitchen, ran the tap, washed my face, rinsed out my mouth with cold water, and poured half a tumbler of Whyte & Mackay and drank it neat. Then I sat down.

'Your face,' she said. 'What's happened to you?'

'A dissatisfied potential customer,' I said, as the whisky ran in my blood and gave me a little false strength.

Sara got up and looked out of the windows across the mews. The only activity seemed to be behind the doors of the garage across the way, where they were rebuilding one of the early Mulliner Continentals in which a property developer had developed himself into a corpse through falling asleep at the wheel on the M4. The fact that he'd been coming back to London after spending a night with his secretary might have contributed to his tiredness, or again it might not. Even his widow would never know, and with the will in her favour, why should she ever care?

'What happened, really?' Sara asked.

I told her.

She shook her head slowly, as though she didn't believe me, or didn't want to.

'Now tell me the truth,' she said.

'I have.'

'Did you know the man?'

'Never seen him before. But I'd remember him again. Pity I didn't see the fellow who hit me from behind, either. I'd like to remember him, too.'

'The Mercedes,' she said. 'Is it so important to you that you couldn't take his money to forget it?'

'Look,' I said, 'I'm in business to sell cars. There's two-fifty iron men of my own on that vehicle, and this fellow Diaz was going to give me three and a half thousand. It's about the market value, maybe even a bit less. And I can get that for it tomorrow, Diaz or no Diaz, from your old family friend, whoever he is, or from someone else.'

'There are some things more important than money.'

'Name me two,' I said, thinking of sex, for one, though the older you grow the less sure you are.

She smiled.

'One day,' she said.

'Well, make it soon,' I said. 'The way things are going, I may not live too long.'

Sara sat down in the chair opposite me, lit a cigarette and then stubbed it out, as though undecided whether to say something or not.

'Why are *you* so keen on that car?' I asked her, to prime the pump. 'How would you get it to your friend now Diaz is dead—if we could find it, that is?'

'Before we think of that,' she replied, 'we have to find the thing. That may be difficult.'

'Life is difficult,' I said, because it is. 'We've got the chassis number and the engine number. I know they can file these

73

off and stamp new ones, but these can be checked. You can take an X-ray picture that shows if it's been messed about with.'

'So what do you think will happen?'

'If it was an ordinary car,' I said, 'even if rare and valuable, I think it would be given new numbers, a new paint job, and then advertised. They'd soon pick up a buyer.'

'Why not in this case?' she asked.

'Maybe in this case,' I said. 'But I don't think it's just an ordinary car. I think there's something special – or something odd – about it. I don't think you wanted it *just* to give to an old friend, too?'

'I don't know you very well,' Sara began.

'There's still time,' I reminded her.

'Yes. But not a lot, perhaps, as you yourself say.'

'What do you mean?'

'I'm not sure,' she said lamely, and I believed her. I wasn't sure myself. I also wasn't sure what the hell was happening.

I lit a cigarette and picked my teeth with the match, and tried to recap events as briefly as possible. So far, I could see nothing to give me any comfort in what had happened, and what was happening, or what was likely to happen. I had paid out £250 without even a receipt, without even seeing the log book, to an old woman who said she owned a car. And me a car dealer! How naïve can you get? What jury would ever believe my story?

The man who had promised to buy the car from me at a profit of £2,500 was now dead. So was the old woman who had sold it to me. I had been beaten up, and the car had disappeared. So what did we do now? Two-fifty quid wasn't the end of the world. I could soon get back that outlay by bumping up the profit on the next few cars I sold. But the potential loss of £2,500 profit was out of the petty-cash league. Also, I'm a stubborn cuss and I don't like bums who come into my garage, con me into looking at some heap they say they want to sell, and then do me up. If anyone is going to do anyone else, I prefer to be the doer and not the done.

I stubbed out my cigarette. The smoke stung the inside of my nose as I exhaled; I was still in pain.

'This old family friend,' I said. 'Who exactly is he?'

'He collects antiques as well as cars,' she said, as though that told me anything.

'What's his name?'

She paused.

'I can't tell you.'

'Why not?'

'It's – it's a personal thing.'

'I see,' I said, but I didn't; people who say, I see, rarely do. I thought my face was also a personal thing. Why should anyone beat me up for an old car? I thought of one or two dealers who might, but not for £2,500. It might be different if you were running a rigged auction and a hundred cars were going through your hands at each sale. But it just wasn't worth the trouble or the involvement for one car, however rare it might be.

'Any ideas on that driver?' I asked her.

'None. I'd never seen him before.'

'That goes for me,' I said. 'But I'd know him again.'

Those broad shoulders under the brown tweed jacket, and that tanned face, might have been a throwback from a film-star profile of the Thirties; it came like an instant-handsome-man kit: small dark moustache, high cheekbones, thick black curly hair. And yet it had seemed somehow incongruous on those shoulders. I thought of a phrase, an old head on young shoulders. This was more like a young head on old shoulders, and if that was my most brilliant thought for the day, I should give up thinking for a while.

'Where does he live, this anonymous collector of antique cars?' I went on.

'He has various homes,' she said vaguely.

'So have I. Here. Rowton House. The Salvation Army Hostel for Downs and Outs. Penny on the rope, twopence on the knot.'

'He's different. He's a rich man.'

'Obviously,' I told her. 'Where is he now?'

'I don't know,' she said. 'He moves about.'

'How nice for him,' I said, thinking how I also moved about between second-hand car dealers in Swiss Cottage and Belsize Park and called that an outing. But that was hardly the kind of orbit for a man who could afford £3,500 for an unrestored old car.

I was irritated with her, and with myself. What were we doing here chatting, carefully telling each other nothing, when the real action was taking place God knows where? I felt like the oozoo bird that flies around in ever-diminishing circles until it finally disappears up its own jack. And who wants to be an oozoo bird?

'Well, we can do two things,' I said brightly. 'First, nothing. Second, we could try and find the car. It must be somewhere.'

'Where do you think it could be?' she asked, as though I knew.

I shrugged.

'It's not the sort of car you could sell easily here,' I said, thinking aloud. 'If I'd lifted it, I'd blow it over a different colour – which is very easily done in half a day in the trade if you know where to go, and you have enough pound notes to put on the kitchen table. Then I'd get it out of the country as soon as possible. Somehow.'

It could be in a packing crate labelled 'heavy machinery', for some new African country that is politically popular at the moment, waiting to go aboard a ship that would considerately stop at a European port before it reached its supposed destination.

'Where to?'

'Best place is Andorra. I'd register it with their local automobile club, then whip it over the border into Spain. Then I'd flog it very expensively to some rich American collector. They've so much money that if you offer them something cheap, they think it's no good. No strain at all.'

Most of the cars that disappear from Britain to the Continent go to Andorra, and then goodness knows where, for no one has ever heard of any car coming back. That is the bourne from which no stolen car returns.

Sara stood up.

'I'd better go,' she said, and meant it this time. 'I feel rather badly about having got you involved in this at all.'

'I feel rather badly myself,' I said. 'In fact, I only feel good when I've made a profit. It's against my religious principles to make a loss.'

'You've got strong religious principles?' she asked.

'The strongest,' I said and watched her go down the stairs, wondering what sort of pants she was wearing. At the bottom, she turned; had she read my mind?

'I'll ring you if I hear any news,' I said. 'Where will you be?'

'The Connaught.'

So she wasn't leaving for Canada just yet.

'Are you staying there?'

She shook her head.

'I'll wait in the bar.'

I'll wait for the second coming, I thought, and watched her walk up the mews. Then I looked at myself in the mirror. I looked even worse than I felt, which was hard to believe. I poured myself another whisky, and dabbed some Milton on my bruises. I always keep some handy, not only for its medicinal properties, but for other, less well-advertised properties it possesses, which, in the used-car business, are sometimes even more valuable.

Say you have a car to sell and you either want it to appear newer – or, oddly enough, in my stretch of the forest, older than it is, because, to be described as vintage, a car has to be registered no later than 1930 – then a little Milton on the registration book bleaches out the date and another one can be written in. Iron the page to put back the shine, and presto, another vintage car has been discovered!

As I dabbed, I tried to piece together any bits in the jigsaw of events, but none seemed to fit. My mind was turning like a fairground roundabout, and questions followed one another like its painted swings. Obviously, someone wanted the car more than Sara did to steal it so openly. But why – and who? Why couldn't they have bought it in the ordinary way? I might even have sold it to them if I had been approached. I'm not one of those people who refuse to believe that everyone can be bought; they can, although not always by money.

If this was a professional car thief, his actions would follow a set pattern, and I might have more hope of finding the car, simply because I knew the pattern. If he was an amateur, then it would all be more difficult.

Most cars that are stolen to resell are driven as quickly as possible to some shed or lockup garage, often under railway arches, where a couple of bent sprayers blow over the paintwork, while other craftsmen grind off the original engine and chassis numbers, and substitute new ones. They can get lists of numbers easily enough from the makers. If the car is still in production, they simply copy the plates of a similar car that's in a local garage for servicing.

Registration books present no difficulty, because you can easily call at your local motor-taxation office, explain that you have lost the book, and the clerk gives you a new one for five bob. You can fill it in there and then. That's if you haven't been prudent enough to steal a collection of books for yourself first from some genuine dealer. They usually keep the books for the cars they stock in a desk or a filing cabinet, and it's no great problem for one apparent buyer to chat up the dealer on the pavement while a colleague works a quick flip through the files. But this Mercedes would be difficult to hide, if indeed they wanted to hide it.

I decided to ask around, for old-car dealing is a small parish. I turned out the light, pulled the curtains, and looked out over the mews. I wasn't so keen on going out again in the dark if any odd characters were hanging around, but the mews was empty. The only sound came from the leather-tipped coachbuilding hammers and wooden mallets over the way. They must be doing a good job on that Bentley, but I still wouldn't like it much. It is with chassis as with people; once bent, they rarely go straight.

78

I had decided to ask Jacko Jackson what he'd do in these circumstances, so I walked up the mews, and banged on the door. A window opened above my head, and a grey-haired man peered out. Jacko's face was always vaguely familiar, because he appears in TV advertisements, sniffing bowls of packet soup as though he hadn't eaten for weeks, or looking up at the light through glasses of dubious wine that has never sprung from grapes. His grey hair was crinkly, like corrugated iron, and he had a grey military moustache, although so far as I knew he had never seen any military service; I think that during the war he was what George would call an Alphonse – a ponce – in Jermyn Street.

On the box, Jackson looked ageless, as men of his looks can sometimes seem. It is only when you're close to him that you can see the fine, wrinkled blue veins on the nose, and the open pores exuding sweat that even pancake make-up cannot entirely conceal. It's only when you see the trembling hands that spill any drink, and the fingers brown with nicotine, that you realize Jacko is not quite the retired ambassador, the man of distinction, the old colonial administrator, the diplomat in eclipse, that he would like to appear.

'Come up for a drink,' he suggested now, for want of anything better to suggest. I could tell from his tone that, in the dim light, he wasn't too sure who I was.

I opened the door, and went up the narrow wooden stairs. He had a one-roomed flatlet with walls of white vertical boards, each tongued and grooved, because this was where the hay had been stored – and within living memory. Wooden pegs still sprouted from the walls for grooms' hats or whatever; some tatty old pictures hung from them now, and the worst areas of blistered paintwork were covered by nudes cut out of *Penthouse* and *Playboy*. Across a huge expanse of pink pneumatic breastwork he had stuck a red label pin: 'Mine is bigger than yours'. I didn't bother to argue.

Jacko was in bedroom slippers, his trousers rather unpleasantly stained around the fly; he wore a filthy old woollen cardigan with a sodden ball of handkerchief stuffed into one pocket. He held a plastic tumbler with gin and tonic in one hand. Drink slopped down over his sleeve; beads of gin glittered like tears on the grubby wool.

'What's happened to your face?' he asked, recognizing me.

'Argument,' I replied briefly.

He grunted, poured some gin into another tumbler for me; the neck of the bottle rattled on the rim of the glass. I hoped it mixed with the whisky.

'I want your advice, Jacko,' I said. 'You know the car business pretty well.'

He didn't disagree, although his view of it was unusual. When he wasn't acting in commercials, he acted out two neat little cameos for the benefit of one or two rather shady car dealers around town. Sometimes they would take into their stock a Rolls that was just too young to be old enough to make a high profit on, but which still might suit a retired colonel in the West Country, or a judge from one of the few remaining colonies who had been so long abroad that he still believed in the honesty of his fellow countrymen.

They would go through the elementary precautions of fixing the car up with a new log book, then tart it up as cheaply as they could, and Jacko would appear as the original owner, who was selling to help pay his son's fees at his old school (frequently, the buyer's old school, if this could be discovered). Time spent in reconnaissance is seldom wasted, even when it's only looking up Who's Who in the nearest public library.

On other occasions, Jacko would put on a blue uniform and a shiny peaked cap he'd once used in some long-forgotten commercial, and had never returned to the costumier, and he'd be the family chauffeur who had been left the car in a legacy from her late ladyship after he had tended it lovingly for twenty years. He was a hit in either part.

'What's the trouble?' he asked me now, looking at me out of eyes that swam like two eggs poached in gin.

'If you had a hot old car, how would you get rid of it quickly?'

'Have you got one now?' he asked me. Water was gathering at the corners of his eyes. It should have been tonic water; he even wept gin.

'No, I haven't,' I said, improvising. 'But I know someone who has. It's probably the only car of its sort left in this country.'

'Then I'd get it out of the country,' he said. 'And bloody smart.'

He raised his elbow and licked the drops off his sleeve with a white and furry tongue; pity he didn't do a laxative commercial. His liver must be like asbestos.

'How – if all the ports are watched?'

'Dismantle the bloody thing. Strip off the body. Then put a truck body on the chassis, and ship it out that way. Then carve up the body and take that out in pieces from different ports in the boots of three other cars. Use kids. The customs don't usually open up cars with lots of kids asleep in the back. No problem.'

'Only if you have contacts,' I said.

He looked at me in amazement.

'Well, you wouldn't get involved unless you had contacts, would you?'

'I suppose not,' I said.

'Where's this car, then?' he asked. 'Who's got it? Anyone I know?'

'I thought I had it,' I told him, 'but when I went back to collect it, I was just in time to see someone driving it off. I don't know who has it now. That's why I'm picking your brains.'

He grunted. He was obviously not convinced by my account. He poured himself another gin, but didn't offer me one. I got the message. He watched me move towards the door and stood, bottle in one hand, glass in another.

'If you want me, you know where to find me,' he announced. 'But I'll be away all tomorrow. Taking a Phantom Three down to Cheltenham. I'm Scrotum, the old and wrinkled retainer. Been with his lordship thirty-five years, and it don't seem a day too long.'

81

The neck of the bottle rattled on the glass. I left him there, starting to sing.

They seemed to have built the stairs more steeply in my flat when I came back, or else I was tired. Hammers beat in my head as they still beat in the mews across the road.

What should I do now? I could, of course, do the easiest thing – nothing – and hope the police would turn up with the car, unlikely as this seemed. I decided to use my loaf and try to find the car myself.

I opened the AA handbook and looked under the section, Ports. There were ports I had never imagined anyone using for cars: Newcastle-upon-Tyne, Weymouth, Stranraer. I felt a nut asking someone at the other end of the line in the middle of the night whether they'd got a booking for any unusual car or lorry with strange bodywork. The man I was seeking might not even be travelling through the AA. What if he was a member of the RAC?

I took them in alphabetical order, starting at Dover. They had nothing there. The man who answered my call at Fishguard said an old lorry had gone across to Ireland with the last vessel. It wasn't old enough – a 1934 Morris Commercial – but I thanked him and rang off. He meant well. At Harwich, a group of students had gone to the Continent in a pre-war London taxi that day, and from Holyhead a very old couple had taken a Weymann-bodied Bentley across to the Isle of Man. Old cars were on the move, right enough, but not the particular old car I wanted.

By then it was after midnight, and I felt too tired and depressed to bother to ring the rest. I would do it in the morning, if I did it at all. I suddenly realized that I had had hardly anything to eat since breakfast. I opened a tin of beans, poured them into a pan, warmed it on the gas stove, and then ate them with a spoon from the hot pan, standing holding it, reading the *Daily Express* on the draining board. Why bother to lay a table with knife, fork, spoon and plate, with all that trouble of washing up afterwards, whereas now all I had to wash up was the spoon and the pan? In the end,

I didn't even do that; I filled them with water under the tap, left them, and then went to bed.

The night was filled with violence, or so my dreams had me believe.

George had been downstairs for two hours before I awoke. My face still felt like someone else's I was trying to break in, and I didn't like the feeling. I reached for the telephone, and dialled Trunks. Lydd Airport had had one or two cars go through which were obviously pre-war; Newcastle-upon-Tyne had seen a 1928 round-tank BSA, and nothing remarkable had been booked or sailed from Newhaven. But at Southampton I got a roar of laughter in my ear.

'You're asking about one old car, are you, then?' boomed some salty voice whose owner had clearly slept better than I had.

'Yes,' I said, holding the phone half a foot away from my year because I wanted to use the drum again. 'Have you had anything through?'

'Anything through?' the man repeated. He seemed to like conducting a Socratic question-and-answer conversation of his own. 'We've got fifty old cars going through now.'

Either he was mad or I was. I swallowed.

'Fifty?' I repeated. 'How?'

'Old-car rally to the Costa del Sol, Spain. As you might have motored thirty years ago. Easy journey, easy distances, new hotel every night, plenty of wine, plenty of sun. What more do you want?'

I could have thought of one thing, but I didn't say so. This fellow might be a lay preacher or something.

'Who's organizing it?' I asked him instead.

'I've the secretary here with me in the office,' he said. 'I'll hand you over to him.'

I heard a click in my ear, then breathing against a distant cacophony of old-fashioned motor horns. A quiet, resigned voice asked me: 'Can I help you?'

'I don't know if you can,' I said. 'To be quite honest, I don't know if anyone can. I don't even know if I can help myself.'

'What do you want to know?' he went on in his tailored voice. He must have thought that here was another one, a right nutter, but this didn't show in his voice. I'd have said he was very precise, very neat, with three points of a handkerchief in his breast pocket, and possibly a six-a-side moustache, if his voice was anything to go by.

'A friend of mine is taking his old car abroad,' I said, adlibbing as I went along. 'An old Mercedes. He forgot to tell me what port he was leaving from. I've been ringing them all.'

'What's his name? As you heard, we've fifty of our members leaving for Bilbao at this very moment. We're going on a fourteen-day run right across Spain and back. Is your friend a member?'

'His name's Jackson,' I said, giving the first name that came to mind. I heard the rustle of paper over miles of wire.

'We haven't any one of that name here. We do have a Johnson, though.'

'No, it wouldn't be the same one. Have you got a Mercedes, then?'

'Not so far as I know. We've got most other makes. Even a Mercer.'

This had been a great rival of the Stutz, another fine American car of the same era. The Stutz owners concocted a rhyme: 'There never was a worser car than a Mercer', and the Mercer owners retorted: 'You must be nuts to drive a Stutz'. Happy days.

'I see,' I said. But all I saw was an ingenious way to push one wanted old car through the customs openly – in a rally of fifty others. No one would look for it there, for it would be protected by its own camouflage, the original mechanical chameleon.

'Is that all?' asked the man on the phone. He must have grown tired of listening to me breathe. Yet once he had gone, I should lose contact for ever. My mind spun like a spin drier.

'Just one last thing,' I said. 'Has anyone cancelled their passage with you? My friend might have picked up a cancellation.'

'We've had one car cancelled, yes. Domestic trouble. I think the member's wife is ill.'

'If I could have his name?' I said. 'He could probably tell me if my friend has taken his place.'

'He's Mr Ruper, Chesapeake Gardens. Somewhere out by London airport. I haven't his exact address. I hope he can help you. Now, I really must go. Goodbye.'

Goodbye, sweet ponce. May flights of angels sing you to your rest, for I wasn't having any. I wondered who the hell Mr Ruper was. The easiest way to find out was to telephone him. I found him in the phone book, and dialled his number. An old man's voice answered with a dead East London accent, suspicious, querulous, slightly edgy.

'I would like to speak to Mr Ruper,' I told the old man's voice.

'Which Mr Ruper?'

I hadn't expected this. I never thought there would be more than one. Who the hell would be a detective?

'The one who is interested in old cars.'

'You're speaking to him,' said the voice. 'Who are you?'

'I'm in the business,' I said. 'Aristo Autos.'

'Well?'

A good question. Well, what? I was watching my face in the mirror across the bedroom. It was also watching me. From its expression, it didn't think much of my performance.

I took a deep breath.

The man repeated, 'Well?'

'I heard you had cried off from the rally.'

'That's true. What's it got to do with you?'

'Nothing,' I replied, honestly enough. 'I was hoping for a place myself. I was wondering if anyone had taken yours?'

'Yes,' he said. 'They have. Anything else?'

'I suppose he wouldn't swop with me?' I went on, optimistically.

'Certainly not,' said the voice. 'Why should he? He's just swopped with me. So I'll bid you good day.'

He put down the telephone. So far so bad.

I looked down under the name Ruper; there was a second number for Ruper's Breaker's Yard. Ten to one it was the same person. I telephoned Jackson, to see if he knew him. A voice, ripe with gin, wearily fighting back the prospect of facing another day driving two tons of towsed-out metal to Cheltenham, said, 'Yes', in my ear.

'Just thought I would see how you were, Jacko,' I said, which wasn't entirely true.

'Christ, I'm bloody near dead,' he said. 'All the bleeding way to Cheltenham with no back brakes, dressed as a chauffeur in trousers so tight they practically castrate me. *Me*. And I might have been where Sir Laurence Olivier is now if I'd played my cards right.'

I thought this was pushing his talent a bit high, but why annoy the fellow?

'Do you know anyone called Ruper?' I asked him. 'Oldish. Got an old car.'

'Ruper,' he repeated the name. It slotted somewhere in the sponge of alcohol he used as a brain.

'Yes, I know the bleeder,' he said at last. 'Crafty sod. A fence. But he's never been nobbled for it. Belongs to about twenty different old-car clubs. Claims to be an enthusiast in each one, so that members will sell him their cars, if they want to sell, at a reasonable price. Then he flogs them off for five times as much next day. I'd do the same myself if I had any sense.'

'If you weren't being Sir Laurence Olivier,' I reminded him.

'Sure.'

He belched into the phone.

'Oh, my guts. The gin you get nowadays. What do you want Tom Ruper for?'

'Nothing, really,' I said. 'Know anything else about him? Is he married, for instance?'

'Was. Wife pissed off years ago. Know nothing good about the bugger. He was questioned pretty closely after both those bullion raids at the airport last year. They got away with the money in a couple of vans. Copper I know said some boy who collected car numbers saw Ruper and some other yob with the number plates in their yard. He made a note of them, but it wasn't conclusive evidence, for the boy was only seven, which is too young for the courts.

'And maybe Ruper leaned on his old man a bit, or got someone else to do so. After all, if you'd a kid of seven, you wouldn't like to have his eyes burned out with acid, would you? That's how my guts feel.'

'Take half a pound of bicarb,' I told him. 'It'll have some reaction,' and put down the phone.

I felt better now something was happening. I didn't know what, but something. I hate inactivity. Let's do something, if it's only each other; let's say something, if it's only good-bye: that's my way of life, anyhow. I don't know about yours.

I had a bath, shaved, ate my breakfast (a cup of black coffee and two Alka-Seltzers) and then took the SS out into the wasteland of dreary semis and characterless concrete cul-de-sacs in search of Chesapeake Gardens. I left the car in the park of a public-house marked 'For patrons only', because it is a bit too conspicuous to leave in the street, and walked into Ruper's yard.

They had a notice chalked up on a blackboard offering best prices for old cars, old car batteries, old tyres. But best for whom – the buyer or the seller? It was like those ads some car dealers run: 'Guaranteed used cars'. All that's guaranteed is that they are used. Or: 'Every car hand-picked', as though they were fruit. And whoever heard of anything being foot-picked?

Behind a shed lay a mass of rotting cars, piled high, one on the other, mostly empty metal shells without windows that once someone, somewhere, had loved. Here and there a loose door banged open and shut wearily in the wind, as though ghostly unseen passengers were climbing in and out for a journey that would never begin. An Alsatian on a short chain sliding along a metal wire bared yellow teeth at me. I bared teeth just as yellow back at him.

On the side of the shed someone had chalked: 'No visitors

beyond here'. Under this notice was a bell-push. I pushed it. An alarm bell sounded somewhere in the back of the yard, and a little old man came towards me out of a forest of chassis members and rusty exhaust pipes.

He might have been heaving coal, his face was so black. He was wearing steel-tipped boots, blue dungarees, and a jacket taken off a rag-and-bone heap. He looked about twice as old as time.

'What do you want?' he asked.

'Mr Ruper,' I said.

'I'm Mr Ruper. Who are you?'

'I spoke to you on the telephone this morning,' I said.

'So did seventy other people.'

'Not about the rally to Spain.'

'Oh, yes. That. Well, what do you want?'

'I want to know why you didn't go.'

'You've got a bloody nerve,' he said.

He put his right hand into his pocket. When he took it out he was holding a King Dick spanner.

'Don't give me that crap,' I said, watching his eyes in case he was going to make life hard for me. I didn't want to stand bantering words with him like a couple of Afro-Asian delegates at UNO: I simply wanted to know the answer to a question.

'You can sod off,' he said. 'Wasting my time. If you won't go, I'll get my brother to you.'

He turned his head over his shoulder to shout.

'Before you do,' I said quietly, 'remember that raid last month? The airport?'

He stopped, swallowed, and turned back and looked at me. His eyes were cold, without expression, like the eyes of a serpent. The yard suddenly seemed very quiet, like a grave-yard; even the Alsatian had stopped whining.

I didn't like Mr Ruper. I had one eye on a six-foot left-over of exhaust pipe to my right; if he and his brother tried anything, I reckoned I could reach that pipe first, but I hoped things wouldn't come to that.

'What are you getting at?'

His voice was softer, as though he were speaking against the wind.

'Just what I say,' I said.

I didn't know anything, except that he was supposed to have had some part in it, but I've always thought I'd have made a hell of a good method actor. Especially when I see the performances put up by some of them.

'I know someone who saw those plates,' I went on. 'Not a little boy, either. A man. Someone who would talk.'

'I don't know what you mean,' he said, but his voice sounded no more convincing than any other fence protesting his innocence.

'There's no reason why you should,' I said. 'I'm just trying to find out who took your place on the boat.'

Then I put a card on the table that he should understand.

'I think it's someone who tried to welsh me on a deal.'

'I want to keep my nose clean,' said Ruper suddenly. 'There's too much violence about. I don't like violence. I told you I had to cry off for domestic reasons. The wife's sick.'

'Balls,' I said. 'You haven't got a wife. Who took your place?'

'I don't know his name,' he said. His voice was stronger now, as though he were on surer ground. He could even be telling the truth.

'I've got a lot of contacts,' he went on. 'You know how it is in this business. Callers. People who have a roomful of old mascots. Some other nutter who's collected five hundred radiator badges or hubcaps. I keep in with all these old-car clubs. I'm a member of several.'

'I know.'

'I was all set for this Spanish rally. Got a friend in Torremolinos. I was going to drop off there on the journey, spend a few weeks with him, and come back under my own steam. You get cut rates if you go even one way with a club.

'Then last night a fellow I've done a bit of business with in the past' – his eyes flicked away from me for a moment –

'this fellow rang me. He'd a friend who wanted to take my place. I didn't ask any questions.'

'How much was there in it for you?' I asked.

'Fifty nicker,' he said, so quickly that I knew he was lying. He probably meant a hundred.

'What car did he take?'

'I don't know. I think he was screwing some girl. He wanted to take her with him. His wife wouldn't go on this old-car rubbish, and she'd never imagine he'd have the neck to take a girl if she stayed at home.'

'That's what you were told?' I asked. 'All you know?'

I didn't believe him, but this didn't seem the time to tell him.

'Yes.'

'Thank you.'

I didn't turn my back on him; he might be a bit too handy with that spanner, although I didn't think so. I backed a couple of paces out of reach and looked into the shed. It was full of old spotlights. Horns and distributors hung in festoons from the rafters like some surrealistic metallic fruit from the nineteen thirties. Perhaps Dali could have done something with them; I couldn't.

As I walked out of the gates, I saw a big man thread his way through the metal shells to Ruper. He had short gingery hair that stood up like bristles from a toothbrush, and amber sideburns. I've never liked men with sideburns; amber sideburns I like least of all. I was glad he hadn't arrived when I was talking to Ruper. Maybe he was his brother. I was pleased he wasn't mine.

I didn't waste time, but hot-footed it back to the car, gave the 'V' sign to the publican who came out and asked me if I couldn't bloody well read. I could read all right, but only danger signals and signs that seemed to lead nowhere.

I was back in Belgravia by noon, having stopped only briefly in Shepherd's Bush to put my card under the windscreen wiper of a parked duck's-back Alvis in case the driver wanted to sell.

'Anything?' I asked George.

'Got a down payment on the Ford,' he said, 'Fifty nicker, if you can do terms.'

'I'll do terms,' I said. I'd do almost anything to be rid of that rubbish.

I went up the stairs. Someone in my room was smoking Turkish cigarettes, which I couldn't afford. I pushed open the door. That someone was Sara. She was curled up in a chair reading *Vogue* but with her legs tucked under her so that I couldn't see anything.

The room looked different somehow; cleaner, for one thing. The bed had been made, the bean pan and spoon which I had forgotten to wash up weren't in the sink; the paint looked fresher: you could actually see what colour it was. I didn't altogether dislike the change.

'Where have you been?' she asked. 'I was waiting for you to ring.'

Of course, the Connaught; I'd completely forgotten.

'I went to see a man,' I told her. 'I rang up the ports last night and this morning. Nothing that could conceivably be that car had gone through, except Southampton. Fifty vintage cars went out there this morning to Spain. A rally.'

'Was the Mercedes among them?'

'I don't know. One man says he was paid fifty quid to drop out. I've just been to see him. I'd say he's a small-time crook.'

But, even as I spoke, I thought of ten or twelve dealers like Ruper whom I'd known over the past fifteen years. Without exception, they'd sold off the couple of acres of wasteland where they had broken up their cars, and now skyscraper office blocks towered above the shabby houses. They were all millionaires, or as near as even an actuary wouldn't dispute.

In the old days, you couldn't reach them on the phone because the GPO had cut them off for not paying their bills. Now, you couldn't reach them because of all the secretaries, personal assistants, and so on they employed to keep callers away. They probably couldn't even reach themselves if they wanted to. And I was the mug, still padding around in a beat-up mews that probably belonged to one of them through a Bahamas holding company. What had they got that I hadn't, apart from brains?

'Fifty pounds seems a lot of money just for a place in a rally,' Sara said thoughtfully.

'Yes,' I agreed. It was a lot of money, period, in my state of financial health.

'Then what are we waiting for?'

'Look, lover,' I told her, a bit of the old Freudian wish thing slipping up from the subconscious. 'Be your age. You may live in Claridge's or the Connaught as the mood takes you, but I don't. I've lost two-fifty quid on this deal so far. My natural inclination is to take off, on the chance that the car *is* on that boat, but I don't know. It's thirty-six hours before the ferry docks in Bilbao. And if the Merc is aboard, how do I prove it's mine?'

She swung her legs down off the seat. I wanted to see that telltale flash of white thigh, but I saw nothing: she was wearing tights. I told you, life's not what it was for the leg-lookers of this world since tights became so popular. You won't find me investing in their firms. I remembered an afternoon in my adolescence, that brief period between infancy and adultery, when I was hanging around a car park in Woolwich hoping to see a few girls get out of cars carelessly, and an old woman came along and thought I was begging, and gave me sixpence. I took it, of course.

'I told you about the car in the first place,' Sara said. 'What if I finance the trip?'

'What if you do?'

'What's the quickest way to get to Bilbao?' she asked.

'Fly to France. Then put the car on the train to Biarritz. Then drive over the Spanish border.'

'Is there much paperwork involved?'

I shook my head. I always keep an insurance green card in case I have to go abroad with a car on business. It would mean taxing the car, though, and I'm one of those motorists who prefer to run a car untaxed with a little 'tax applied for' sticker on the windscreen. Why waste £25 when there's no need?

'It's only a matter of ringing up the airport to see if they've got a place,' I said. 'Then try French Railways. The numbers are on that board above the desk.'

But Sara was already picking up the telephone.

I went downstairs and had a chat with an undergraduate from Sussex or somewhere, who was trying to flog me an early Jowett Jupiter in British racing green.

It had to be that if it's green, I thought. It's a safe bet that any green open sports car offered for sale, whether it's emerald, pea-green or near-black, will be diligently described in the advertisements as British racing green, BRG. In fact, there ain't no such colour *as a colour*.

Racing cars first wore national colours in 1900 for the Gordon Bennett race. The organizing committee specified blue for France, yellow for Belgium, red for the United States, and white for Germany. Britain hadn't any colour allotted to her.

British racing cars were painted green officially for the first time three years later, when it was decided that Britain would defend the Gordon Bennett Cup over the Athy circuit in County Kildare.

Count Zborowski, the older, suggested that the British team should paint their cars green, 'as a tribute to the Emerald Isle'. So British racing cars have been green ever since – of one shade or another.

Whatever the shade of the student's Jupiter, he wanted too much money for it, and, anyhow, I wasn't in the mood. My mind was elsewhere; about twelve feet above me, in fact, where Sara was still holding her skirt casually with one hand. She wasn't giving away a thing, this girl, which was how I liked them.

'There's a flight at six,' she said. 'Shall I take it?'

'That's up to you,' I told her. 'You're paying the bills.'

She made a face at me and went back to the telephone.

I asked the student for his name and address, and said I

would be in touch if I found a buyer. I wrote his name down on the pad I keep by the telephone. The name above his was Diaz, Highland Brae Hotel. Diaz. I'd forgotten all about him. Now, I remembered.

I called up the stairs, 'I'm just going out for half an hour. Got to see a man.'

I didn't add that he was a dead man, and I wouldn't see him, but I had an idea in the back of my head, and the only thing to do when you've got an idea in the back of your head is to get it out of your head altogether and see what it amounts to. That's my great thought for this page. If you've got a better one, then write it in the margin. There's no charge.

'We'll have to leave by half past four, because of the traffic,' called Sara, as though I didn't know that myself. Already, I noticed, she was tending to take charge; like all women, she liked authority. And like all I've met, she'd be more amenable if she were smacked down. Nicely, you know, but just hard enough to show who's boss. It could make an entertaining way of spending an evening.

'Get yourself packed,' I told her, 'and be here then with some money. I'll be ready. And if you've got a warm coat and some woollen combs, put them on. This car's terribly cold for a long journey.'

'Haven't you anything else more comfortable we can use?' she asked. See what I mean? Complaining's another habit women drop into very quickly.

'Nothing here,' I told her. 'Anyhow, there's quite a market for SS100s on the Continent. I could even sell it there.'

I had done this sort of deal before. You don't need a carnet for France, so there's no record that the car has crossed the frontier. Then you give the overseas buyer a bill of sale for, say, three or four hundred pounds less than he's actually paid for the car so he doesn't have to pay the full import duty on it, if the customs ever discover the car is there at all. That helps him. He helps you by giving you the difference in some useful currency that Her Majesty's Government's Inland Revenue people know nothing about. I've got bank accounts in Paris, Bonn, Rome and Madrid through these deals – and not in my own name, either, just in case some bright currency boyo in the Bank of England's investigation department ever came across them. If you don't look after yourself in this world, no one else will, and I'll give you that in writing.

I picked up a cruising cab outside the mews, and told the driver, King's Cross Station. I dropped off at the traffic lights at Midland Road and Judd Street and crossed the Euston Road into the hinterland of private hotels on the other side. Cars and coaches were parked end to end outside the little bed-and-breakfast honeycombs that had once been private houses.

A few bore discreet signs in the windows: 'Vacancies, H and C all rooms'. Some were shabby, with coloured men standing in doorways picking their teeth and looking for bewildered immigrant families; others glittered with a plastic smartness. Fluorescent tubes flickered through door fanlights, behind unlikely names, chosen to make raw Northerners feel more at home.

The Highland Brae was halfway up a side street, no better and no worse than the others. It had a huge purple thistle stencilled in the middle of the front glass door, so that Scotsmen, staggering back after a Burns-night booze-up, would not walk through the glass door without opening it first. The hall smelled of wax polish and Jeyes fluid. I didn't like the smell much, but then I didn't like the place. I wondered if Diaz had liked it, either. He'd seemed a fairly natty dresser to me; I couldn't place him in this particular part of Failuresville.

A porter was reading the racing news behind the Formica counter to the right of the door. He had cross-eyes and smoked a cigarette, tapping it out in a china ashtray stamped Negresco Hotel, Nice. He wore a dirty white jacket, opened at the collar. He looked up as I came in, and then went back to his reading. Behind him hung a row of keys beneath pigeon-holes with room numbers, and little cardboard tags bearing the names of guests. I saw that Mr Abdul

Amir was in Room 12, and Mr Fort in Room 2; Mr and Mrs Hassall (with child) were in Room 18. Now who or what were they? Amazing, the number of people I didn't want to meet, I thought.

I would have read more, but the porter folded up the newspaper with a big sigh, and reluctantly asked: 'Can I help you?' with an Irish accent, as though he feared he might be able to.

It seemed a fair question. To show that, in certain circumstances, I could also help him, I took out a pound note, held it up against the light, then folded it in two and pushed it underneath the ashtray. He looked at it as if he had never seen a pound note folded in two, pushed under an ashtray before. Perhaps he hadn't, but I'd give him the opportunity of seeing another, if he'd help me.

'There's the same again if you can tell me a few things,' I said, so he realized I was in the market.

'Such as what?' he asked. 'Are you a reporter?'

I shook my head.

'No. Just a friend of Mr Diaz. He died here.'

'Oh, yes. Poor Mr Diaz.'

He made the sign of the cross and watched me out of his left eye to see how I took this religious procedure, while his right eye appeared to be watching a fly crawl up the window of the door.

'What about Mr Diaz?' he asked, focusing both eyes on me; maybe the squint was just a party trick.

'I've been away for a few days,' I said, which was quite true; I had been away to Kent, for example. I don't like the lie direct, but sometimes one can bend the truth into more satisfactory shapes.

'We did business together,' I went on. 'I don't know if he's got anyone here to settle up his bill?'

I let my voice tail off. I didn't want to offer to pay the bill myself, I just wanted to see it.

'That's very kind of you, sir,' said the porter. 'That's very Christian. You should really see the proprietor, Mr Bairns.'

He pushed a card to me. On it was written: Mr and Mrs R. J. Bairns, Res. Props.

'Where is he?' I asked.

'Out,' said the porter, drumming his split fingernails on the counter top. I was glad he wasn't the cook. Or maybe the cook's nails were worse?

'I won't be in London that long,' I said, putting my hand in my back pocket and leaving it there. 'Could you just check through the bills and see whether it was settled?'

'I really shouldn't,' he said.

'I know that,' I agreed. 'But I'd appreciate it. There are a lot of things we shouldn't do. But if we can help a fellow man through life's lonely journey . . .' I stopped for I didn't want to overplay my part, and also, I wasn't entirely certain what my part was.

He glanced down at my hand in my pocket. I rubbed two sides of a pound note together. He heard the noise: it's one I like hearing, too.

He made his great decision. 'I'll do what I can, sir,' he said.

He went into an inner room, came back with a buff folder, opened it. I read, upside down, a badly typed letter to the Brazilian Embassy explaining that Mr Diaz, a Brazilian subject, had died suddenly of a heart attack, and asking if they would meet the cost of his hotel bill. Underneath, was a carbon copy of the bill.

'There seems to be some correspondence about it,' said the porter. He couldn't read very quickly. He hadn't got beyond the letter heading.

'Let's see the bill, anyhow,' I said.

He handed it to me. The Highland Brae Hotel didn't go in for adding machines; it was all written out in a neat spidery hand. Seven and six for early morning tea; five shillings for newspapers; telephone calls, four pounds eighteen shillings.

'That seems a lot,' I said. 'Who did Mr Diaz telephone?' I tried to look as though I wasn't very interested in the answer.

The porter pulled out a ledger marked 'Telephone' from the counter drawer and began to thumb over the pages.

'Diaz. Diaz. Here we are. It's a foreign call.'

'I thought so,' I said, although I hadn't. 'He was probably trying to contact me. What was the number?'

'Here it is. Salamanca 543541. In Spain. Was that you, sir?'

I didn't answer the question, but pursed my lips and looked grave; he could take it either way. He snapped the book shut.

'As the Embassy seems to be dealing with this, I'd better not get involved,' I said. 'I'm sure they'll take care of everything very well. Tell me, how did he have his heart attack?'

The porter leaned towards me; I could smell his breath, sour as an open sewer.

'He fell, sir. The maid found him in his room. He'd hit his head somehow as he fell.'

'Poor Mr Diaz.'

'God rest his soul,' said the porter piously, focusing his individualistic eyes on the ceiling.

'Amen,' I added, for I thought something was due from me.

I took out the other pound note and laid it on the counter. His hand covered it instantly. We understood each other. He smiled. I went out, down the steps into the street, repeating the telephone number to myself until I was out of sight and could write it down on an envelope.

What exactly had I discovered? Simply a telephone number without a name, for an exchange I didn't know. Presumably, this could be the man for whom Diaz was buying the car. So what should I do now? Telephone him? Then I realized I didn't even know his name, and so I did the easiest thing – nothing.

I had a cup of coffee in a café on a corner, and took a cab back to my mews. George was wiping his hands on a piece of rag. I'd forgotten it was nearly lunchtime.

'Where's all the action, then?' he asked, as if I knew.

'You tell me.'

He came out of the garage, stood in the sunshine, his head on one side and told me.

'They've been here again,' he said conspiratorially. 'Grasshoppers. Coppers. Told 'em you'd be back in a few moments.'

'Where are they now?'

'Coming down the road behind you.'

Two men in light mackintoshes were walking up the mews. One was in his thirties, the other a bit older. They walked slowly, in step.

'You want to see me?' I asked the younger one.

'Pure formality,' replied the older man. 'We'd like a statement from you about what happened at Grange House.'

'That's no problem,' I said. 'Come inside.'

I led them upstairs. They sat down side by side on the edge of the bed. I pulled up the only other chair, offered them a drink. They refused it.

'Not while we're on duty,' the older man explained. 'Now, if you will just tell us what happened. In your own words.'

I couldn't tell them in anyone else's. The younger man took out a notebook; I could see he wrote shorthand. I told them what had happened. He read it all back to me.

'To save a lot of messing about,' I said, 'there's a typewriter over there, and paper and carbon. Bang it out now and I'll sign it.'

'That's very kind of you. You're being very helpful.'

'Why shouldn't I be? Is there any watch out for that car?'

'We haven't ascertained yet that there was a car.'

'Oh, my God,' I said; this was almost where we came in. 'Anyhow, start typing. If you won't have a drink, have a cup of coffee? Be my guests.'

I brewed up three cups of Nescafé. The policeman wouldn't have won any prizes for typing; like me, he used two fingers, and I could put two fingers to a better use. I went downstairs before I did so. In between all this dodging about, I was supposed to be making a living.

I checked through the proofs of what we term a call-bird

advertisement I was going to run in some provincial evening papers. This advertises a car that doesn't exist at a price that is just too good to be true. Then, when you get a dozen eager calls, you tell each one that that *particular* car has just gone, but you've got an even better one in stock, or just coming in.

The caller is keyed up for what he thinks is going to be a good bargain, and his natural avariciousness carries him over the hump of disappointment at losing it, so that he's pleased at being offered another.

Some dealers even print photographs of cars they don't own, so long as they look exotic enough, and if the owner sees them, what can he do? I got to the bit I put in the American adverts, 'rebuilt with loving care by old-English craftsmen, working not against the clock or down to a price, but up to a standard', but I wasn't even convincing myself.

My heart just wasn't in describing an MG Tigresse that didn't exist. I rather wished it did, for I've always had a soft spot for MGs and their octagon badge which Cecil Kimber, the man behind them, chose to distinguish them from the humbler Morrises on which they were based. He ordered instruments in this shape, choke and throttle control knobs, sidelights, even the oil filter on top of the camshaft cover. And in the MG works I'd heard that the directors had octagonal napkin rings in their dining-room and even octagonal-shaped electric-light switches. Other car makers had used similar shapes – Packard, a hexagonal on its hub-caps, and SS, a six-sided badge, and even, in some models, the same shape around the instruments, but none to the same extent.

I moved over to George, thinking of car badges, and symbols, the heraldry of the twentieth century. The Pierce Arrow motif that started out simply enough as an arrow through a wheel, and ended as a naked archer crouched uncomfortably on the hot radiator cap. The blue-and-white-chequered circle of the BMW, chosen in the Bavarian colours to represent a spinning propeller in the days when they made aircraft. The prancing horses of Pegaso and Ferrari; Lamborghini's bull; the cross and serpent of the Alfa Romeo – the arms of Milan, where it's made, with a laurel wreath added in 1925 when their P2 racing cars won the equivalent of the world championship; Peugeot's lion; the goddess' helmeted head on the Minerva, the knight's helmet used by Cord, the Marmon 75, and the Lammas-Graham; the crown and sceptre of the Reo-Royale, Maserati's three-pronged fork; the fasces of the old Chrysler Imperial . . .

'When you were down with Mrs Meredith, doing up that Merc,' I said to George, bringing my mind back, 'where did you work?'

'In the garage at first, simply because the car was too heavy to push out. When I fired up the motor, I drove it into the yard and did the rest there. Why?'

'When I looked in her garage yesterday, it was full of junk. Chairs, tables, rubbish of every kind. Even cobwebs. You wouldn't have thought anyone had been in the place for years, let alone worked there this week. The coppers didn't believe there was a car at all.'

'Are you serious?' asked George, his face squeezed up like an oyster when you drop lemon juice on it. I told him I was. He went upstairs. The policeman was still typing, his tongue out.

George said, 'I know there was a car, for I worked on it for two days. I've brought back yards of old wire from it, and some bulbs. Bosch originals. You can see them downstairs.'

He turned to me.

'And while we're on the subject of wiring, the whole thing needs going over. I've only done the sidelights and the horns. It looks a rough old job. I had to use what wire I had – all white plastic, even for the horn earth.'

'What sort of car was it?' interrupted the older policeman.

'Mercedes. Five point four litres. Two-seater. Supercharged.'

'Look,' said the policeman, as though speaking to a backward child. 'Both of you say there was a car there, and so does the lady, Miss Greatheart. But *if* there was, *and* it was driven out on to the road, what happened to it? Somewhere between the house and the roadworks, it disappeared. No doubt there *was* a car, sir. All I want to know is where it is now.'

'So do I,' I told him. 'And I want to know that two hundred and fifty pounds more than you.'

The man at the desk pulled the sheet of paper out of the typewriter.

'If you would sign this,' he said.

I read it through. It was much as I had said, although the punctuation wasn't all I would have wished. I thought of adding a bit of spiel about consulting my lawyers, and then I thought I wouldn't. After all, what could the lawyer do, but charge me 'for taking client's instructions', or some such crappo, when, of course, the whole reason for involving him was to find out *his* instructions.

I signed the top copy and kept the carbon. The two policemen went down the stairs and along the mews, still walking as policemen do, slowly, and in step. George lit a cigarette.

'You say there were cobwebs in that garage?' he said.

'Yes.'

'That's not hard to arrange.'

'What do you mean?'

'Be your age,' he said. 'You know that fellow at the end of the mews who makes a living turning out antique rocking chairs and coffee tables, all with genuine wormholes bored into them? You can buy an aerosol now to spray on the cobwebs. Just as we use an aerosol to put back the smell of new leather when all we're using is plastic.'

'But why should anyone do that?'

George gave me an old-fashioned look in lieu of anything else and went downstairs.

I would have followed him, or shouted something, if I could have thought of anything to shout, but I couldn't, so I poured myself three fingers of Whyte & Mackay (it sounds better than two fingers, which could be misinterpreted) and added a bottle of Coke from the fridge.

Then I folded up my advertisement, pushed it into an envelope, stamped it, gathered together a few things I would need; an international green card insurance form, the SS log book, my international driving licence, passport, and twenty £10 notes.

I rolled the money up in a piece of polythene, slipped an elastic band round it, put it on one side. I would slide it into the hollow part of the frame at the front end of the chassis where the jack fits. There's a rubber plug to keep out the mud, and I'd never known the customs look inside, although they might deflate your spare tyre just to see if it is stuffed with notes.

I went downstairs with these things, put the papers into an AA folder, and that into the pocket of the driver's door. Then I took out five more tenners, placed them flat on the top of the battery cover, snapped on a slightly larger cover above them – they would never think of looking there, either.

I stuck a 'Visitor to Britain' Union Jack sign on the windscreen, because all kinds of officials are more helpful to you if they think you're a foreigner, poured a pint of oil into the sump, and checked the water and the tyres. Then I remembered I only had a 'tax applied for' piece of paper on the windscreen, and the customs people might want to know whether the car was taxed – and a glance at the log book would show it hadn't been taxed for years.

None of the old cars in my garage had licences on them, but an old Morris Minor outside, had. It belonged to a commercial traveller I knew slightly, well enough to know he was away on business for his firm for a week. He wouldn't need the licence, and I'd be back before him.

I peeled it off his windscreen, used some Milton on the ink, wrote in 'SS', instead of 'Morris', and my car's number, and stuck it in my own licence holder.

George watched my preparations with a beady eye.

'What's it you're after, then? Money, or just spade and pail? Tail?' he asked me.

I didn't answer him, because I didn't know the answer myself, and I couldn't admit this to George.

The odd thing was that I wasn't thinking so much about the money as about the girl, which is crazy if you're in business to make money, and not girls.

'Spain,' said George lugubriously. 'Spanish fly.' He held up the middle finger of his right hand. I could follow how his mind was going. I'm sharp on the uptake.

'Do some business down there,' he suggested. 'As well as the other thing.'

I nodded. There might be some deal to be done, at that, for old cars last far longer in a warm country. Most of their bodies have wood frames, and in damp climates they rot and crumble, but I've seen Cloverleaf Citroëns and ancient Amilcars in the South of France in use every day, just as they were thirty-five or forty years ago.

'You've got the chassis and engine numbers of that Merc handy?' I asked him.

He nodded and picked up a little red exercise book from the bench.

'I always write them down for every car I work on,' he said reproachfully. 'You should know that.'

I did, too, but I'd forgotten. He gave me the numbers. I wrote them with a Biro on the spine of the yellow AA folder.

'What do you think my chances are of finding the Merc?'

He made a long face.

'Once it's out of this country, you'll never get a whiff of it. You know that as well as I do.'

'There's always the exception to prove the rule,' I told him.

He said nothing.

I went upstairs, threw some underclothes, a couple of shirts, a turtle-neck sweater, and a pair of Terylene trousers into a holdall, for there isn't much room in the SS for suit-cases, and I didn't know how much Sara was bringing. My experience with girls in the past is invariably that for even one night away they need three suitcases, a beauty box, and so forth.

The phone rang three times, but none of the callers was Sara. The first was a nutter who'd just come off the train at Paddington from Bristol and seen my address in an advertisement. Somewhere between these two stations, he said, he'd glimpsed an old car parked in a field against a haystack. He didn't know whose it was, or what make, or even whether it was for sale, but he thought I might be interested. Of course, he hadn't any address, and wasn't sure exactly where it was near, but if I was interested, I could easily find all that out, couldn't I?

The second caller offered me a 1935 Squire two-seater with a special body. Only thing, he said, the car was up in Preston, and I'd have to go there and see it. I told him not to worry, and rang off.

I'd have loved to find a Squire, a beautiful and expensive sports car, made by a tiny firm in Remenham, outside Henley, in the mid-Thirties. But only seven were made before the firm folded and I know where they all are. I guessed that the caller was a crook who hoped I'd hare off up North, and then he'd call around in his own time and whip whatever he could of my stock, or any odd lamps or horns or mascots he could carry. I tell you, mine's an easy way to make a hard living.

The third caller offered me a Seal, the car not the animal – or so I thought. I was interested, for the Seal is about as rare as rump steak in a Chinese nosh-up. It has three wheels, and at first sight it looks exactly like a motor-bike and side-car – until you have another look and discover there's no saddle or handlebars; the driver sits in the side-car with his passenger, and steers with a wheel.

I said cautiously that I *might* find a buyer, and then the caller got all het up and began making odd noises. He'd cleft his palate from the difficulty I had in understanding him, but gradually I realized my error.

My phone number is only one figure different from the

telephone of London's most exclusive house of ease; this character wasn't offering me a Seal – he wanted a feel.

'Not in my state of health,' I told him sternly, and put down the telephone. Aren't men beasts?

I poured myself another whisky and thought about the sadness of the human animal – especially when, like me, he also owed money to the bank. I thought how wonderful it would be to be rich. I thought about Sara, and then she arrived.

She was wearing slacks, low-heeled shoes, a heavy black sweater and skiing anorak. She went up in my estimation because she had only brought one bag, a soft leather affair, rather like mine. I wondered if she'd brought her equipment with her; it didn't matter if she hadn't, I was taking my own precautions.

I put her bag with mine behind the seat, buttoned down the tonneau cover, and we were off.

CHAPTER FOUR

I don't know what Sara did, but I dozed all the way over the Channel.

We were in a BUA Bristol freighter, and the crossing was calmer than if we'd been in one of the toy ships far beneath us. The SS was lashed down behind the cabin with two other cars. The other drivers, a couple with a baby, and two women on their own, chewed sweets and pointed out the boats to each other.

I might have stayed awake if this had been my first trip, or if I had been crossing when some of my cars were young, in the days when you didn't need a passport, but you made sure you had a box of golden sovereigns and a Stepney wheel and cans of petrol (for the car tank had to be drained) plus, of course, a chauffeur with a plentiful supply of spare goggles.

But, in this case, we were over the Channel in minutes. What had once been a great adventure, an important part of the grand tour, had dwindled to something as insignificant as a wait at a country level-crossing. We took the train to Biarritz, and slept in couchettes that didn't give much chance for anything but sleep, and not too much of that. However, I thought philosophically (Spinoza should be my middle name), at least I was getting my strength up. But for what – and when?

The road south to the Spanish frontier was surprisingly empty. A few bright blue and orange tents blazed on summer grass. The French do these outdoor things so well; portable washbasins, collapsible kitchens, folding chairs and tables, whereas on my own camping trips I've often taken a bar of soap to a stream and washed myself in the running water, crouching down like those characters in the Old Testament.

The road beyond San Sebastian in northern Spain was even emptier; the few vehicles were lorries with green tail-lights they flashed obligingly when it was safe to pass them.

Bilbao didn't impress me much, but then there was no reason why it should. The streets were narrow and crooked and crowded. Huge chimneys poured out black smoke that drifted towards the cone-shaped hills behind the town; clouds rested on their dark green peaks as though they were too tired to move.

The ferry, the Swedish-Lloyd *Patricia*, was already in the harbour, and cars were coming off, stopping briefly at the customs, then moving on. We bumped over railway lines, past a rusty hulk of a barge where men with acetylene torches swarmed amid showers of sparks. I wanted some-where to park where we wouldn't be seen, but I was in the docks before I realized it, so I parked up behind a vast yel-low container waiting to be loaded on some vessel, and went in search of anyone who spoke English. Sara stayed in the car, making up her face in the driving mirror.

At first, the cars were all modern, with a caravan or a Dormobile here and there, and a single-decker bus with the blinds down and a sign in front 'Charter Homes for Blind Children', then a motorcycle and side-car and, finally, an old car, a Frazer Nash, twitching along, its chains and sprockets growling away like an angry animal imprisoned beneath the rear tonneau. It was off up the road with a roar from its Anzani engine, and to a faint cheer from those pro-fessional spectators who always crawl out of the woodwork to watch anything faintly unusual. Clearly, I had arrived just in time.

Behind this came a dark red Lancia Lambda, like a huge bath on wheels, and then something else I wasn't sure about, also open, with a Grebel searchlight by the passenger's door, possibly put there by a former owner – I guessed a maha-rajah or other Indian princeling – to facilitate the dispatch of tigers on shikar. These characters didn't need tigers in their tanks; they preferred them in their sights.

An Englishman in a sports jacket, with a blue, official-looking band around one arm, was waving the cars on their way, and ticking off names and numbers on a typed sheet clipped to a board. He had a fancy striped tie. If I'd been smart, I'd have found out what school he went to, and bought the same tie myself; but if I were that smart, I'd also be rich.

'Excuse me,' I began.

'Please,' he said, frowning at the interruption. 'If you're the Press, I'll see you in a moment.'

'I'm not. Just an enthusiast. I was wondering who took over Tom Ruper's place?'

'Tom Ruper?' He glanced down the list. 'A Mr Woodward.'

'What car is he in?' I asked.

'Doesn't say. Ruper was bringing a Clyno, if he'd come.'

'Any Mercedes going through?'

'One,' he said. 'But he's on his own. Not with us.'

He turned away to wave at the driver of an Alfa, who gave him a cheerful 'V' sign in response. The cars all glittered with polished paint and nickel. The older ones among them wore polythene bags around their silver-plated headlamps to protect them from scratches or flying stones. Some went by in silence, a dignified feather of smoke at their exhausts; others, in jerks that spoke of straight-cut gears; still others, with a purr from twelve-inch fish-tails.

I almost wished I was on the rally myself, for I really like the cars I sell. In fact, sometimes I like them so much I can hardly bear to sell them. Paradoxically, the other side of me wished I could get my hands on them professionally; with that lot, I could have retired. I was lost in a dream of admiration and envy, which is as good a basis for dreams as anything else.

Then I felt a hand grabbing my arm. I thought at first it must be a creditor, for I was so engrossed watching the cars going past I had forgotten all about Sara. She nodded towards the next car coming up the ramp from the ship to the customs post. My heart gave a small thud; it was a Mercedes 540K. It appeared – as I would have said in my advertisement – immaculate. It was exactly the same model as the one I had seen in Mrs Meredith's garage – but was it the same car? That had been red; this was white, the German racing colour.

Under the hard Spanish sun, the plating and the paint shone like jewels. A man sat at the wheel. He wore a fawn alpaca jacket, wash-leather gloves, dark glasses, and a white leather helmet of the sort that used to be the fashion at Brooklands before the war.

He glanced from side to side, supremely confident; others might think they had the best car in the rally. He knew he had. Then, with a bellow from the exhaust about as wide as a chimney pot, he was through and away. The huge, eared hubs revolving slowly in the centres of the giant wheels. What a car! But – whose?

The registration number was different, so was the colour: the only thing the same was its make. My first instinct was to follow it, but this was impossible, for the cars were running in line, nose to tail, through the narrow streets, and I couldn't squeeze in between any of them.

I should have shouted or waved to the driver, but I was so amazed at seeing the car that I just stood there like any other gaper and let the moment go. I waited until all the cars had passed and saw the secretary climbing into an old Humber, one of those with the Weymann body, which have a tiny skylight about four inches square in the roof to let out the heat. It didn't seem all that successful. His face was incandescent.

'Is that Mr Woodward in the white five-forty?' I asked him.

He focused his eyes on me without any pleasure.

'You again,' he said. 'Why are you so keen on it? I don't know whether it is or not. I don't know him at all. I told you, the car's not on the rally anyhow. Must be coming for the ride. We always have one or two like that.'

He wiped a speck of dust or a fly out of his right eye. The heat was telling on him, I thought. He must be drowning in his own sweat inside that herringbone jacket. It was suitable for the Scottish moors, or to wear while staring up a ghillie's backside, fishing on the Dee, but ludicrous in this heat and dust.

'Well, that's that then,' I told him, because he was obviously so involved with problems of his own that he couldn't spare time for mine.

I went back to the SS. Sara was already in her seat, a map unfolded on her knees.

'Do you know where the rally cars are heading?' she asked me.

I didn't. I should have asked. All I knew was that they were heading in the general direction of the sun. I would have to follow them until they all stopped and I could ask the secretary. The road through Bilbao was so narrow that I couldn't pass any of them, but, equally, neither could the driver of the Mercedes.

Old houses, all dusty concrete and faded brown paint, leaned across the road, over deep, wide gutters. Their front doors had ancient knockers, shaped like hands, with a ring on the little finger. The air felt gritty with coal dust, sour with the smell of gas. Everything seemed old and rusty; even the trees grouped around a square had nobbles in their trunks, like arthritic joints.

We passed a stream of girls on their way up the hill to school, and a stream of boys in grey short trousers and white socks, coming down. The road bent and turned as though it hated the hill, and some of the older cars were breathing hard on the incline, and didn't like it, either; the crunch of tortured gears echoed back from leaning walls. On the left lay the sea, and on the right a deep gorge with a river at the bottom pouring itself sluggishly over masses of orange mud. Pink blossoms fluttered from the trees.

I hadn't much time to note all this, because the cars ahead were bunching up, and my own SS was growing a bit warm at all the slow running. I watched apprehensively as the temperature-gauge needle climbed up the dial, but just as it crossed the 200°F mark, the hill flattened out and the cars ahead began to go faster.

The town suddenly fell away, and its smoke and grime were behind us. Ahead, the road lay straight as a fallen arrow across the open country; empty, save for our convoy. Huge advertisements sprouted out of fields: a giant black bull in silhouette; the blue-and-white Pegaso horse; the injunction, Beba Fanta.

We trundled on; I couldn't see much pleasure myself in this sort of run, just jogging through a rather drab country. I prefer some sort of definite excursion to the vineyards of France, the taverns of Alsatia, a trip where the wine is so cold it puts a mist on the glass, where they cook the lobster with saffron and the girls look at you as though they know you've not just got it to pee with.

This was all a bit proper and dull, and life is too short for any of it to be wasted in dullness.

I was thinking about all this, easing my weight from one cheek of my bottom to the other, for the SS seats felt as hard as sitting on a marble slab, when I saw tail-lights flicker towards the head of the column. I didn't have to be a senior wrangler to realize we were stopping; no doubt some thimble bladder up there was bursting.

If he was, he didn't tell me, because just around the corner the cars were pulling off the road into the car park of a restaurant. The flags of half a dozen countries flapped from white posts; behind them stood a long low building with green trelliswork on its walls, and behind that, the grey bald rock of the foothills. The secretary was marshalling the cars in rows, but the Mercedes was not among them. Ergo, he must still be ahead, on his own. I waved to the secretary for want of anything better to do and accelerated along the road, empty now except for a couple of lorries coming towards me.

There's no seventy-mile-an-hour limit in Spain, thank goodness, and I turned up the wick as far as it would go; ninety-five in this case. This wasn't much, I know, but it was the best the car would do on the rising incline, and, as things turned out, it was enough.

The road burned on across the plain, banked up with soft

reddish earth on either side. Ahead, over the folds of distant hills, we could see it rising and falling, merging into the green horizon. Maybe the Romans had been here, to build it so straight; I wished I'd paid more attention to my history lessons as a boy.

The cornfields on either side were bleached pale as a blonde's tail feathers. I was brooding on the colour of various tail feathers and the whys and wherefores of it all, for if you want to know the natural colour of a woman's hair, look at her eyebrows – which she nearly always forgets to dye. If you doubt me, prove it for yourself.

We came up behind a MAN lorry, high as a haystack, and we were so low on the ground that I was grateful for the green light, on the left-hand side, that the driver flashed to show us we could pass. The sun felt warm on my face; life seemed very pleasant. And then, as we accelerated away from the lorry, I saw a white dot, miles ahead. The Mercedes.

He was driving fairly fast, but his car was so heavy that it would be far easier to control than mine, which leapt about like an itching grasshopper. Even so, he hadn't much time to look about him, and was obviously not keeping a watch in his mirror.

I came up within fifty yards of the Mercedes' tail and blew my horns. He swerved to the right in the dust at the side of the road, and then back out into the middle.

Now I saw his head turn, and I waved. If he saw me, he took no notice. I blew my horns again and flashed the headlights. His response was to move towards the middle of the road so that it was impossible to pass him. I might have risked it in something modern, but not on the SS cartsprings. If I put a front wheel on the soft shoulder at the side, I was afraid I might somersault. Also, up ahead of us I saw some Spaniards jogging along on the backsides of donkeys and I daren't risk it.

I dropped down a gear and wound up the engine to four thousand revs so that when or if I could see fifty yards clear ahead, I'd pass him, or at least draw level and persuade him to stop. I began to edge up on his left. Then a big Saurer lorry swung towards me and was past, horns blaring, the driver waving his fist out of the window at me. I sympathized with him.

The Mercedes driver glanced sideways and saw how close behind him I was. I must have been much closer than he realized, for he leaned forward, and then the exhaust pipe sprouted a white beard of smoke and the high scream of his supercharger cut into the thrash of our engines like a whip.

I had dropped down to third, and doing eighty, but for all practical purposes I was alone. The Mercedes was already five hundred yards ahead and still accelerating, its rear tyres painting black rubber lines on the road. I slipped back into top and the revs fell. I couldn't match his speed, but then the supercharger on that model was only intended for sudden spurts of acceleration, and he couldn't hold it for long. The crankshaft just wouldn't stand up to that treatment; the con rods would start making holes in the sump. I could still catch him if this happened.

The road now began to turn and dip and the hills fled away. Shepherds wearing dyed furs on their backs against the wind stared at us in amazement. Their flocks, terrified at the noise, blundered blindly into longer grass.

My wrists felt as though they had been beaten with hammers, holding the jerking steering wheel. I realized I was also holding my breath. I don't like pushing an old car or myself to the limit, so I let out my breath and eased my foot off the accelerator; there was no point in killing ourselves.

'Do you think it's the car?' I asked Sara, when we could hear each other speak.

She shrugged her shoulders.

'You said it was red.'

'Maybe it's been repainted,' I said. 'But if it isn't the one, why the hell should he act like this? Why can't he stop?'

'Perhaps he thinks you're just playing boy racers.'

The Mercedes grew smaller and smaller, miles in front of us. Then it overtook a string of lorries running together and was away.

We passed houses perched on hilltops, and peasants carrying bundles of wood, who stood by the roadside patiently until we had gone. Ageless women with, no doubt, rose-red titties, half as old as time, shielded their faces under black head coverings until our dust had settled. Statues stared stonily at us from village shrines; and once, an eagle, great wings extended, soared above us, so close that I could see individual feathers sticking out from its wings like fingers. We overhauled a train pulling a hundred yards of trucks, and then another, pulling only itself. And then we came to a village with three main roads running out from its centre. I slowed to a fast walk.

'Where now?' asked Sara.

'Depends on your money,' I told her.

'I have enough,' she replied.

'Well, that's something,' I said. In fact, it was the only thing I could think of to say, which shows the state of my mind; I felt diabolically tired. 'Do we call it a day?'

'Do you want to?' she asked me.

'My wants and needs are simple,' I told her. 'Three meals a day, a bed at night, a bit of this and that if one can find it. Presumably one can. The Lord is often good to His followers.'

'I hope you're a follower, then,' she said, 'because I want to find that car.'

'It's probably the wrong car,' I said.

'Give it two more days,' she said suddenly, as though making up her mind. 'And if we don't come up with something then, it's back to Biarritz and home. OK?'

'OK,' I said, but it wasn't really OK. Not entirely. 'What about my two-fifty iron men?'

I felt mean asking her the question, but then if I didn't, no one else would. It wasn't her fault that I'd lost the money, but then it wasn't mine, either.

'Don't you insure against bad debts?' she asked me.

'In the used-car business?' I asked incredulously. 'Think again.'

She thought again.

'Let's discuss that at the end of the two days,' she said. 'If we don't come up with something. Meanwhile, I'll pay everything else.'

'You've got a deal,' I said. It wasn't much of a deal, but at least I was covering my losses with regard to food. And if we had no luck with the Mercedes, or if it turned out to be a different car, I might still sell the SS, or even find something else to buy. Also, if I couldn't lay Sara in two days (with two nights attached to them), I only deserved to sell new cars and not old ones.

We drove through the village, keeping to the main Burgos road, for this led to the largest town. The scenery was bleak at first, but then the empty grass spaces on both sides of the road began to fill with olive trees, thousands and thousands of them, all in rows.

Ahead of us, a lorry pulled out of a grove of these trees, laden down to its old flat springs with twigs and branches, looking like an enormous hedgehog weaving along the road. I flicked my lights, blew my horn, trying to pass, but the driver could obviously hear nothing and see less. I might be behind this for thirty or forty miles, unless he turned off. The only thing was to turn this hold up to my own advantage, and let him go. I kept on for about ten miles until I saw a suitable place to stop, then pulled to the right of the road under some trees, switched off the engine and climbed thankfully out of the car. It was bliss to stretch my legs and arms and straighten my back; I felt like the model for Rodin's Thinker, all hunched up permanently. After the boom of the exhaust and the roar of the wind, the only sound was the fading beat of the lorry's engine. It is extraordinary how peaceful silence can be, and yet, in England, even in the so-called countryside, a couple of trees away you're almost certain to find a new town or a motorway or the bulldozers carving away at the earth for a housing estate. And even if you escape all that, you can never really escape from the airliners. In the west, they start to come down from the sky for London airport before they reach Bristol. From the north, they're beginning to lose height somewhere over the Orkneys, so how can you ever get away?

Deep inside the olive plantation, perhaps a quarter of a mile away, a shepherd, wearing a coat of sheepskin dyed brown, squatted on a tree stump, while sheep tore hungrily at the scrubby grass.

I glanced at my watch: one o'clock. We would have to find somewhere soon for lunch. A car came along the road, going north, spoiling the silence. It was a little Renault, with the driver in shirt sleeves, probably a commercial traveller. I stood and stared at it, as though it had no right to be there. Then a donkey cart clip-clopped past, and behind that, in the distance, growing louder, I heard the groan of an old-fashioned engine finding the hill an ordeal.

Sara climbed out, and disappeared into the bushes to have a slash. It always amazes me how women out in the country walk so far away, continually stopping and looking over their shoulder to see if they're observed. They overdo the modesty chat a bit, I think. I peed against a tree and the shepherd looked at me, a bit surprised. Maybe he thought I was being unnecessarily modest, too.

I was doing up my fly, trying not to look too obviously in the direction Sara had taken, when the bus I had seen coming off the boat, the Charter Home thing, crawled over the rim of the hill behind us.

Bloody awful to be blind, I thought, imagining those kids in their hot private world of night behind those shades on the windows. The old cocktail-party argument about whether it is worse to be blind or deaf never swayed me; I'd shoot myself if I knew I was going blind. I simply wouldn't have the courage to keep on living.

I watched the bus grow larger. The right indicator light began to flicker, and the driver pulled off the road under the trees about a hundred yards behind us. Driving that old AEC, some throw-out from a beat-up provincial bus company thirty years ago, must be very hard labour. I could imagine the heat in the cab, the sickening smell of burning oil, the aching arms after holding that unpowered steering on a reverse camber. Sara came back through the bushes. I lit two cigarettes and handed one to her.

The driver was climbing out of the cab behind me, flexing his arms, running his hands through his thick hair. He was in his shirt sleeves. He wiped his face with his handkerchief, glanced at himself in the big outside mirror and then began to walk towards me. Damn this, I thought. What the hell does he want? This was as bad as having a picnic on the Brighton road; a shepherd watching us from a tree stump, now a driver with a busload of blind children wanting to get into the act. He was short, but very broadly built, with a pleasant, country sort of face; it wasn't hard to imagine him in a blacksmith shop or driving a tractor somewhere in the Shires, wrapped up in sacks against the rain.

'Afternoon,' he said, cheerfully.

'Afternoon,' I replied. After all, this didn't commit me to anything.

'Wonder if you could help me for a moment?' he went on. 'I've a bolt loose under the driving seat and it's murder. Got to keep bracing myself against the door all the time. I asked a couple of people parked a mile back up the road, but they're in modern cars and the only tools they carry are bits of bent tin they think are spanners. In this vintage thing, I should think you've got a King Dick adjustable, haven't you?'

'I have,' I said, thinking how old George would rhyme King Dick.

'Thought I had myself,' the man went on glancing at Sara and nodding to her. 'Someone must have swiped it back at the garage. I don't like to intrude, but if you could spare me a minute to hold the bolt-head while I tighten the nut...' He paused.

'Sure,' I said. This was little enough to ask, and I might break down myself any time and be glad of someone else's help.

I lifted up the front seat, took out a couple of King Dick adjustables, replaced the seat, slipped the ignition key on to my metal key chain, and we all walked towards the coach.

The sun felt much hotter now, beating down through the feathery leaves of the olive trees. The burnt grass beneath them stretched away into a hazy infinity. Everything seemed unbelievably quiet; even the sheep weren't baaing. I remembered George's definition of a virgin sheep – one that runs faster than the shepherd.

We might have been a thousand miles from anywhere. The world could have stopped turning; probably the spring was running down.

'You weren't on the boat with the other old cars, then?' the man asked me.

'No,' I said. Then I asked whether he'd seen the white Mercedes.

He nodded.

'Lovely job. Good-looking bloke had it. Not with the other crowd, either.'

'Didn't know where he was going, I suppose?'

He shook his head; he obviously wasn't interested.

We reached the bus, and the driver opened the cab door.

'Now, where's that loose nut?' I asked, opening the jaws of the spanner.

'I'll show you.'

I followed him up into the cab, which felt as hot as I had imagined it would. He had a route map clipped to the spokes of the steering wheel and a vase of plastic flowers held by a sucker on the windscreen, next to another holding a packet of Senior Service on a wire clip. A canvas roll-up curtain screened the cab from the rest of the bus.

He moved over to the passenger seat, and then bent down.

'Here,' he said, pointing to a loose bolt-head with a circle of rust around it, under the driver's seat. It didn't look like a Whitworth, but was possibly an American or even a metric size. No wonder he needed an adjustable spanner. I pushed the seat, and it slid round for two or three inches; it must have been murder driving with it like that.

'If you can get your spanner on that bolt, I'll get mine underneath,' he said.

I bent down under the steering wheel as he climbed out of the passenger door.

'Shout when it's tight,' he called from somewhere beneath the floor. I heard him move about under the bus, then the tap of his spanner on metal. The bolt-head moved as he gripped the nut with his spanner.

I tightened mine on the bolt, and held it firm.

'Now!' I shouted. I felt the bolt move against my spanner as he began to turn the nut, and suddenly the whole world exploded into light. Then came darkness and a long valley of almost unbearable pain. Then I felt nothing, nothing at all.

I swam back wearily between shimmering layers of light and darkness, like a fish surfacing through a deep-green sun-striped sea. I opened my eyes. I wasn't underwater, I was lying on my back, on something rough, and my fingers felt canvas at their tips.

I moved my head, and it almost fell off my body, so I moved it more slowly and saw I was lying on a dirty, grey canvas stretcher. What the hell had happened? Had I been in an accident?

I closed my eyes for a moment and tried to wind my mind back like a clock, but the springs felt rusty and the key was loose. I vaguely remembered a man walking across the grass under the olive trees and asking me for a spanner. I wondered whether he had hit me with my own spanner, which was ironic. No, he couldn't have done, because I had been holding it myself: I could see the rusty bolt as clearly as if I was still holding it. And the man who had asked me to help him had been under the bus when *someone* had hit me – so it couldn't have been him.

Who was it, then? Sara? I glanced down towards my feet and again my head lifted a few inches. A strap was buckled across my chest holding my arms to my sides. I tried to move my feet but they were strapped above the ankles. We were bumping along in semi-darkness, the air heavy with the smell of oil and petrol.

I was in the bus, of course; the blinds were pulled down. That acounted for the semi-darkness.

I moved my head slowly to the right. It was inches away from a damned great tyre stamped Engelbert, but this had nothing to do with Humperdinck; it was only the make of the tyre. I moved my head round another half-inch and saw the gigantic eared hubcap, the cylindrical balance weights on the spokes, the three-pointed star in the centre. Of course, the Mercedes. I had found it – or perhaps it would be more accurate to say that it had found me.

From where I lay I could see the white overspray of paint under the vast curved wing. The painter must have worked in a great hurry or he would have masked it better, but if this was the car I sought, he would have had to work against the clock. The bus creaked and bumped and once, on the overrun, the exhaust backfired angrily beneath me.

I moved under my straps, and turned as much as I could on to my right side, peering between the huge chassis member and the floor, to the other side of the bus. Sara lay on a smaller stretcher, tied like me. Something like relief flooded through me; at least she hadn't hit me.

So who the devil had?

I shouted: 'Hoy!'

It wasn't a very good thing to shout, because the top of my head again lifted six inches and then came down slowly, like a flying saucer landing.

About four feet above me, the man who had asked me for the spanner said, 'So you're awake, are you, buster?' His voice didn't sound friendly now; it sounded contemptuous.

I swivelled my head round slowly, until I could see his shoulders above the back of the cheap rexine seat. I watched his face looking at me in the driving mirror. I didn't like his face. If he hadn't hit me, then, no doubt, he knew who had.

He grinned at me, maybe guessing my thoughts. His teeth, even in the driving mirror, were yellow, uneven stumps. I would be doing him a favour if I knocked a few out, I thought. I'm not the sort of nut to stand aside from doing anyone a favour like that.

I said nothing.

'We want to talk with you, you bastard,' he went on. 'You and the girl.'

'Who's we?' I asked.

'Me and my friend,' he said, and, watching in the driving mirror, I saw his eyes flicker momentarily to whoever was in the other front seat. From where I lay I couldn't even see the back of that seat, let alone who was sitting there.

'What about?' I asked. 'And what the hell do you mean by kidnapping us in this way? Who are you?'

'You'll know,' he said.

'So will you when I get free,' I told him. 'You've got a bloody sauce. You ask for help, and then you knock me out and kidnap us. What do you expect – a ransom? Who do you think I am? A millionaire?'

'Don't give me all that aggrieved crap,' he said. 'Why were you following us?'

'Why did you steal this Mercedes?' I countered.

'So you recognized it?'

'It's a different colour,' I said. 'But I guessed it might be the same car. Now, I know.'

'What do you know about it?' he asked.

'Nothing, except there's two-fifty quid of mine on it. It's mine.'

'Why are you so keen on having it?'

'It's my living, that's why. Any more questions?'

'Plenty, but they'll wait.'

'For what?'

'Until we reach a place where we can stop and get some straight answers. That's what.'

I lay back on the stretcher; there wasn't much else I could do. Also, it was more comfortable lying than trying to sit up. I glanced about for some sort of weapon but, even if I found one, I wasn't very well placed to use it with my hands at my sides. And I didn't find one; I couldn't see my spanner, and there was no wrench or crowbar that always seems to be so conveniently lying about in fiction, but never in fact.

The only weapon I had was what George would call my Dirty Dick, and right now, even this seemed out of place, which shows you how lousy I was feeling. I felt so low that a snake could have walked under me with a top hat on and I wouldn't even have noticed the movement.

If this was a book or a film, I thought wearily, I'd have had a knife sewn in the seam of my trouser leg, and then I could snip the strap and let it lie across my legs so that the driver wouldn't realize it had been cut.

I would then lever my feet out of the bottom strap, and with one enormous leap, clobber the driver on the loaf of bread and leap smartly out, pausing only to run a light finger or two over Sara's sweater as I freed her, too. But this wasn't fantasy, this was fact. And that made a difference, for I had no knife. Also, I felt like death. The only thing fusing fact to fantasy was that I wanted to clobber the driver. I put my right hand in my trouser pocket, my mind miles away on these mad schemes.

'Don't try anything, buster,' warned the driver over his shoulder. 'Big brother's watching you.'

'I want a handkerchief,' I said. 'My nose is bleeding.' It wasn't, but it felt as though it might – and who was this crud-cutter to tell me what to do? I pulled out my handkerchief, but I couldn't reach my nose with it because of the straps. This was a lot of no good. I slithered down the stretcher a couple of inches until the top strap was above my elbows. The driver glanced back at me again.

'Just stay where you are,' he advised. 'Let your nose bleed. It'll get a bit of practice for the main event.'

I looked up at the roof; a plaque had stamped on it: 'Tom Ruper, general dealer, cars transported, bought, sold, broken up'. That about covered his activities, I thought. I also thought that the driver might be Mr Woodward, so I asked him.

'Woodward?' he repeated, and grinned. 'Who's he?'

I pushed my handkerchief back into my right-hand trouser pocket, because I couldn't reach my nose with it, for all my squirming around. I didn't like the look of things, the feel of things, or the prospect of things.

I'm no hero. If I were, I would have been wearing a midget transmitter in a bootlace that could send messages out to half a dozen colleagues ahead of us, who would set up a roadblock. I'm not, so I did nothing.

My right hand was still in my trouser pocket, so I began to feel for anything remotely useful to me, and don't let's have any smart gags, either. The results were not immediately encouraging. Three keys on a ring with a bright metal tag bearing the SS number, joined by a flexible gold-plated chain about eighteen inches long to a button on my belt loop; a small felt-tipped flow pen, and an old, thin sixpence I use as a screwdriver on electrical circuits, or to fool parking meters. It's just the right thickness to operate the mechanism and then drop out of the rejected coin slot. I know, for I filed it flat myself. With such meagre equipment for escape, even Houdini would have handed in his cards.

I lay with my eyes open, looking at the pattern of light flicker on the roof as the bus bumped over the road. The old blinds rattled against the windows. Well, at least I'd discovered how the Mercedes had disappeared so completely from Grange House. This bus, converted by Ruper into a car transporter, must have been hidden round the corner at the end of the lane. The handsome man who had driven the Mercedes out of its garage must have run it up a ramp into the back of the bus.

You can always see at least half a dozen of these buses converted into transporters at any vintage-car meeting at Silverstone. Sara and I were on the stretchers that the mechanics or the owner used as beds by the side of their cars, after they'd prepared them for the next day's racing. The idea of labelling the bus as an outing for blind children provided a perfect excuse for pulling down the curtains, and would also gain sympathy for the driver and his companion on the journey.

I didn't like the prospect of the discussion the driver promised me, for what had we to discuss? I knew nothing about the Mercedes except that I wanted to shift it at a profit. I looked across it, under the chassis, towards Sara. She was lying on her side, looking at me. The thought crossed my mind that it would be rather fun to try it like that, sideways, on a narrow stretcher in a dim light, bumping along the road. What would add to the zest would be to know the driver was aware what you were up to, but would be going berserk with the knowledge, for he still had to keep driving, both hands on the wheel. But what use are thoughts when you need action?

'How are you?' I asked her.

'I'm all right,' she replied in a very small voice.

'Well, that's more than I am,' I replied. 'These buggers been knocking you about?'

'No. Not really. And you? How are you?'

'Terrible,' I said, but an idea was just beginning to sprout like a tentative bean shoot in my mind. Montaigne once wrote that adversity is the time for philosophy, and I wouldn't quarrel with that viewpoint, if you mean to be done and let everyone walk over you. But if you want to get up and out from under, you've got to do more than philosophize! you've got to act.

I've told you, I always thought of myself as a natural actor, but someone would have to write me a script here – unless I wrote my own. I had to make do with what I'd got. And what I'd got, I thought now, was a chance, small and thin, but there. I had realized this when I was looking across at Sara and saw the white earth wire from the horn relay that George had taped to the chassis.

'I wonder what's happening about the old SS?' I asked her, to keep some sort of conversation going. At the same time, I pushed the cap off my flow pen, held the body of the pen in my palm and took it out of my pocket. While I did this, I kept looking at Sara, holding her eyes with mine, trying to will her to look down towards my hand. I moved my head very slightly. I saw her eyes move, too. With the end of the pen I wrote as best I could on the side of my new Dacron trousers one word: *Shout*.

Her eyes moved back to mine; she raised her eyebrows questioningly. Did I mean she was to shout now? I shook my head carefully. She hadn't answered my question about the SS car. So I asked it again. I cleared my throat, which had suddenly gone very dry; and my tongue seemed to fill my mouth like foam rubber.

If this failed, everything failed. I had to be sure of my timing, for there wouldn't be a chance of a second attempt. It was all or nothing, now or never. The clichés in my mind multiplied, and, with them, my fears.

I lay back with my shoulder blades pressed down against the canvas of the stretcher, waiting for the slight slope of the springs, for the angle of the floor to change, that would tell me the bus was going into a corner, when the driver would have least time to glance in the mirror at me, for he'd be using all his energy to keep the front wheels on the hard centre of the road.

I saw his left shoulder droop and the note of the engine rise slightly as he eased out the clutch. As he slammed the gear lever into third, the whole bus trembled. This was it.

I said to Sara in a voice I didn't recognize: 'I wonder what's happened to it – *now?*'

She picked up her cue and screamed.

'*Yaahh!*'

In that same moment, I pulled the key ring from my pocket, jabbed the metal number tag against the white-covered wire from the horn relay, and sawed furiously.

Someone in the passenger seat was shouting something against Sara's screams, and against the rising roar of the engine as the bus went into the corner. It lurched slightly to the left and right, and then my tag cut through the thin plastic insulation of the wire and gouged a scratch on to the chassis. The circuit was complete, and the points of the relay switch clicked together.

Then the brass-lunged blast of the three-foot Stentor horns on either side of the Mercedes' radiator drowned out all other noise.

'What the hell?' shouted the driver hoarsely, without finishing the sentence. The unexpected bellow of these horns literally only two inches from his ears, had destroyed his concentration. From his situation, it must have sounded like all of Herb Alpert's Tijuana Brass.

His grip on the wheel slackened momentarily, and halfway round the corner the bus reared on its springs like a bucking stallion. My fingers tore as quickly as ten blunt thumbs at the buckle on the belt around my chest, and when that was open, at the one around my ankles. And then I was up, steadying myself against the white bonnet of the Mercedes with my left hand as the bus lurched and the tyres squealed on the bend.

Against the bucking of the bus and the thresh of gears, the driver had no chance to stop me. He crouched over the old-fashioned, bakelite-covered, four-spoke steering wheel, for we were halfway through the S-bend.

Through the windscreen, over his hunched back, I saw the road narrow and flat and grey, and on either side a strip of yellow earth, and then a drop of several more feet to the flat green plain. I also saw his head, vulnerable under its hair as a naked egg.

For a second, I watched it. I enjoyed that second; it should have been longer, for there is something in revenge that is sweeter than rich wine, something elemental and supremely satisfying. Then I brought my left hand across the front of my body and struck the driver a scything blow on the back of his neck at the base of the skull. He fell untidily across the wheel. As he sagged, I gave him another blow just to remember me by, with my right fist on the side of his head, behind the ear. It would clear the wax, I thought.

His right foot jerked out over the accelerator pedal in some nervous reflex, the bus surged forward in low gear on to the soft shoulder of the road, dipped to the right, and then ran gently down the embankment. We ploughed on through the grass and then stopped, the back wheels spinning uselessly in the loose earth.

I put my right forearm around the driver's neck, under his chin, pulled back his head over his shoulder, leaned across him and switched off the ignition. There was no sound from whoever else was in the front seat, which saved me having to deal with him – or, maybe, he with me.

I could see now that another older man with strong shoulders had slumped over the dashboard. The windscreen was divided down the middle. His head had hit the pane in front of him : the glass had splintered into an opaque sheet. I let him lie there; he wouldn't be waking for a while.

I climbed over the Mercedes, released Sara from the buckles. She seemed too dazed to realize what was happening, and after that fanfare from the horns, my ears still rang like bells. I glanced round for a weapon. There was nothing.

'Open the back doors,' I told her. 'We've got to get the car out of here before anyone comes along.'

This was easy enough to do. The doors were unlocked; metal stays obligingly held them wide open. The Mercedes' wheels were in two scooped metal runners, and under the back axle a sliding ramp clipped into the rear of the bus. I didn't know how long I'd have before the two men in the front regained consciousness, or before some other car passed us, but I knew I had to have the Mercedes out before either of these things occurred. I didn't know whether they were being followed, or whether they were on their own, and so I worked like a one-armed paper hanger when the paste is nearly gone.

I kicked away the wooden safety chocks behind the rear wheels, then jumped in the Mercedes' driving seat. The ignition key was in the lock. I switched on, and pressed the starter. The huge engine began to turn, and then fired up, the air intake hissing like an asthmatic serpent. I backed the car down and out on to the grass, and accelerated up the ridge to the hard shoulder, before the wheels could lose traction. Then I turned the car round so that it was facing the other way, and parked it about fifty feet beyond the coach under the olive trees. Anyone coming along would think that we had just stopped on our way north, when we'd seen the accident to the bus travelling south.

Sara seemed to read my mind. She threw the ramp into the bus and shut the back doors. Then I went round to the driver's door and opened it. The driver lay where he had lain minutes earlier; I pulled him out on to the grass. I turned him over on his back, restraining an inclination to kick him in the crotch as I did so. The quality of mercy is not strained, I know, but my feelings were, and so far as I am aware, Shakespeare hadn't been slugged on the head when he wrote that.

It wasn't my innate decency that stopped me, but the fact that I had so little time. The road was almost empty, but I still did not know whether anyone might be following us. Maybe another shepherd was somewhere in the trees, watching us. The forest could be full of eyes.

I felt in the driver's pockets, as I had seen people do in films. He had a small automatic, rather like a starting pistol, in the right-hand pocket of his jacket. I didn't know whether it was loaded or not, so I fired it into a tree to find out. It was loaded, so I put it in my own pocket. Then I stretched him out flat on his back so that it would look to anyone now arriving that I had been trying to bring him round.

I shut the door on his side of the bus, went round to the other side, felt the pulse of the man in the front seat. At least, I tried to feel the pulse, but I wasn't exactly sure where the pulse should be, and I couldn't hear anything with my own heart thumping like an old Knight sleeve-valve engine, out of oil, going up a four-in-one hill.

This wasn't surprising. I'm generally a mild character, but I do hate being tricked. I pulled him out of the door. He fell to the ground because he was too heavy for me to let him down gently, and, let's face it, I didn't try too hard. I shut his door, knelt down beside him, went over his clothes for any weapon. So far as I could discover, he was unarmed.

He was a big fellow, wearing a lightweight summer suit. The backs of his hands were wrinkled and very brown, as though he had lived in the sun for years, yet the skin on his face belied his age. It was smooth and creaseless, the face of a young man. Some tiny splinters of glass had detached themselves from the shattered windscreen pane and stuck like fine diamond fragments in his forehead. Yet, almost unbelievably, he was not cut.

I'd seen him somewhere before, I was sure. The set of his shoulders, the bull-like build of the man; these things were familiar, but not his face.

I lifted up his right eyelid. The eye stared out, seeing nothing. I was suddenly reminded of Mrs Meredith's dead eyes.

The back of my hand was on the skin of his face, and, at the touch, a shudder went down my spine. There was no texture in his flesh, no warmth; it felt as cool and impersonal as plastic.

I opened his shirt collar to give him more air. The grey hairs on his chest, the dark brown, old man's flesh beneath his shirt, contrasted strongly with the pale young smoothness of his neck and face. I could see a line of something that extended around the base of his neck. No wonder his face was unlined and free from all traces of age. It wasn't his face at all.

I looked at Sara.

'He's wearing a mask,' I said.

She said nothing. She just stood, staring at the blank handsome face, as if mesmerized. I took hold of the bottom edge of the mask, where his neck joined his body, and pulled gently. It was beautifully made, of very thin material, either polythene or some plastic compound, tinted like young flesh, yet so fine that some of the colour of his real skin came through. It was easy to move, fine as a balloon when filled with air. I rolled it up over his neck, over his face, or rather what had been the face.

The moustache came with it, so did the perfect nose, the gold-rimmed sunglasses and the two plastic ears which provided an anchor for the spectacles. Beneath, the old skin lay mottled and purple, a mass of surgeon's stitches, of blueish weals and rough fleshy excrescences; a blueprint for a human face rather than the finished product.

There was no nose, only two oval holes, damp and streaked with mucus. His skull lay as smooth and hairless as an ostrich egg; the roots of his hair had apparently been killed with whatever had blown away his face. His right ear had gone completely; the flesh was creased and folded and sewn together; the left was only a thick piece of gristle, pink and somehow obscene.

In addition to being knocked out, kidnapped, plus the reaction to my escape, this was just too much. I stood up shakily, crossed over to the bushes and vomited. I have always hated the sight of blood, especially my own, and although there was no blood here, I coudn't stand this grotesque parody of a face.

After I was sick, I still felt like death, but at least I had discovered something; this must have been the man who had driven the Mercedes out of Grange House. His handsome face had not been the work of nature, but of man – and a pretty expensive piece of work, too.

'He must have been wearing a different mask,' I said to Sara. 'I thought I recognized those shoulders, but not his face. He's probably got half a dozen different masks somewhere.'

'What are we going to do with him now?' asked Sara. 'Will he live?'

I shrugged; would any of us? The question was unanswerable. Everything was only a matter of time. I knelt down by his side again, keeping my eyes deliberately away from the tortured pulp of flesh, and felt his pulse for the second time. There seemed to be some faint throb, or maybe I was imagining it. As I stood up, I heard the beat of an engine far up the road. A grey Volkswagen van was coming towards us. On the impulse, a sort of reflex, a need to get someone else involved, I waved frantically. The driver pulled over to the side of the road, and cut his engine.

He came down the bank towards us. He was a young man with spiky black hair that he kept pushing out of his eyes with his right hand, and a sharp nose, thin as though he'd had it squeezed when he was young. I couldn't speak any Spanish, but he was better educated; he managed some English.

'He is dead?' he asked. 'No?'

'No,' I said. 'Unconscious. Can you get an ambulance?'

His English didn't run that far.

'Please?' he asked again.

Oh, hell. I thought. This is ridiculous. Why hadn't I learned Spanish at school instead of that useless la-plume-de-ma-tante crap from a master who had never even been to France?

He came around the side of the bus, and knelt down by the side of the unconscious man. Then he saw his face and winced and swallowed and turned away. I thought for a moment that he was also going to be sick, but his stomach was stronger than mine.

'We'll have to get him to hospital,' I said.

He understood this. He nodded and stood up quickly, understandably eager to be away. Plastic surgeons may grow used to this sort of thing, but not the rest of us.

'I'll telephone from the next village. It's only two kilometres away.'

'Where's the hospital?' I asked.

'Please?' asked the man again. I had a Spanish phrase book in my car, but that was miles back up the road.

'I will telephone, señor,' he said. 'Will you wait here?' He turned to walk up the embankment, and I suddenly remembered the driver of the bus.

'There's another man,' I began, but I was too late. The Volkswagen engine was already roaring on full throttle. The van reversed smartly, its wheels spraying out a fusillade of stones as the driver accelerated. The Spaniard looked at me in bewilderment.

That bloody driver. I had been so concerned with the passenger, I had forgotten all about him. He must have only been pretending to be unconscious on the grass, on the other side of the bus. I told you, I'd be no good as a cop.

'I'll drive you,' I told the young man, who started to run towards the Mercedes. Then I paused. A motorcycle patrolman in black glasses and crash helmet, peering like a plump Martian through the wide, round windshield on his machine, was slowing down to a stop just by the car. He switched off his engine. The young man began to shout excitedly at him in Spanish, presumably explaining what had happened.

The policeman moved very slowly, like a heavy clockwork man. I almost expected to hear him whirr. He pulled off his gauntlets, laid them down deliberately, one on top of the other, on the black tank of the Sanglas, swung his leg over the saddle, pulled the bike back up on its stand, took off his glasses, put them away in his top pocket, and then came ponderously down the bank towards us, unbuttoning the black flap of his crash helmet. I didn't know what to do, so I made a vague gesture of salute. The policeman could speak English and proved it by speaking some. He listened to what the young man had to say in Spanish with lots of gestures and fingerwork, and then turned to me.

'First, I will radio for an ambulance. And then I would like to ask you some questions. You saw the accident, señor?'

'Not actually *saw* it, officer,' I said, being truthful as ever. 'We arrived here very shortly afterwards.'

Which, to my way of thinking, was also true, or very nearly true.

The policeman looked at me for a long minute; he was nobody's fool. Policemen are like egg sexers; they grow to recognize a bad one straight away. I hoped he wasn't recognizing one in me. He looked inside the driver's cab, and then walked round the bus. It might have been my imagination, but I was wondering whether he was looking for tyre marks. The grass was spongy; none were visible from the Mercedes, at least.

'Your papers, please,' he said to me. 'It is only a formality.'

I hoped it was. I put my hand in my jacket pocket and pulled out the oilskin pouch which contained my passport and international driving licence.

'That is your car?' he asked, jerking his head towards the Mercedes as he handed me back the pouch.

'Yes,' I said. Obviously, it wasn't the district nurse's.

For a moment, a terrible moment, which seemed beyond all normal measurement of time, I thought he was going to ask to see the car's papers; because if he had, I would have been sunk. I didn't know where they were, and in any case, the green card wouldn't have been in my name. But he didn't. After all, the car was pointing the other way, and fifty feet down the road. It wasn't as though we had even been going in the same direction, and I could conceivably have been trying to overtake the coach.

He nodded and walked over to the man on the grass.

'He is English?' he asked.

'I don't know,' I said, and I didn't. 'It's an English bus. Got a GB on the back, anyhow.'

The young man said, 'The man who escaped in my van. Was he driving the bus?'

'Yes,' I said. 'We got him out of the seat. I think he must have banged his head pretty badly.'

I didn't mention my efforts to ensure he'd bang it as hard as I knew how.

The policeman nodded understandingly.

'We'll pick him up. It's probably the shock. Much the same thing happened to my brother-in-law after an accident in Malaga.'

He didn't elaborate about his brother-in-law's accident and I didn't ask. I didn't want to hear about his troubles; I had too many of my own.

I opened the bus door, leaned in behind the passenger seat, pulled out a suitcase.

'This, I think, belongs to him,' I said, nodding towards the man on the ground. The policeman turned over the luggage tag. It was one of those expensive cases with two little plated keys and a little mica window. Through this I read the name and address: Rudolf Kellner, Schloss Urnberg. Hindelang, South Germany. Villa Mataxa, Famagusta, Cyprus.

'You are staying in Spain?' asked the policeman.

'Possibly,' I said. 'For a few days. We're just travelling around.'

'If you are needed as a witness, what hotel will you be at?'

'You have my name,' I reminded him. 'Try the British Embassy, Madrid. I have no fixed plans for hotels here.'

I didn't add that I had no fixed plans for anything, because policemen don't like that sort of remark; it's too near to no fixed abode, which is like being described on a charge sheet as a model or a journalist, which means damn all.

He made a note in a little black notebook and nodded a dismissal to us both.

'I'll give you a lift up the road,' I told the young man.

'Please?' he asked, but this time he got the message, for he climbed into the Mercedes and sat between Sara and me. Speaking frankly, and as I say, why not be frank, for there's no extra charge, I would rather have had Sara's thigh against mine than his, with the possibility of my hand casually resting on it as I changed gear, instead of this character breathing chives at me; but it seemed mean to think thoughts like this about a good Samaritan, and I tried not to. The journey wasn't long, and I don't think we said a word between us. We dropped him off at the next village, outside the post office, and then I beat it back to the SS.

Sarah didn't say anything until we reached the olive grove. The car was standing where I had left it; only the shadows that had swung round it showed the passage of time. I glanced at the instruments; the engine temperature was still a hundred degrees. I felt we had been gone for a lifetime; in fact, we hadn't been away long enough for the engine to cool completely. It all depends how you measure time; by incident, or the hour. I felt in my trouser pocket for the key ring. Sara said suddenly, like a child at a party who has had enough of paper hats and ice-cream cornets, 'I'm not going on with you'.

'Not going on?' I repeated. 'But why not? All we've got to do now is deliver the car to your family friend, and you've done your good turn, and I've made my profit.'

'No,' she said. 'I'm frightened. If we hadn't got away just now, what would have happened?'

'God knows. I'd have been roughed up a bit, I suppose. But why bother with hypothetical events? If the drag link goes on your car at sixty, ten to one you're dead. If a tiny wire, as thick as a hair, shorts in my electric razor, I'm dead. But they haven't yet, touch wood.'

'It's no good. If *you* want to, you go on. Take your profit, but mind you don't pay for it with your life.'

'My life?'

In the late afternoon quietness, with the shadows stretching long dark fingers towards me across the grass, the words had a chill about them I didn't greatly like. My heart jumped as though I'd stepped under a cold shower, which is something I do only rarely.

'What do you mean?'

'What I say.'

'But why kill someone – me, for instance – because of that car? It's bloody ridiculous.'

'Maybe. But that business of the bus, and that awful man without a face, frightened me. Come back to London with me. I'll see you won't lose.'

'How?'

'I'll pay you that two-fifty. And your expenses.'

'It's not enough,' I said, trying to convince myself. 'I'm interested to know why someone wants this car badly enough to steal it, then attempts to carry it across Spain in a bus, then kidnaps us, too, to go along with it. There must be something very special about it. Don't you agree?'

'Yes. And I want no part of it, whatever it is. I simply meant to do an old friend a good turn. And look what's happened so far. His agent in London – killed. The owner of the car – dead. The car itself – stolen, and we're incredibly lucky to be unharmed here now. Enough is enough. Now, are you coming with me?'

'No. I'm delivering the car first. Never a backward glance. Tread swiftly on the heels of him who goes before. That's my family motto – or it should be, if I had one. But if you're serious about going back, you can take the SS, and I'll press on in this great white chariot.'

'I am serious.'

'So it seems. Well, thanks for everything.'

'I haven't given you much.'

'There's still time,' I told her. 'Another time, another place.'

'Where do you want me to leave the SS?'

'My mews. I'll ring George and tell him to expect you.'

'I should be there tomorrow. I'll drive up to Biarritz now and try to get on a plane.'

We shook hands. It seemed all formal and wrong, and if we could have spent the night together, as I'd intended, shaking hands would have been ridiculous and quite unthinkable. She climbed in behind the wheel. I waited until she started the engine and turned out on to the road. She waved once, but she did not look back; maybe the car was so strange that she needed all her concentration.

I watched its little green shape grow smaller and smaller until it took the crest of a hill miles away, and was gone. For a few moments afterwards I still heard the faint beat of the exhaust, and then that died, too, and my ears filled with silence.

I wasn't wholly surprised at her decision; it was only idiocy that kept me there. If I'd had the brain of an ant I'd not only have gone with her, but suggested that we drive into France together and try to find some old cars to buy. But if I had that sort of brain I wouldn't still be working in a mews; I'd own the whole damn block, and the skyscraper on top of it as well.

I lifted the boot lid of the Mercedes. The boot loomed large as a cupboard beneath the stairs. I threw my holdall into its dark mouth, closed the lid, climbed in behind the wheel. The car felt strange and heavy. Before, I'd cursed the cramped cockpit of the SS often enough; now, I missed it.

I started the engine, drove up on to the road. I wanted to get out of the olive grove. Somehow, in the gathering dusk, it didn't look so friendly as in the sunshine.

I'd aim for Salamanca, find a hotel with a lockup garage if I could. Then I'd ring the number I'd taken from Diaz's bill. With luck, and I figured I could use a bit of luck on this deal now, I should be finished by the following evening. Then I'd beat it back to Belgravia like a pigeon homeward bound.

I was ten miles up the road when I saw the ambulance coming towards me, its blue light flashing on the roof.

CHAPTER FIVE

I pulled in to the side of the road to let it go, and sat watching its white outline shrink like a diminishing toy in my driving mirror. Then I switched off the engine, and climbed out of the car.

I opened the bonnet and checked the engine and chassis numbers with those that George had given to me. Then I looked at the oil, because these big old cars can drink the stuff, but the sump was still full, and the oil on the dipstick looked clean. George had done a good job in the time available at Mrs Meredith's house. Remembering her I also recalled her death, and the death of Diaz, and who the hell was the driver of the bus and Kellner, the man without a face, and how were they involved?

I felt like a fly in the middle of a spider's web, or a man lost in Hampton Court Maze. Everywhere I turned was marked No Way Out. The only link between these events was the Mercedes, and the sooner I could shift this the better (and the safer) for me.

One or two cars passed me as I stood there, commercial travellers or doctors on their rounds, and one man in a little van from a grocery store in Salamanca. I supposed they also had their problems, but surely none were so complicated as mine.

I climbed in behind the wheel, and did a quick check with the AA foreign-touring guide, to see where I was, for I'm not one of those people who can tell their whereabouts by the sun; I find it hard enough to do even with a map. However, it wasn't too difficult to discover that, as near as damn-it, I had forty miles to cover to reach Salamanca.

I decided to cover them as quickly as possible, before anything else could go wrong. Then I'd book myself in at any hotel with a garage, because I didn't want to leave the car in the street where it would only gather crowds. Then, after a bath and a meal, I would telephone Salamanca 543541, the number Diaz had rung, and we could take it from there, because there wasn't any other point we could take it from or to.

Salamanca. Until I read the name on the map and the signposts, it had mainly meant to me a special type of body, very popular on Rolls chassis in the late Twenties and early Thirties. The passengers sat under cover in the rear, snug as in a stagecoach, while the hired hands, chauffeur and footman, sat, as of old, up front 'on the box', protected only by a windscreen.

English coachbuilders called this style Sedanca de ville, but the American firm of Brewster, which built lots of these bodies, preferred the title Special Salamanca.

It was special, all right, but some later models, as a reluctant concession to changing times and moods, incorporated a kind of horizontal roller blind that could be unrolled over the servants' heads and so protect them from a direct downpour. Then, his master's voice in the speaking tube by his ear, the chauffeur stoically steered the huge car at its prescribed velocity – for owners in those days frequently fitted dual speedometers, one in their own rear compartment, so that they could personally control any tendency of the driver to 'scorching', or 'furious driving', while not, of course, having to sit by his side. After all, the man *was* a servant.

Incidentally, as a motoring and social footnote, during the depression of the Thirties, when revolution, even by footmen, seemed not impossible and the rich felt ostentation to be unwise, this same fine old firm of Brewster, alive to the needs of the hour, designed their own car on a Ford chassis. The Brewster was cleverly made so that from the outside it appeared ordinary and unlikely to arouse the anger of out-of-works, but inside, ah, inside, it could be as sumptuous as the owner's purse was deep.

Only one thing detracted from the ingenuity of this scheme: the body style chosen was the Salamanca, that remembrance of more spacious, less democratic days, with the driver out in the open as of old, a style that had never appealed to Henry Ford as much as it had to Sir Henry Royce.

It was one of those days in early summer when the air looks luminous, and I experienced a strange feeling of timelessness and unreality as I drove. What was I doing trundling along in a thirty-two-year-old car that didn't belong to me? There must be other ways of earning a living.

I glanced at two horses pulling a wooden plough through a field on my right, at stone Saviours in their roadside shrines and felt I could be living in almost any century; and if I'd had a choice I wouldn't have chosen the twentieth.

In what other century save this, for example, would any reasonably normal red-blooded male be alone with a girl in a foreign land, and almost one hundred per cent certain he was going to get a bit of the other – only to find at the last moment that he wasn't?

Such behaviour was, in my view, against all the laws of God and man; and beast, too, I shouldn't wonder. Yes, most certainly against the laws of beast.

Had Sara decided to go home because she was frightened – or was there some other reason? Could Kellner have warned her off or had she recognized him?

This last possibility didn't make much sense to me, for it would be difficult to recognize anyone with a face so mutilated. On the other hand, she might have recognized his voice in the bus, and I hadn't heard him speak because he hadn't spoken since I regained consciousness. Or perhaps she had just cleared off because she didn't believe in the hereafter, and she'd no intention of letting me have what I was here after? This didn't make any more sense than the other possibilities. But then life is full of oddities. Fact is always infinitely stranger than any fiction, for fiction only holds the mirror to life.

I thought back over some of the odd happenings that friends and I had experienced in the old-car business. I thought of some of David Scott-Moncrieff's stories. As 'purveyor of horseless carriages to the nobility and the gentry since 1927' – and if you doubt me, read his ad in *Motor Sport* for yourself – he is the doyen·of all dealers in rare cars.

After Wellington and an engineering degree at Cambridge, he says that the reason he went into the motor trade was simply self-defence; he saw how little other engineers were paid, and, like Morris, he realized he could always pay himself more than anyone else would pay him.

Indeed, while serving his time as a patternmaker in an engineering works, the foreman told him that, in his opinion, 'all you'll be good for is knocking out knots from deal boards to make arseholes for rocking horses'.

This was not a very accurate prophecy, for David now lives in magnificent style in Staffordshire, with peacocks roosting in derelict Rolls about his four-hundred-acre estate, while I limp along, like the webfooted peasant I am.

Scott-Moncrieff started in our business at a time when gentlemen didn't talk about money; you either had it or you hadn't. If you hadn't it, you married it. His clients in those days were mostly extremely rich – like the Cambridge undergraduate, with an allowance of £1,000 a quarter, who bought a Delage off the stand at the 1932 Motor Show to drive back to his college. On the way, he decided he didn't like the car's colour, so he pulled into the yard of the nearest pub, and deliberately set fire to the Delage. Then he rang Daimler Hire to send a car and a chauffeur to pick him up, and sat quietly drinking until they arrived. Try doing that today and see the grief you'd bring on yourself.

I recalled the occasion when he had bought a hearse from an undertaker, meaning to fit a new, more lively body on the chassis. Then the undertaker chased him halfway across the East End to demand the contents of the hearse which he had omitted to remove, to wit, one coffin, containing one corpse.

The old Rolls was certainly a flyer, and although Scott-Moncrieff had barely two minutes' start, he'd reached Tower Bridge before the man caught him up.

Scott-Moncrieff reminded the undertaker that it had been

definitely agreed that the bargain was that he took the Rolls strictly 'as is', so he refused to hand over the contents.

He didn't quite know what he could get for a second-hand coffin on the open market, but he thought that someone with a macabre sense of humour might give him a good price to use it as a cocktail bar. The corpse would be worth £15 from any teaching hospital for medical students to dissect.

The undertaker was in a great state of anguish at this and declared that it would ruin his business if news ever leaked out he'd sold one of his customers, so Scott-Moncrieff relented and sold him back both coffin and corpse for £15. The late lamented, the former loved one, was then pushed unceremoniously into a Bedford van that smelled strongly of formaldehyde and driven away.

Then there was the day, long ago, when he sold an SSK Mercedes to a ponce, a right Alphonse, as George would describe him. This customer paid him in notes, but was thirty-eight quid short, so he offered him a cheque for this amount. He wasn't the sort of person from whom anyone would accept a cheque, so a deadlock was reached in the deal. Finally, the ponce came up with a solution; he drove the Merc round the beats his various tarts were making, until the £38 deficit was made up.

I thought, too, of some of the odd people I'd known myself in the business. There was the character I'll call Cuthbert, who lives permanently in the South of France, where he is generally regarded as a fine old English gentleman, a sort of present-day C. Aubrey Smith. He keeps two accommodation addresses in London, one near Grosvenor Square, the other off Bond Street. The first is ostensibly a firm that deals in rare and exotic books; the second, apparently, a 'specialist repairer' of Rolls-Royce, Bentley, Jaguar, et al: by appointment to His Grace the Duke of Fornicator, or whoever. At least, that is what appears at the head of his two sets of expensive notepaper.

Cuthbert works for an hour a day reading obituaries in *The Times* and *The Daily Telegraph*. When he finds one for a suffragan bishop or a retired colonial judge, he writes to the executors on his first letterhead and begs to bring to their attention the fact that his late lordship had neglected to settle a bill of £53 5s in respect of certain erotic and obscene books and pictures. Nine times out of ten, the executors pay up at once and destroy his bill, lest the news of the bishop's foibles should become public, and his dear lady wife (who's rising a hundred and four, has tits like strops and a guardsman's moustache) should suffer pain. Which is jolly decent of them; decent, but dumb.

The tenth time, however, a sharp-eyed lawyer may remember that he has seen a similar bill addressed to a general's estate he wound up only months before. And he replies tartly that there must have been a mistake, because the bishop had been blind for the last five years of his life.

A rebuff like this would make a lesser character than Cuthbert fall about, but he simply sends a second letter with a different signature on the other notepaper of his non-existent car company. In this, he begs to bring to the notice of the executors that the sum of £103 14s 10d is still outstanding for the specialist work done on the bishop's Silver Wraith. Obviously, the executors think this must have been overlooked and a cheque arrives within a matter of days.

Then there was the Indian maharajah who ordered a special body to be built on a Phantom III chassis, which eventually passed through my hands. He kept visiting the coachbuilders almost daily, suggesting continual alterations and modifications: opera lights on each side; a glass roof; mother-of-pearl inlays; gold handles and so on. The result was a coach-built abortion, so vast, so flamboyant, and in such execrable taste that the managing director of the coach-building company decided to deliver the car to the maharajah himself, in case he shared his horror at the result, and refused to accept it.

But not so. The maharajah was as delighted as a child with a new and expensive toy, and over a magnum of champagne in his suite at the Savoy, he explained that he would not wish to see another similar car on the road.

The managing director readily agreed, although for different reasons.

'Then,' replied the maharajah, 'I would be obliged if you would ensure that the designer does not live too long, *in case* he decides to make another.'

The managing director bowed understandingly.

'This has already been taken care of, Your Highness,' he assured him blandly, and poured out more champagne.

When the bill was delivered by messenger the following day, the seventeen pages of modifications had one additional paragraph: 'Item: To bow string, for designer's throat . . . 90 guineas.'

The messenger returned with the maharajah's cheque.

Behind each great man there is supposed to be a woman, pushing him along, and behind each great car that's ever been through my hands, there's an odd story, but, even so, I'd never been involved in anything like the succession of events surrounding this Mercedes. The more I thought about it, the stranger it seemed.

A girl asked me to sell a car that wasn't hers, to a family friend whose name she wouldn't tell me. I was to use an intermediary for this, but then the intermediary was found dead, so was the woman who owned the car, and here I was, out-of-pocket, out-of-mind (because no one with any sense would get involved this far), driving through Spain to an address I didn't know, in the only car of its type left this side of the Atlantic – and which wasn't really mine to drive. How would this story sound to a jury of retired tobacconists and counting-house clerks? I shuddered at the idea and tried to think of beautiful things, like girls with long legs, and mini-skirts barely an inch below see level.

I was coming into Salamanca now, anyway, and the time for thought was passing. The telegraph poles at the roadside had single 'T' pieces on top, like the cross on which Christ died, and the shepherds in the fields wore woollen helmets against the driving wind. Outside some houses, with white walls and blue-edged doors, several sheepskins, dyed red and blue, were hanging up to dry in the afternoon sun.

I picked the easiest hotel to find, the Monterrey. A porter was opening the car door even before the car stopped, and he guided me into an underground garage farther down the street. This garage was dark and smelled of exhaust smoke, but not to worry, I wasn't to stay there; only the car. I parked in the farthest corner, rolled up the roof, locked the doors, took out my bag and followed the porter back to the hotel.

The tourist season hadn't properly begun, so I booked a room easily enough, and a bathroom just as big, with huge bath and old-fashioned nickel taps. I ran a bath and shaved, took a couple of Alka-Seltzer to steady my head after all it had been through, physically and mentally, rang room service for a bottle of Fundador, because I always like the wine of the country: Coke in the States, beer in Germany, brandy or sherry in Spain. Then I lay on the bed, thinking. That's an exaggeration, really, for what thoughts I had just chased themselves in and out of the emptiness of my mind, what I call my empty quarter.

But, after a couple of brandies, I felt a little more like a human being, and asked the telephone operator what was the delay to London. She said, hold on, there was no delay. So there I lay on the bed, propped up with pillows, listening to Spanish and French voices, and then an English voice from the international exchange, and then George.

'Hello there, cocko,' I said. 'Where's all the action, then?'

'Action?' he repeated. 'It's as quiet here as a lean and lurch. Church. Only thing, had a couple of Brightons in over that Burney.'

'Brightons?'

I couldn't follow him.

'Yes. Brighton piers. Queers. Said they wanted it for a film. Would we hire it?'

'Of course. On a good deposit, though. And at least twenty quid a day when it's in their hands. Whether they're using it or not.'

I had painful memories of a film company that had hired an old Panhard from me for the same fee. They had kept it for six weeks and then only paid me for two days, because our agreement said in minuscule print that they only paid me for time 'in shot' and the car had only been used in the scenes for two days. Never again.

'You know that bugger, Ruper?' George went on. I knew him. I could still see his plate on the roof of the coach. But I didn't know his sexual interests and I didn't care. He could be a taxidermist, a man who mounts animals, in George's definition, so far as I was concerned, which you can see, wasn't very far.

'Funny thing happened to him the other day.'

I could think of many things that could happen to Ruper, but none of them funny. George went on: 'Apparently, some nutter got his name from some other old-car dealer up West and wanted a car shipped out of the country quickly. Ruper hired him a driver and the bus he uses for transporting his old cars around the country. He was going to take the car out openly in some rally, but had the bus along to whip it inside if need be.

'Anyway, the car they were trying to get out had to be resprayed in a hurry, so the buyer put up at some pub while this was being done. So did Ruper's driver. Next morning, the driver wasn't there, but another driver was. In his place.'

'Why?' I asked, thinking of half a dozen reasons and none of them carrying any comfort. Maybe the first driver had been ill, maybe he'd had bad news, maybe anything. 'Why?'

'Because Ruper's man was tied up like a turkey on his bed. That's why. They didn't discover him until after lunch, when someone went to do his room. He was nearly dead. Half suffocated. And do you know what the car was?'

'I know,' I told George. 'The Mercedes.'

'Well, I'm damned,' said George.

'You will be, later, but right now I've got that same actual, physical car in an hotel garage here in Salamanca.'

'So what do you make of it?'

'It's a hard way to make an easy living,' I said. 'That's what. But, with a bit of luck, and I could use a bit now—'

'You could use a bit *any* time,' interrupted George. 'So could I, I tell you. A real good old-fashioned Colonel Puck.'

'Never confuse business with pleasure,' I told him. 'With a bit of luck, I'll have shifted that Merc tonight, and then I'll catch a plane home. Probably tomorrow.'

'Anything else?' he asked.

'One thing.'

I had almost forgotten about Sara. 'The girl's on her way home in the SS. It's too complicated to explain why here. If she can catch a plane from Biarritz, she'll be back some time tomorrow. Any other news?'

'Yes. Had a Duke of York – talk – with a fellow I met in the pub. Newspaper reporter, from Maidstone. I gave him a spiel that I was an old family friend of Mrs Meredith. He'd got a tip from the slops – cops – that she'd died of a heart attack. Could be natural causes. No sign of violence, anyway.'

'Maybe the character who stole the car frightened her?' I suggested.

'Could be,' said George, and we left it at that because we could do nothing else with it.

'Anything else?'

'Fellow offered me a Delaunay-Belleville. Otherwise, nothing.'

'That could be something,' I agreed, although it wasn't my car. The only Delaunay I'd like was the 70-hp one the Czar of Russia had owned in 1910, which was specially fitted with compressed-air starting – in case a backfire should make His Imperial Highness think he was being shot at by an assassin.

'This call's costing me money,' I said. 'And I can't afford more until I've sold the Merc. One last thing. Stay around this evening, and I'll ring you to let you know how I get on. Ciao.'

I replaced the receiver, drank another Fundador, and looked at my face in the mirror, picked a blackhead and examined my tongue. It was furry as a bear's backside. I pulled down the skin under my eyeballs to see if they were

as yellow as I thought. They were. Then I asked the operator for Salamanca 543541. As I heard the bell ring in my ear
while I waited, I hoped that whoever answered the telephone
could speak English, and that they also wanted the car I
had to sell. What if the number only turned out to be Diaz's
girlfriend, or his wife, now his widow?

A woman's voice answered with a long screed in Spanish,
which I couldn't understand. I let her say her lines, and then
I said, 'I would like to speak to the señor', for presumably
no woman would want to buy a car like this – if, indeed,
anyone did. There was a bit more in Spanish, which I could
just follow; she was explaining that she couldn't speak English. The connexions clicked in my ear.

I said, 'It's about the Mercedes car', and a man's voice
in English, but yet not English, asked: 'What about the
Mercedes car?'

This could be the day, this could be the man. I took a
deep breath, poured myself another brandy. I told you I'd
make a good method actor, and this was my method of
creating the right impression on my audience of one.

'I run Aristo Autos in London,' I explained in my rich,
dark-brown fruitcake, port-wine voice. 'We deal in old cars.
I understand from your agent over there, Mr Diaz, that you
are interested in a 1937 Mercedes two-seater, 540K model?'

A tiny pause in which anyone dropping pins could have
heard them. I hadn't said that Diaz was dead, for it wasn't
for me to pass on bad news and perhaps prejudice the deal.
My business was strictly with the living. The dead had had
their deals.

'Mr Diaz told me on the telephone he had met you,'
agreed the man cautiously. 'You have such a car?'

'Yes.'

'Where is it?'

'Here,' I said. 'In Salamanca.'

'In Salamanca?' he repeated, as though he had to be
sure. 'Where are you speaking from?'

'The Monterrey Hotel.'

'Really.'

Surprise overlaid interest in his voice, like rich veneer over lesser wood.

'Would you like to see the car?' I went on.

'I would be much gratified,' he replied, which made me certain he wasn't English, for no Englishman would use such a phrase, even if he were. The phrase sounded as stilted as that ancient dialogue between client and whore : 'Thank you for having me,' says the client, and, ever polite, the whore replies, 'Thank you for coming'.

'Where can I bring it?' I asked him, freewheeling back to the present.

I would rather see him at his house than try to deal in a corner of an underground garage with a lot of Spaniards looking on, scratching their jacks and picking their teeth and saying olé to each other, or whatever Spaniards do say on such occasions. You have to set the scene. Casanova couldn't do his best unless the background was right; why should I be different?

'Never been here before in my life,' I told him, and judging from my recent experience, I wasn't too keen on returning.

'It's really very easy to find my house. You take the Caceres road, and about fifteen kilometres out, on your right, you will see it.'

He spoke as though there was no other house within miles; I didn't realize then how right he was.

'How will I recognize it?' I asked. Hadn't the house a name?

'Everyone knows it,' he replied, as though I should do the same.

'It is of stone and has a farm attached. And, on the roof of the farmhouse, you will see a stork's nest. What time can I expect you?'

I glanced at my watch. I would have liked to have eaten first, but in Spain they never seem to dine until half past nine, which would make me late setting out. But, on the other hand, all my instincts reminded how prudent it is to sell a second-hand car in the evening, when fading light is kind to old paint, with one vital proviso: never try to sell one under a sodium-vapour street lamp, because these lights show up every blemish as cruelly as magnifying mirrors enlarge the wrinkles on an old woman's face. Best of all, I like to flog old cars on a rainy evening, for rain makes the dullest paint gleam like new, and the buyer can't see an old tired engine pouring out its smoke screen, for it's far too dark.

None of these points really applied in this case. I would make do with a quick snack of paella or whatever I could snatch, and take the car over to him as soon as possible. Like the barrowboys in the Old Kent Road, I didn't want to be here today and gone tomorrow; I wanted to be here today and gone today – if I could.

'I'll be with you in a couple of hours,' I said.

'What is your name?' he asked.

I told him.

'Then I look forward to meeting you.'

'I hope you'll be looking forward to meeting me with the equivalent of three thousand five hundred pounds. Preferably in American dollars or Swiss francs. No horsing about with pesetas or pounds.'

I heard him chuckle.

'I will have that amount ready. If the car is what I want.'

The phone died on my ear, and I suddenly had a horrible thought. What if he were a nutter and had no money whatever? However, that was another problem; I could deal with it if it ever arose.

I brushed my hair and walked downstairs. I knew it was too early for a meal, so I went into the bar. This hadn't moved into the nineteen fifties, let alone the Sixties. The huge mirrors and marble floor, with candelabra cascading like a phony foaming fountain from the high ceiling, seemed as dated as brown-and-white shoes and trousers with twenty-three-inch bottoms.

A barman in a white jacket was setting out bowls of cherries and crisps on circular tables. He looked a bit dated, too. Another man in a white jacket was polishing glasses at the bar. I would have liked a whisky, but I thought it wouldn't mix with the brandy too well, so I ordered another Fundador, and asked him what he'd have. He replied in English that he'd have the same. We made the sort of small talk that barmen and customers make in foreign bars when they find they speak the same language. Was I a tourist? No. Just passing through on business. Did I like this lovely old city? Charming.

And then I had an idea.

'Pretty bad accident a few miles up the road early today,' I said. 'A bus skidded down among the olive trees.'

He nodded and leaned on the bar.

'Terrible, señor,' he said. 'I did hear about it. Truly, it was fortunate that no one was killed.'

I thought that truly it was fortunate that I wasn't killed, never mind the others, but I didn't say that. Instead, I looked sympathetic and tut-tutted, and sipped my drink, and then said: 'I passed shortly afterwards and some poor fellow was being taken off in an ambulance. I saw a GB plate on the back of the bus. It must be terrible to have an accident in a foreign country, and maybe not even speak the language. Where would they take an injured man here – what hospital? I've got a few hours to spare, and I thought I might look him up to see if I could help in any way. Maybe send a telegram to his wife, or something like that. It's the least one can do. The good Samaritan.'

I felt in my pocket to see if I'd got a small note, but not too small, found one, took it out, folded it double so that it would look more important than it was, and pushed it over the bar to the barman. His hand came down over it.

'Ah, señor, you have a kind heart,' he said. I didn't argue the point.

'I shall only pass this way but once,' I told him, and believe me, I meant it. 'Could you find out where they've taken him?'

'It would take time, señor, but it should not be difficult. There are three main hospitals around here. The Convent of the Wounds of Christ, another run by the Sisters of Mercy. The third is the Hospital of the Pierced Heart.'

'Please do what you can,' I said.

'I promise you, I will do my best, señor. Always I like to help the English. You know, I once worked in a club in London. All those girls in their mini-skirts.'

'Ah, yes,' I said. 'Where are they now?'

I thought that most of them were probably married and living in Pinner and Surbiton and Penge and Dulwich Village, because no one stays young for ever; and probably no one really wants to. Then I finished my brandy, walked out into the dining-room.

As I thought, I was too early for a meal, but an off-duty waiter very civilly arranged for me to have a plate of cold chicken. Then I walked up the road to the garage, pressed a hundred-peseta note into the willing palm of some web-foot who was hosing down the floor, for him to hose the car as well. It seemed sufficient, for he grinned at me and started work at once.

I emptied everything out of the door pockets, and the tools out of the boot, for why sell more than you have to? I'd have had the swivelling signpost lamps off, too, but I was afraid that Diaz might already have mentioned them to his principal, so I reluctantly let them stay.

There wasn't much in the pockets, actually: a couple of cinema tickets for some unknown town years ago and a few sweet papers, and the registration book. I left the tools in their box with the hall porter, and then took the Caceres road.

The same countryside, the same olives, the same endless plain stretched to infinity, an empty landscape without people, without life. I drove carefully, because I didn't want an accident now I seemed to be so near to making money; also, I could lie out at the roadside all night if the car left the road, for I passed no other travellers.

I found the man's house easily enough. It looked like a stage-set, and I wondered who on earth could have built it. Someone's mother must have been frightened by a Norman castle or a Victorian folly, for it had turrets and round towers, all in grey stone, and grim as Dartmoor prison, and then, next to this, as an afterthought, long farm buildings with red tiles, and a chimney stack topped by a stork's nest.

I passed the house deliberately without slackening speed and went up the road for another half a mile, until it was out of sight, before I turned. I stopped the engine and listened; a dog was barking a warning somewhere. Anyone who lived so far from a town or village would have a dog of some sort to deter strangers, I told myself, but from the deep baying of this beast, it must be extremely big, maybe a Doberman pinscher. I started the engine and drove back slowly, and turned in at the gate.

The drive was short and circular, made of marble chips, the sort we only see in cemeteries in Britain. The stork took off as I arrived, spreading great wings like dark sails against the sky. I had never seen a stork that close before, although I've had a few near misses in a mis-spent life, but now I could believe the basis of legend that they actually brought babies; they were certainly big enough to transport twins. I recalled George's definition of twins: womb mates who later became bosom pals. After you with that bosom, pal.

The only stork I'd had any personal involvement with was the famous stork mascot that Hispano-Suizas wore on their radiators. During the first war, a Swiss engineer, Marc Birkigt, designed aero engines that were fitted to many Allied fighter planes. They powered the fighter squadron of a French ace, Georges Guynemer, whose insignia was La Cigogne Volante.

After the war, when Birkigt went on to produce the Hispano-Suiza – literally, Spanish-Swiss, because his backers were Spanish and he had been born in Geneva – he chose this emblem for the marque.

In front of the house, carp swam lazily in a circular pond. The front door was of dark, oiled wood, studded with black bolt-heads. It opened before the car had stopped, and a man came down the steps.

I had no doubt he was the buyer. Some people, who should know better, say that the only difference between rich and poor is that the rich have more money. That's a lot of old chat. The rich have an air of opulence which goes far beneath the skin: it comes from right inside them, from months or years, or maybe centuries of giving orders and not taking them; of using other people for the irksome jobs, as a boat uses rollers to slide down a beach to the sea. The difference between this man and me was that while we might both have started life with nothing, I'd still got it.

He wore a wristwatch which would represent to me the profit on half a dozen cars. His lightweight suit looked as though it had been pressed an hour before, and probably had, while I felt I had crawled through a bird's nest backwards.

He was of medium height, but heavily built, wearing glasses with tinted lenses; la vie en rose, I thought, which shows I learned some French at school. As we shook hands, I could smell his aftershave lotion, which wasn't the sort I'd buy in my local supermarket, but which the man who owned the supermarket could probably afford. Then I saw his fingernails. He was wearing them long, perhaps like an old-fashioned Chinese mandarin, to show he didn't need to work with his hands.

'So this is the car,' he said, and walked round it slowly.

I had half expected him to kick a front tyre in the way dealers do, to try and draw attention from a fault the buyer is going to see, or, if they are buying, to con the seller into thinking that there's too much play in the kingpins. But he didn't, so I didn't either.

He was smoking a cigar as big as a bull's tool. I felt good just breathing in the smoke. That's another quality the rich possess; they make you feel you're one of them – until they sigh away in their air-conditioned Continentals, and we find our own level, waiting for a bus, usually in the rain, with the dampness seeping up through the soles of our shoes, and an east wind making our gums ache. Altogether, this set-up seemed to me the sort of place where in days long ago the servants would touch their forelocks (or their foreskins) according to age, sex and inclination, as the young master passed them by.

'It seems in good condition,' he allowed, breaking into my thoughts. 'Is the paint original?'

'It's had a quick spray,' I told him, but not the reason why.

'You did that?' he asked.

I shrugged. There wasn't any mileage in going into reasons at this point.

'I thought you would like to see it in its original German colour,' I said, ad-libbing, because no one but a flathead or a webfoot would try and sell a car of this class, at this price, with a cheap respray.

He opened the doors and glanced inside casually. I expected him to raise the bonnet and peer at the massive engine lurking there like a monster in its metal cage, but he didn't.

'One of the original left-hand drives,' he said musingly. 'How rare. I thought that all Mercedes exported to England before the war had right-hand drive?'

He was right. And some exported to the States even had wooden tyres, to be replaced on landing, because in those days the Third Reich was using rubber for more martial purposes.

'This wasn't built for export,' I explained. 'The original owner was probably German.'

'Ach so,' he said softly, and I knew his nationality.

'Three thousand five hundred pounds? Or, rather, its equivalent? Yes?'

'Yes,' I said. 'And cheap at the price. I'm not charging you anything for bringing it over. But, as I said, I would like it in cash. I don't understand cheques.'

'You're very wise,' he said, looking at me through his pink glasses, as a scientist might examine some midly interesting specimen of pond life through a microscope. 'I often think the value of a cheque has only the value of the stamp on it.'

'My bank manager thinks the same about mine,' I told him.

'I have the money inside. You have all the papers for the car?'

I took out the log book. He glanced at the name of the last owner: Richard Julian Meredith, presumably Mrs Meredith's son. I kept the green card, for it hadn't my name on it, and this might make him ask questions I didn't want to answer. He'd have to pay duty on the car if he kept it in Spain for more than a year, but that was his problem. I didn't think it would worry him.

There are many ways of avoiding such irritations, and if he didn't know them all himself, he'd know someone who did. Even I could tell him two. First, the Spanish customs people usually look only at the registration number of a car, and not at the engine number. So, after you've brought a car into Spain on a green card, which allows you to keep it there for twelve months, you drive it out before the year is up, fit on a new set of numbers – any set you like, for it's most unlikely you'll run into another car with the same combinations – and drive back again. Then you've another year ahead of you before you need to repeat this performance.

If you've an American friend out there, then you make the car over in his name, and the state of Virginia will very obligingly register the car abroad for him, and each year you've only to spend one day out of the country in it, so that you can recross the border with a new number. This is especially useful in Portugal, for after you've owned a foreign car for seven years out there, it can stay in that country for ever without attracting any duty.

But back to the action, as the Duke of Wellington said, or would have, if his speech writer at Waterloo had thought of it.

'Come and have a drink with me,' the man said. 'We will settle up and my chauffeur will drive you back to Salamanca.'

Like the cigarette ad says, the hall was cool as a mountain stream, but rather more expensively furnished. A great Seville lantern, all gold and glass, with about a hundred bulbs inside it, hung from the ceiling. Mirrors stretched to infinity on the walls, and I could tell that the paintings were originals, because you could see the thickness of the paint and the brushmarks and so forth. No giveaway art-bookclub prints, here.

A butler soft-shoed in after us, carrying a silver tray with glasses. The room we were in was no larger than a small lawn, marble-floored, with tapestries and curtains on the walls, and a polished desk with the leather top, richly tooled as the antique dealers like to describe these things. I'd lay this character was richly tooled, too, and he looked as though he'd know how to use it, and I suddenly wondered whether he was Sara's type, and whether she'd appeal to him.

We sat down in leather wing chairs. Through another window I saw a lawn of surprising greenness for Spain, where the grass grows yellow and dry, but here sprinklers played endlessly on it. A peacock fanned its tail, and its thousand feathered eyes regarded us through the arched windows.

'Nice place you've got here,' I said, as though I was referring to a new semi-detached bungalow on some Essex estate, specially designed for young executives; the type you see advertised in the Sunday papers.

'It's quiet,' he agreed. Silence is another quality much esteemed by the wealthy. I don't mind it myself, either.

We sipped pink champagne that had probably lain for years on ice and tasted none the worse for that.

'Funny thing,' I said, as though I was going to laugh, 'but I still don't know your name.'

'Ackerman,' he said, as though this was unimportant.

'Like the inventor of the steering gear?' I said.

'Precisely. Perhaps he was an ancestor of mine.'

'Perhaps,' I said; he certainly hadn't been one of mine.

That Ackermann had been apprenticed to a coachbuilder in the late seventeenth century, and then grew interested in publishing and selling books, and finally came from Germany to London to concentrate on both careers, designing coaches, and selling prints in the Strand.

In 1817 he established art lithography in England, and in

the following year he patented the system of pivoted steering axles which actually had been invented by another German, Lankensperger, and which every car uses today.

This Ackermann stood up, went to his desk, unlocked a drawer, took out a manila envelope and opened it. Half a dozen bundles of dollar bills, each bound with elastic bands, cascaded on the leather top, with the lovely sound that folding money makes, especially when it's coming your way.

'At the present rate of exchange, here is the sum you ask for. Nine thousand dollars,' he said. 'Allowing some for your running expenses on top of our agreed price.'

I got up from my seat and fanned through the bills. I didn't think he would screw me with the odd hundred-dollar bill folded double, but I've been done so often that I'm too old to take any chances where counting money is concerned, even in a bank. Ackermann sat back in his chair, the points of his fingers pressed together, smiling at me as I counted.

He hadn't screwed me. He picked up the notes, put them back in the envelope and handed it to me.

'Do you want a receipt?' I asked.

He pushed over to me a piece of paper, which was already typed in English. I signed it, folded up the envelope and squeezed it into the inside pocket of my jacket. It felt good there. For the first time since I'd become involved, I also felt pretty good myself.

'Tell me,' I went on, pouring myself some more of his champagne – I live by the Spanish proverb: wake up and drink, you've centuries to sleep – 'Why do you want the old car? You didn't examine it closely; you didn't ask for a trial run, or even try to bargain.'

His eyes flickered for a moment, behind his glasses.

'Why does anyone want anything?' he said, which was no answer.

I said nothing; after all, it was no concern of mine; he had paid his money. It was a lot of money, but he wasn't the only one who would have bought that car. As always, when I've done a reasonably good deal, I wondered whether

I could have done better if I had waited a bit longer, if I had played things this way or that. Are you the same? It comes of being born under Sagittarius; you're never satisfied. And why should we be satisfied? If our forebears had been satisfied with their set-up, we'd all still be living in caves and eating dinosaur steaks. Only good thing would be, they wouldn't be deep-frozen.

'I suppose,' Ackermann went on slowly, as though he were trying to find a reason for wanting the car, either to convince me or to convince himself, 'I suppose it's really for sentimental reasons. You, as a dealer, will know how collectors seem to favour the type of car that impressed them when they were at an impressionable age. And in Germany before the war, when I was in my late teens, this was to me the most exotic car of all.

'I know we had the Horch and the Maybach, but so far as I personally was concerned, they stood in the same relation to the Mercedes 540 as your English Daimler or your Sunbeam stood to your Rolls. Good, but not quite equal. And, of course, they don't make them like that any more.'

'Have you any other old cars?' I asked, before we set sail on a tide of psychological urges and wish fulfilment. Never ignore any chance of doing a deal; you may not have another. I shall not pass this way again, etc.

'One or two,' he admitted. 'But nothing like this. Although I have had in the past.'

'Do you want to get rid of anything old now?' I asked him. The past was past; I couldn't make a profit out of that.

'No, nothing. But if ever I do decide to sell any of them, I know who I can contact. Yes?'

'Yes,' I said. We stood up simultaneously.

He pressed some hidden button, and the butler was also standing at the door. We made a fine upstanding trio, I thought. I shook hands with Ackermann, and followed the butler across the hall. A Volkswagen, with a driver at the wheel, and the engine already running, waited for me at the bottom of the stone steps. The driver didn't say anything to me; I said nothing to him, but he had been briefed where to take me. Maybe Ackermann had checked where my telephone call had come from; the rich have their reasons, just as they have so much else.

I told the receptionist at the Monterrey Hotel I wanted a safe-deposit box, and I locked away the money and kept the key.

'How can I get out of here quickly to London?' I asked him.

'There's a train tonight to Madrid, señor, and perhaps you could catch a plane tomorrow. Or you could take a train, go north.'

He gave me the number of the local travel agent. I went up to my room and rang him, but it was too late; the office was closed. I'd try again in the morning.

I poured out another Fundador, lit a cigarette and stood at the window looking at the wall of a house across an alley, which is where all my hotel rooms seem to look. I never have the room with the view over the hills or the sea that appears in the hotel brochure, but if there's a lift shaft around, or, as here, an outlook over an alleyway, that seems permanently reserved for me.

I glanced at my watch: half past eight; still an hour before dinner. I wasn't feeling very hungry. Instead, I felt a certain flat reaction. Somehow, I had expected more than a straight deal, maybe some mystery, some excitement after all the coming and going, and just to be given my asking price seemed a letdown.

Why should a rich expatriate German pay so much for an old car someone else was willing to steal? Was the man who had stolen the car working for him, for himself – or for someone else?

There was obviously more in this than just buying an old car for sentimental reasons, but what, and how could I find out? And if I did, what use would the knowledge be to me? Could I make a bit of money out of it or not? Knowledge for itself isn't power, no matter what Thomas Hobbes said, unless you can use it to do you a power of good.

There are always more questions than can ever have answers, and this looked like one of the questions whose answer I would never learn.

I stood, looking out over the alley, wondering what to do. I don't know about you, but when I am in an hotel on my own in a foreign town, I soon grow bored. I sit about, or walk the streets aimlessly, or eat a meal I don't really want and then crawl into bed a few hours nearer the grave with nothing attempted and no one done.

This time, the same restlessness was already infecting me. I didn't fancy a cinema, I wasn't really hungry, and it was too early for sleep. I knew what would be fun, but it's against my principles to pay for poon; if I can't get it for what is laughingly called love, then I'll do without.

I went downstairs to ask the receptionist, who spoke English, what he would recommend in these circumstances as a cheap, decent, yet acceptable way of spending the evening, when suddenly something made me glance over my shoulder.

A man was reading a newspaper on one of the settees in the hall. He lowered the paper briefly to turn a page, then went on reading. He was like any city Spaniard, with big-rimmed glasses, a sallow face and dark waxy hair. The only reason I noticed him at all was that he was the man who had driven me in from Ackermann's house. Now what the hell did he want?

I didn't even approach the receptionist at his desk, for I had decided how to spend my evening. I walked past the driver slowly, and out through the swing doors into the street. The evening had that gritty, sun-dried feel of central Spain; after a long, hot day, all the fresh air had been used up. All around me, the thick stone walls were thankfully returning to the night the heat the day had forced upon them. A stream of mopeds, without silencers, swarmed down the road; the shops were shut, but lit up brightly from inside.

I walked up against the traffic, crossed the square, edged

with arches, each hung with lights, and went down the first narrow alley I saw. It was barely wide enough for a car, with cobbles and doorsteps a foot off the ground in case of flooding. I climbed up to the third doorstep, then stood flat against the unpainted door, feeling the wood warm under my fingers. I hoped the householder didn't come out, or I'd have to say I was the White Tide man, or the man from the Pru.

The driver hurried past me, his newspaper folded under his arm. He walked quickly, head pushed forward slightly, as though worried in case he had lost me. The purple dusk poured down the street after him.

I gave him a minute's start by my watch, and then came out of the doorway and walked back into the main square and stood about on a corner, hoping an interesting car would drive by, but none did, so I returned to the hotel. The driver padded in ten minutes after me, out of breath and looking worried until he saw me. Then he sat down again, opened his newspaper, and tried to look unconcerned.

So Ackermann wanted to know where I was, and what I was doing. Perhaps he really didn't believe I was a dealer in old-fashioned cars? Perhaps he thought I knew more than I did, which wouldn't be difficult. Why else should he send the driver to watch me? If I was harmless, and spent an evening on the town, all right. But if I wasn't quite so simple and met someone else, or went back to his house, for whatever reason, he would like advance warning.

I walked into the lounge, sat down and looked at a Spanish newspaper I couldn't understand. The Mercedes. It all came back to that car. He must be doing something to it or looking for something hidden in it, something that perhaps the man without a face had also wanted desperately to find. If there was a deal in it for them, I might get my share. At least, I would find the answer to my question, and it would not return to vex me.

I threw the paper to one side, and walked out into the bar. The same barman was polishing a glass – possibly the same glass; it gets a habit with them.

'Ah, señor,' he said, as he saw me. 'I have much news.'

He obviously had, because it poured out in a verbal Niagara before I could even order myself a drink.

'That man in the coach, señor. You were wrong – he wasn't English. He was German.'

'Really?' I said, and nodded towards the Fundador bottle. He produced two glasses. We toasted each other.

'He's now in the Convent of the Wounds of Christ.'

'How did you find out?'

'This is a small town, señor. I have many friends and many relations. I have a cousin who works there, in the nurses' home.'

'Nice work if you can get it,' I said, and this cousin had got it, and was no doubt getting it, too.

'Yes. His name is Kellner. He appears to have lost his memory at some time and they think the accident has brought back parts of it. He became delirious. They actually had to hold him down at one point.'

I nodded gravely, as though this was what I had expected, although it wasn't at all. But then what had I expected to hear?

'He was raving like a lunatic, señor,' the barman continued. He obviously relished his story, and I didn't find it so uninteresting, either, although it wasn't adding too much to human knowledge, or to mine.

'What about?'

'The war. Actually, the very end of the war. Apparently he was there with Hitler in the bunker in Berlin during those last days.'

'How does your cousin know this? Does he speak German?'

'Of course, señor. But then so many of us do. He served with the Blue Division during the Spanish Civil War. The Germans fought with them. Remember?'

I remembered now, but I had forgotten. There have been so many other more desperate, more professional wars since then: the Second World War, Korea, Vietnam, the Middle East. By their more refined standards of carnage and cruelty, the Spanish Civil War was just a dress rehearsal; but not if you lived in Spain.

'What else did he say?' I asked him. 'Did he mention anyone else?'

'Yes. There was a colonel. Kellner had to drive in a truck to some house to deliver a box of papers. Then someone shot him in the face, and he was left for dead. A man called Diaz was involved. He saw him in London a few days ago, apparently – quite by chance – but mostly it was shouting, reliving the past. They'd given him sedatives, but apparently, apart from mild concussion when the bus turned over, I don't think he is badly injured.' The barman sounded a shade disappointed; there's nothing like a slow decline to an early death for sharpening a gossip's tongue.

'There's no point in me going on to see him, then?'

'Not really, señor. The hospital will put him in touch with the German consul if he needs any help from his own countrymen.'

'That's very kind of them,' I said, and it was.

So, I'd learned something, but was it really important? It didn't seem so to me.

As I stood, thinking, someone else came into the bar; a girl. She walked past without looking at either of us, but we looked at her, because she was worth looking at. She sat down at the table in the far corner and the waiter brought her a sherry. I stood watching her because I had nothing else to watch, and this was no strain.

She was in her early twenties, with a wonderful pair of bristols; I could see their outline, firm and round, against her dress. She crossed her legs and I caught the merest flash of white thigh above the top of her stockings; no messing about with tights and rubbish of that kind. This could be interesting.

An idea flew into my mind like a swallow from Sardinia. I'd pick up this girl – God knows who she was – and we'd have a few drinks. Then I'd swing the conversation round to cars. It was a thousand-to-one chance she'd never seen a Mercedes 540, so I'd take her to see the one I'd just sold.

We could hire a self-drive from somewhere, and I'd leave her in the car on some excuse, say to make sure the garage was open, and then, if Ackermann found me, I could say I hadn't wanted to disturb him, but my girlfriend was most anxious to see this car. At least I'd see whether he was dismantling the car, and maybe even the reason why. Then back to the Monterrey, and to the real business of the night.

In Belgravia, I frequently had rubbernecks digging around my old cars on thinner excuses, and I put up with their visits with a good grace, because they didn't mean any harm. Ackermann was almost certain to do the same. I felt a bit mean using this girl as a stalking horse (mare?) but not mean enough not to do it.

The bar was empty except for her, so I sat down at the next table, and ordered a Fundador. Then I glanced boldly across at her. She looked up from her book, as though irritated that someone had broken her solitude. Maybe she was an intellectual. I raised my glass to her.

'God bless the Prince of Wales,' I said, 'and all who sail in her.'

She looked puzzled, but she raised her glass. She wasn't all that puzzled. Her mouth was the sexiest thing I'd seen in a girl's face for a long, long time; somehow it reminded me of a lapel badge I'd seen earlier in the year, on Broadway in New York: '69. A midnight snack fit for a king.' Maybe I'd be a king this midnight? Better than being a queen, I thought, as the old Fundador began to warm my blood. Happy soixante-neuf!

And I was fit enough, too, wasn't I? Fit for what? For anything.

'Over here on holiday?' I asked her. How's that for an original approach? I tell you, when I'm bad I'm unbeatable.

She nodded.

'Sort of. I'm in Spain for a year to learn the language.' She had a deep Southern American accent, the sort that should be asking for mint juleps and Uncle Tom's cabin – though why Uncle Tom should stay in his cabin in the heat they have there, I don't know. He's probably on a civil rights march somewhere these days, anyhow.

'What have you learned?'

'That depends on who's teaching,' she said.

I felt I could give some tuition to this girl.

'I'm a little deaf,' I told her. 'Do you mind if I sit nearer you?'

'How near?' she asked without any trace of a smile.

'Like this near.'

I sat in a chair right opposite her where I could get a pants-watcher's view if she crossed her legs again. She did. Maybe she felt nervous. A glimpse of thigh, so quick it was hardly there. Tight white pants. I could get interested in her, so I ordered another Tio Pepe for her, and one more Fundador for me. At the rate I was drinking the stuff, they should give me a discount. Anyway, what the hell: it was deductible; entertaining on an export trip. Entertaining for research, I'd put it down as.

By now, I had no doubt about the outcome of the evening. You have your bad luck, and you have your good, and this seemed like one of the latter times. As the song said, this was a lovely way to spend an evening, and it would grow better. In fact, it seemed such a lovely way that it was rather a waste going over to see the Mercedes; my interest in it had suddenly diminished greatly.

There's an old family motto: never mix business with pleasure, and this could be interesting business. Her name was Ingrid, and from Memphis she'd moved to Freehold, in New Jersey, a little town I had once visited when I was buying a couple of Stutz Bearcats in the days when those strange spidery little cars, with their single windscreen worn like a huge monocle on the steering column, were not as pricey as they are now.

We had a couple more drinks. By then it was after half past nine, and a waiter came in and asked if we wanted places for dinner, and we looked at each other and said we did. Usually, in Spain, there's half an hour between each course, so by the time you have finished eating, it's almost time to start again, but here they were quick, and we were through by ten.

Somehow, I can't remember how, maybe I mentioned the Bearcats, I steered the talk round to cars. She'd got a Wolseley Mini. She thought the transverse-engine idea was new, but I told her about the Wolseley racing car that had a transverse engine way back in the early nineteen hundreds. It drove the rear wheels through chains. The American Christie of the same period went one better, with a transverse engine driving the front wheels. Progress? I tell you, we're like the Udu bird that flies backwards because it doesn't like the wind in its eyes.

Not that she seemed much interested. Anyway, from this favourite theme of mine, but obviously not of hers, we talked about other old cars, and I told Ingrid I sold them, and she said that when she was very small her father used to run an Hupmobile. I said how cars of each country seemed to bear their country's characteristics. The Honda, and the Toyota, were neat and small and impeccable, like the Japanese who built them, while at the other end of the scale, you have the Toronado for the straight American highways, or the little Fiat for the Italian hills, and you have all the German precision and thoroughness in the BMW and the Mercedes.

I gradually steered the conversation round to Mercedes, in a way I didn't hope was too obvious, and then, as though I had just thought of it, I told her how I had sold a very rare Mercedes, that same day, and should we go round and see it?

'Is it very far?' she asked, without any enthusiasm whatever. 'I never like driving after dark in a strange country. And I had hoped to get to bed early.'

So had I, but not for sleep. But then, there was still time – for both. So I said: 'I'll be with you all the way. You have nothing to fear, except my eighteen hands. We could be there and back in an hour, and you'll never see a car like this again.'

I don't think she wanted to see a car like that at all, ever, period, but I bored away and finally I convinced her. We finished dinner and I signed the bill with my room number.

'Do you want to spend a penny?' I asked her.

She shook her head.

'Well, I'll just nip up and put on a sweater,' I told her. Actually, thimble bladder, London, should be my cable address.

'Where's your car?' I wouldn't have to bother with hiring one, if we could use hers for free. Why throw money around?

'In the garage,' she said. 'The street's too narrow here for me to leave it outside.'

'Give me five minutes,' I said.

'I'll get the car then. See you at the front door.'

That suited me. I went up to my room, picked up the telephone and asked for George's number. There was no delay at this time of night, and George's voice was speaking in my ear sooner than if I had been ringing from one of those new call boxes that only take sixpenny pieces back in England.

'Where are you now?' he asked.

'Still in Salamanca,' I said. 'But I may be moving out. I want you to do something for me that won't cost you anything. First, check watches.'

'Five past ten.'

I checked with mine; he was right.

'Did you sell the car?' he asked.

'Yes. And got the money.'

'Harry Nash?'

'Yes,' I said. 'Cash. Look, I'm in a hurry,' I went on, 'and I can't say much. But at exactly five minutes to eleven I want you to ring me person to person at Salamanca 543541. Book the call now, so there's no delay. Don't be surprised if I'm not able to say much.'

'What if you're not there?'

'Say there's been a mistake. Or put the phone down. Nothing else?'

'Nothing,' he said. He was too old a soldier to waste breath asking questions I didn't want to answer.

I replaced the receiver, had a pee, pulled on a black roll-top sweater which was warmer and lighter than my jacket, then ran down the stairs, and jumped into Ingrid's car at the door.

I let her drive. I liked looking at her, seeing those fantastic charlies pushing out her sweater, like she was wearing a pair of pointed Israeli melons on her chest. I once saw an ad in New York for some furniture – 'genuine tree wood, hand-rubbed'. These would be hand-rubbed, too, by this loving, lustful, old-English craftsman as soon as we got back. It was going to be a wonderful way to spend an evening.

The road was completely empty. Now and then, the eyes of some night animal glittered like beads from the bushes, and once something with a furry tail, perhaps a fox, fled across the road in our yellow headlights. Then, in the distance, on the right, I could see a glimmer of light from one of the farm buildings.

'We're nearly there,' I said.

'Where do you want to stop?' she asked.

'I'll tell you later,' I told her.

'I didn't mean that,' she said quickly. 'I meant where shall we park? Do we drive right up to the house?'

'No,' I said. 'I don't know the fellow well, and don't want to disturb him. Turn out the lights and stop this side of the house in case the noise of the car sets his dog barking. I'll walk along on my own and see whether there's a light in the garage. If there is, I'll come back and you can peep through the window.'

'You sure it's all right?' she asked dubiously. I guess they didn't do things like this too often in Freehold, NJ.

'Certain,' I told her.

The lights died. She drove off the road under the trees and cut the engine.

'Now don't be too long,' she said. 'It's spooky here.'

'Give me five minutes,' I told her. 'Lock your doors, if you like. And keep your knees together.'

I climbed out of the car. The night was cooler than I had imagined, and beneath the trees as dark as an elephant's armpit, and, frankly, no more inviting. I took a few deep breaths, and a few long steps and visibility improved, for the grass between the olive trees was frosted with moonlight.

I was about two hundred yards from the house, and I kept in what shadow I could find, which wasn't much. About a hundred yards nearer the house I saw in the moonlight a glint of a parked car. A small car had been driven into a thicket of trees and then the branches pulled over the windows to minimize any risk of reflection. It seemed a long way out of town for lovers. So who else would want to conceal a car in this lonely place?

I stood still listening for any voice. I didn't want to be taken for a Peeping Tom, but there was no one to take me for anything. I walked up to the car; it was a SEAT 600, really a Fiat built under licence in Spain, and it was empty. I felt the louvres over the engine at the back; they were still warm, so it hadn't been parked for long.

If lovers hadn't driven out here, then perhaps poachers might have used it. I wasn't sure whether they'd find any animals worth hunting in the olive groves, and I realized that I was subconsciously trying to find some safe and harmless reason for a car to be hidden barely a hundred yards from the only house in miles, a house that I was convinced held a secret that others besides me wanted to solve.

I stood, irresolute and uneasy, then I did the only thing I could to influence further events. I lifted the engine cover, and felt carefully among the hot pipes and leads until I found the distributor.

I thought of removing the rotor, but this would mean that someone had deliberately taken it – a definitely hostile act. I thought again, and left the rotor, but loosened the nut holding the low-tension wire to the distributor body. I undid this wire and wedged it down against the bare metal. As soon as anyone switched on the ignition, the wire would short the circuit, but it could easily be put right, and, also, it could conceivably have come loose on its own.

I went on through the olive grove, and worked my way round to the side of the house. I could hear nothing, and I was listening especially for the sound of the Doberman pinscher. Under the chill of moonlight, the place lay silent as a tomb. I repeated that to myself; I didn't like that word tomb. I prefer a house that is noisy, full of people and laughter, where children call to each other, and there's music; a house that lives and is alive, not just a shelter from the elements. A house needs more than money to make a home.

A three-strand wire fence marked the boundary. I held the barbed wires apart and climbed between them carefully. Still nothing. I was now facing the window of the study where Ackermann had given me the money. The grey walls stood cold as steel. An owl hooted once or twice; I thought this might be a signal, as it is in thrillers, but it wasn't a signal to me. Maybe some other nut got the message? I was still in the shadow of the trees, and not really anxious to come out into the moonlight where any watcher could so easily see me. Yet I had to move soon, for Ingrid would be wondering what the hell had happened to me, and wasn't I rather dramatizing the whole thing?

Above me, high up on the wall, the ivy rustled and rattled. A bat or bird of some kind flew out only feet above my head. I glanced up, and stayed looking up because a thin straight stick about three inches long was quivering in the dry, glittering ivy leaves. It hung, and would have dropped, but the barb caught a tendril, and the arrow trembled slightly and hung, tail feather down. Taped to the shaft I saw a small black cylinder about as thick as a flow pen.

Now who the hell had fired this, and why? Could it be some poacher who had arrived in the SEAT? Was he after the bird that had flown away – or was he seeking more dangerous game?

The sooner I got out myself, the better, I thought, but

before I went I wanted to peek at that car. I began to work my way around the side of the house to the garage.

The doors were shut and a side window reflected the moon as though from a large mirror. No lights were on inside, so I pressed my face, cupped in my hands, against the glass, and could make out the dim shape of the white Mercedes.

The roof was open and the trim panels from the door farthest from me had been removed, so that I could see the rusty inside of the metal streaked with sound-absorbing paint, and the big cogged wheel of the window winder. Was Ackermann already starting to restore the car by removing the upholstery?

I moved closer to the middle of the window to try for a better view from a different angle, and as I moved I heard the crunch of a twig behind me.

Something round and very hard was pressed into the base of my spine, and not at all the weapon a lover from the SEAT might use. This was metal. I turned slowly. No one had ever pressed a gun into my back before, but there is always the first time, and this was it.

A man about the size of Billy Walker, but with not such a friendly face, looked down at me. He was smiling; I didn't like his smile. In his right hand he held a revolver that must have taken the biggest bullet ever to go up a revolver barrel. I was glad it wasn't going up my backside. At least, I hoped it wasn't.

I tried to speak, but no sound came. I cleared my throat and tried again. My voice had shrunk and shrivelled into a thin whisper.

'Just to look at the old car,' I said, in unrecognizable tones.

'Inglés?' he said, raising his eyebrows.

I nodded.

'Señor Ackermann . . .' I began, but didn't go on; what was the use if he didn't speak the language?

He jerked his revolver towards the front of the garage. I walked round that way in front of him. The arrow still hung from the ivy, almost vertical now; it had dropped slightly. A gust of wind would dislodge it. He didn't appear to notice it, and it wasn't any part of my duty to tell him. We went in through the front door. I was surprised that so many lights were lit in the house; the windows were fitted with interior wooden shutters so that, from the outside, it could have been deserted.

Ackermann was standing in the hall, wearing a velvet smoking jacket, and chewing a cigar as long as a policeman's truncheon, and they are wearing them long this year. He'd got his glasses on, too. He looked very rich and very much at ease and also very amused at seeing me.

'So,' he said. 'The English car dealer. What brings you back here?'

I had a horrible feeling that he guessed or knew, but I did what I could with the material I had.

'I met a girl in the hotel. We were talking about old cars, and I told her about your Mercedes, so we drove out here. I was just looking through the garage window to make sure the car was there, for I was going to show it to her.'

'Why not come to the front door?' asked Ackermann practically. 'I would have been pleased to show her. Where is she now?'

'A few hundred yards down the road in a Mini,' I said. Maybe we were going to have a nice cosy evening after all, talking about old cars. My heartbeats were coming back to normal. Maybe Ackermann would offer me a drink and a cigar and we would all part friends. Or maybe nothing.

He took his cigar out of his mouth and looked at the end of it, and then turned slightly.

'Are you sure?' he asked.

A girl came out of a door. Ingrid. She smiled at me, but rather as the big man had smiled. Contemptuously. I was the little fellow in a big man's world, out of my league, and out of my depth. As the old-fashioned writer of boys' stories I used to read before my voice broke would put it, I blushed to the roots of my hair. My pubic hair, too, I shouldn't wonder, for I felt a right nit.

'What are *you* doing here?' I asked her as cheerfully as I could, which wasn't very cheerfully.

It wasn't very original, either, but I genuinely wanted to know the answer, although what good it could do me was difficult to see.

Ingrid didn't even bother to reply. She simply crossed the hall and went into another room. What a Charlie I'd been, and I'd felt so bright, picking up a girl to use as a cover for coming here, but, in fact, she had picked me up. The hunter had been hunted, and worse than hunted, caught.

'You stick to your story?' asked Ackermann quietly.

'Of course.' What else was there to stick to? as the bill-poster asked the man who owned the wall. Then I had another idea.

'Actually, I wanted to take a telephone call here. There's a delay at the hotel. My man is ringing me from London.'

But Ackermann was not listening. He kept looking at his cigar as though he hadn't seen it alight before; and I suppose he hadn't. At least, not that particular one.

Ingrid came out of the room and handed him a piece of paper with a few lines of typing on it. He turned his back on me to read it. Naturally, I tried to see what it was over his shoulder, but all I could make out were three lines in close-typed capitals, which I couldn't read. The one word I could read was GENEVA.

'Tell the pilot to get the plane ready,' said Ackermann, folding the paper double and double again. 'I'll be wanting it later tonight. And book me a suite in Geneva.'

Then he turned to me, put the cigar back into his face and blew smoke into mine. So we weren't going to have a genial host and guest relationship, then.

'I think we'd better have a little talk,' he said quietly. 'Don't you?'

I didn't, just for the record. I'd rather have been on my way, but the voting was against me.

The guard opened the study door and motioned me in with his revolver. The room inside, except for a brass desk lamp with a dark green glass shade, was in darkness. The door closed silently behind us, and the guard stood inside and against it, his arms folded, the revolver still in his right hand, like Sean Connery in the ads for the Bond films. Ackermann sat down behind the desk, and turned the lamp so that it shone on me.

'Now,' he began, as though he was a schoolmaster and I a sixth-former found smoking pot behind the bike sheds. 'What *really* brought you back?'

'I told you.'

'You persist in that ridiculous story?'

'It's the truth.'

At least it was part of the truth, and if Pilate didn't know what truth was, how could I?

'Well, we shall see. I am sorry I have little time tonight for talk as I have to leave unexpectedly, so this interview may be painful.'

He paused to let this sink in. It sank. At that moment, someone knocked on the door and opened it. Ingrid was holding the arrow I had seen in the ivy. She said something to him in Spanish, which I couldn't understand. She was a well-educated lady, this one, and I suddenly and quite irrelevantly remembered George's definition of a well-educated lady: one who only swears when it slips out.

Ackermann took the arrow from her, and turned it over and over in his hands, examining the thin black cylinder. Ingrid went out and he looked up at me.

'A transistorized transmitter,' he said as though it was the one thing he expected to find tied to an arrow. 'Yours?'

I shook my head. I'd no one to transmit anything to, and my thoughts weren't worth transmitting, even if I had.

'Now, why did you come back?'

'I've told you.'

'You have told me lies. If you didn't fire this arrow, then who did?'

I couldn't help him there, and worse, I couldn't even help myself.

Ackermann gave a nod in the guard's direction. The man hit me suddenly where it hurt, right over the heart, so quickly I had no time or chance to duck. I went down on my hands and knees and the floor obligingly came up to meet me.

I don't know how long I stayed down there. It could have been a century, or only ten seconds, but somehow, holding the side of the table, I dragged myself on to my feet. The guard watched me with amusement, his gun lowered.

I tried to throw the table at him, but it was too heavy, and I only staggered, and he hit me again. Ackermann laughed as I crawled up for the second time. The walls of the room were now behaving oddly, going in and out like bellows. I could see not one Ackermann but three, and all were out of focus, just as I seemed out of luck.

'Now, will you talk?' asked three Ackermanns with one voice. The guard brought up his right hand slowly to influence my reply. I could see the grooves on the side of the barrel, the rifled muzzle, the tip of the foresight set in the classic position between the shoulders of the backsight. I saw the hammer rising. Surely he wasn't going to kill me? I watched with my mouth open, leaning heavily on the table, my heart banging like an old side-valve BSA engine. As I watched, the room swam back into focus; the hammer went on rising.

'No,' I said. 'Don't shoot!'

I felt sweat dampen my hair; my flesh crawled as though it wanted to leave my bones. I would have done anything, said anything, admitted anything, if only he would lower his revolver. Time stopped as we stared at each other.

At that moment, there was a *phut* like the puncture of a cycle tyre. The guard opened his hand slowly, as though he no longer cared, and when I looked at his face, I realized he didn't. His eyes had closed. The table splintered under his weight as he fell across it, and I went down with it and him. From my hands and knees, I looked up in amazement.

The curtains to one side of Ackermann had parted. Between them, back against the panelled wall, stood the bus driver, an automatic in his hand. It wore a long black snout, which I recognized, from umpteen TV films, as a silencer.

'Stay exactly where you are,' he told us both in English. 'Don't either of you move.'

I was in no position either to move or argue, and the way things were going I was thankful for the rest. I felt sick inside, with a kind of weary apprehension. Oh, to be back in Belgravia, where one's only risk was that a cheque would bounce, or a buyer might discover the size of my mark-up between buying and selling – as when the customer who had just paid me £2,500 for a Lago-Talbot with a Figoni and Falaschi body, found my letter offering £250 to the previous owner still in the dashboard cubbyhole!

'Who are you?' Ackermann asked the driver, and I had to give this man full marks for coolness. He'd have made a mint selling cars, for if I'd been in his position, I'd have done my nut. As Ackermann spoke, his right hand reached out casually towards the desk, apparently to straighten the blotter.

'Fold both your hands behind your head,' the driver ordered him, and ripped up the blotting pad. A button for an alarm bell was recessed inside the desk top.

'Smart boy,' he said. He turned to me. 'And you, buster, you'll never learn.'

'Teach me,' I said. 'Tell me, for a start, what goes on around here?' Relief was flooding through my veins instead of blood; I could have wept with reaction. I might not be a hero, but at least I was alive.

The driver turned back to Ackermann.

'You don't know me,' he said, 'and you never will, but, like you, I'm German. And I want to know something that only you can tell me. What you were doing in that Mercedes outside – or one like it – twenty-four years ago?'

Ackermann's tongue moistened his lips.

'I don't know who you are,' he said at last, as though he and the board of directors had been studying the matter and had finally reached this conclusion, 'and I don't greatly care. But, just for the record, I was never in that car twenty-four years ago. And if this is an attempt at a holdup, you have no possible chance of success. There are other guards outside. And guard dogs.'

The driver allowed himself a smile. He could have allowed himself anything so far as I was concerned, for with each minute that passed I felt a little more like a human being – and more able to make a dash for freedom if I saw half a chance. Or even a quarter.

'You *were* in that car, or one very like it. Your name then wasn't Ackermann, but Horstmann. You were a young captain in the SS. Correct?

'With another officer you drove to a house on the outskirts of Berlin. There was some shooting. Then you drove off in the car, leaving the other officer for dead.

'A few kilometres up the road by the side of a lake you learned you were about to meet American tanks. You had something in that car which should have been hidden in that house. Instead, you dumped it, whatever it was, in the lake. Then you gave yourself up.'

'Very interesting,' allowed Ackermann, drawing on his cigar as though he was watching something on the box, which didn't affect him at all. 'Do go on.'

'I intend to. We know all this because that area is now in Eastern Germany. We have interviewed everyone we could find – people who saw the car, who tended the wounded officer in hospital and so on – just as the Russians have taken back to Hitler's bunker every member of his staff they captured to try and reconstruct exactly what happened in the last hours, and how and where Hitler died. If he died – *then*.

'After you served a token sentence for war crimes, you came back to the lake – apparently as a skin-diving instructor for the troops' leave centre that had opened there.

'Every day that you could, for months, right up through the summer of forty-eight, you dived until you found whatever you were looking for, and then suddenly you disappeared. We lost track of you, but we never lost interest.

'Then a collector in Spain started to buy every Mercedes car of a particular type – the type that is in your garage now – the type you took on that drive in 1945.

'The buying was done through a firm in Hanover – Tobler Autos – so we looked into this firm, and discovered that the owner had *also* been with you then.

'What did you bury in the lake – and why do you want this car so badly?'

Ackermann smiled again.

'Since you will never leave this house alive,' he said quietly, as though this were the most casual sort of remark to make, like, do you prefer two lumps of sugar to one, 'I'll tell you what I threw into the lake. Money. Dollar bills. A box packed full of them.

'I dived for them, as you say, and I found them, and I invested that money in land in the Costa Brava.

'You could buy half a mile of coast a few years ago for a few thousand dollars. It's worth almost as many millions now. I bought miles of beach. As for anything being hidden in the car, that's absurd. I'm purely a collector of antique automobiles – like our English friend here.'

He nodded towards me. I almost felt I was a friend, and then I thought again. If this was how Ackermann treated his friends, who would want to be his enemy?

'I'll have a few minutes with you, too,' the driver told me. 'I think you are more than just a used-car dealer. I want to find out how much more.'

I opened my mouth to reply and the telephone rang. It sounded so near and so shrill and unexpected, that we all jumped. I glanced at the wall clock. Five to eleven. Good old George; right on the nose.

In the shock of that first peal of bells, the driver's arm jerked slightly. For a second, his gun wasn't pointing at me. In that second my right hand whipped down for the dead guard's revolver on the floor beside me. I fired once, twice, barely taking aim.

The kick of the thing almost broke my wrist, but the second bullet broke the driver's. His automatic clattered on to the floor, and his right hand went round his left, his face a gargoyle of unbearable pain.

As he bent forward in his giant agony, Ackermann drove up his right fist into his face. He might have driven his left too, or both his feet, for all I cared, because by then I was out in the hall and away. I threw back the bolts in the front door, slammed it shut behind me and was down the steps, and running like an eight-legged stag being pursued by the Rochdale Hunt.

Men were shouting and dogs were barking, but mercifully not in the front garden. I reached the road without anyone coming after me, and then started to run towards Ingrid's Mini. As I passed the clump of bushes that shrouded the SEAT, I heard its starter whirr and then stop and whirr again, but the engine didn't fire. It wasn't likely that it would, either, so long as that wire stayed wedged beneath the distributor.

In happier times, I would have stopped to see who the driver was, but now I had problems enough of my own; I hadn't got time for the waiting game.

Ingrid's Mini was locked. I smashed the driver's window with the butt of the revolver, jumped inside, ripped out the two ignition wires from the back of the switch, wound their bare copper strands together, pulled out the wire for the starter solenoid, and jabbed its end against the metal of the dash to earth it. The engine started instantly.

I swung around in a wide circle, without lights, and then accelerated along the cold, moonlit road towards Salamanca for half a mile before I switched on the headlights. I thought that we had driven out from Salamanca fairly quickly, but I tell you, going back I clipped minutes off our outward time.

I arrived at the Monterrey and left the car in the street outside, because I hadn't time to put it away, and anyway where did it go? A night receptionist was totting up bills on an adding machine.

'Room seventeen,' I panted at him. 'I'm leaving now – unexpectedly. I've got some money in the safe-deposit and a box of tools. I want to pay the bill as soon as I've packed. OK?'

'Sí, señor.'

I went up in the lift, and let myself into my room. I was ready for anything now, and beyond all surprise, excepting the surprise that faced me.

Sara was lying asleep on my bed.

CHAPTER SIX

I switched on the main light and shut the door behind me. Sara struggled awake and sat up, shielding her eyes from the brightness of the ceiling bulb.

'I'm leaving,' I told her, just in case she cared, thinking what a pity it was that she hadn't been in the room a couple of hours earlier. I could have spent a more entertaining evening with her than fighting my way out of some nutter's castle – and I still hadn't fought my way out completely. I had to be over the border before the police discovered I'd shot a man, before they could circulate my description – which Ackermann would certainly give them.

I thought of the unknown in the SEAT; he'd face a long walk home, if he wasn't caught by Ackermann's guards. Maybe he was one of them? Or maybe he was simply a poacher who, like me, had strayed out of his league.

'Where to?' asked Sara, wide awake now.

'The first plane for England. That's where.'

'But I've got the car, the SS,' she said. For the moment I'd forgotten she'd taken it.

'Why did you come back?' I asked her over my shoulder as I crammed in my few belongings from a drawer into my bag, and then went into the bathroom for my electric shaver and toothbrush.

'I had to.'

'Why? You only left this afternoon.'

'I'll have to tell you the whole story,' she said. 'It goes back a long way.'

'Tell me in the car, then.'

I hadn't got time to listen; I hadn't all that much interest, either. It might have helped if she'd told me more when I'd asked her first, back in my mews. But now I couldn't see how anything she might say could gain me friends or influence anyone, and right then I dearly wanted both.

I zipped up my bag.

'Are you staying or coming?' I asked her, thinking that this sounded rather like the first line of a limerick.

'Coming.'

'Right. Then just to fill you in, I've sold the Merc. I've got the money in cash, and I want to stay alive to enjoy it.'

'How will we get to England tonight in the SS?'

I paused, remembering what the clerk had told me earlier. I could drive to Madrid and catch an early plane, but I'd rather be out of the country before morning with the safety of the frontier behind me.

'Biarritz,' I said. 'Then up by train to the car ferry. They'll have a flight.' Or, at least, I hoped they would.

I picked up my bag, and opened the bedroom door. Sara followed me out into a room across the corridor and collected her bag; I noticed she had not even unpacked.

'Where's the SS?'

'Down the road. In the garage.'

'I'll settle up while you get it,' I told her. Nothing like giving women work to do. So long as they're busy they've less time to find fault with what you're doing. I'd leave Ingrid's Mini where it was; that would give her a little aggravation later on, explaining why it was blocking the road. It was the most I could do to annoy her.

I carried down our luggage, paid my bill, took the money in its brown envelope from the safe, opened my bag and wrapped it in a leg of my spare trousers so that it wouldn't be seen if the bag was opened for a cursory customs examination.

By the time I reached the door, Sara had the SS outside, the engine running to warm the oil. She slid over from the wheel, and I climbed into the familiar cramped cockpit, threw my bag and the box of Mercedes tools into the back, slipped off the handbrake and accelerated away through the sleeping town. Our exhaust beat back from shutters where countless summers had powdered the paint from stone buildings grey with age. The clock tower was still lit up; a few cats prowled alleys that had been old when the Saracens were young. We drove over the cobbles, past little batches of shrubs, with stone statues, past the bull ring. Then the town fell behind us, and we were out on the empty road, night moths drifting across the long path of our P100s. The luminous centre line of the road glowed yellow in their glare. At intervals, in the fields, advertising reflectors glittered red and blue eyes at us: Pegaso, Beba Fanta. Another time, I thought, I'll drink Fanta. Another time, I'll make home base. Maybe.

I turned to Sara.

'Now, why did you come back? The truth. All of it.'

She began to speak, her voice so soft that I had to throttle back to three and a half thousand revs to hear her at all.

'It's a long story,' she began hesitantly, and I knew she didn't want to tell it.

'We've a long ride,' I reminded her.

She said nothing for at least a minute, and then she began.

'My name originally wasn't Greatheart, it was Grossherz. I was born in Germany. When I came over here after the war, Greatheart seemed the best translation.

'Both my parents were killed in the war. In Cologne. The first thousand-bomber raid. Then my uncle adopted me. He was a doctor in Berlin. He and his wife had a son about my own age and they couldn't have any more children. They were very kind to me.

'At the end of the war, my uncle was anxious to escape from Berlin before the Russians came. He wanted to take us to relations in South Germany. Uncle had two cars, a little thing he used for his practice, and the Mercedes he'd bought cheaply early in the war, as an investment, I suppose. The little car wouldn't run – I don't know why – so he couldn't take that. He'd saved petrol from what he was allowed for his practice, and we were going in the Mercedes.

As things were, money had little value then, but this car might conceivably be sold to some American soldier for food if we grew desperate.

'We were leaving when two Gestapo officers arrived and said they had to requisition this Mercedes. My uncle protested, and I remember a lot of shouting. The officers rushed off in the car – and ran over my cousin. My uncle nearly went mad. He hit one of the officers, who pulled out a gun and shot him. Dead. All this in the very early morning when we were packed to go, and we were terrified. Later, some orderlies came and cleared the bodies away.

'My aunt and I stayed in the house, for we couldn't possibly reach her relations without a car. The Russians came to Berlin, and officers kept on visiting her, and asking questions about our Mercedes. The SS officers had used it for some journey connected with Hitler. They wanted to know what, but of course my aunt had no idea. The Russians were polite, so far as I remember, but very insistent. They kept asking the same questions over and over again. They seemed convinced that Hitler wasn't dead. If he hadn't escaped in this car, then at least it had had something to do with his disappearance. We didn't even know where the car was – and, of course, we knew absolutely nothing about their theory.

'After a while, the Russians seemed to believe us, and left us alone. Then East German police – our part of Berlin was in East Germany – began to call on us. And they asked virtually the same questions.

'Finally, we were allowed to come to England. It was easier to get out then. My aunt worked as a housekeeper, a companion to old women, anything to give me a home. She was working for Mrs Meredith when she heard quite unexpectedly from the Control Commission people in Germany that our Mercedes had been found. This would be some time in the late nineteen forties.

'My uncle's name was on a plate under the bonnet, and we'd been traced. Anyhow, it would be shipped to us, if we would pay costs.

'The car was useless to us, of course, for we couldn't afford to run it, and with petrol still rationed, no one wanted a car that size. However, it *was* ours, really the only expensive thing we owned, and my aunt got it back. She sold it to Mrs Meredith's son when petrol came off the ration, and he ran it for a bit.'

'Was he killed at Suez?' I asked, remembering the police inspector.

Sara shook her head.

'No. Mrs Meredith lived in a dream world with her birds and her memories. She'd ring for servants who weren't there. She imagined her son had died a hero, because in reality he was a no-good.'

I knew many people who lived in dreams because reality was unbearable. In my own mews I knew a man who made his living boring thin holes in phony antique furniture, to make buyers think it had woodworm. He had a limp which he told me was a result of frostbite on the Arctic convoys during the war. That was his dream. In fact, he was pissed one night in the blackout, and fell down the stairs of Theobalds Road public lavatory, where he'd followed a coloured airman who he thought was gay.

And at the other end of the mews I knew a man who dignified himself in his dreams by imagining he was a writer. In reality, he'd hang about Brighton front during the off-season and pick up girls. If he made home base, then he had it off, Speedy Gonzalez fashion, under the pier. If they ran away screaming, as they sometimes did, then he stepped smartly into the nearest telephone box and became a writer. He rang all the London newspapers, reversing charges, of course, to give lurid details of this dastardly incident. Next day, they would carry such headlines as: 'Brighton sex-maniac's attack foiled'. They paid him, too, never realizing that the story was the same each time; the names were the only things that changed.

The wish to rise above reality was also the same; only the dreams were different.

'Anyway,' Sara continued, 'my aunt remarried and emigrated to Australia with her new husband. I went to Canada and worked as a secretary for three years, got my citizenship and then came back to England. I went to see Mrs Meredith – she was about the only friend I had there.

'She'd grown very odd and vague. I don't even know if she remembered my name, but she remembered me, and said that some German had been looking for me, only months after I'd left. He'd left her a telephone number – she'd forgotten my address in Canada, or lost it, so I rang him out of curiosity to see who he was. We met in London, and he told me he was working for the East German Government.

'They believed that someone in Spain who was collecting Mercedes cars – he'd placed advertisements in motor magazines all round the world through a go-between – wasn't a genuine collector at all. He really wanted one special car for some secret reason, a car he had driven from Berlin at the end of the war. Ours.

'Then this man made his proposition. If I'd somehow manage to get this car into the man's hands, they'd follow it through and discover why he wanted it.'

She paused.

'What was there in it for you?' I asked, negotiating an unfenced level-crossing ten miles an hour too quickly. No one did a deal unless there was something in it for themselves; if not money, then pride, or satisfaction, even revenge.

'He said that my cousin, Toni, hadn't really been killed. He was still alive. In Leipzig. They'd give him an exit permit and his fare to anywhere he liked. After his accident he had been a cripple.'

'Did you believe that?' I asked her.

'They showed me photographs. He *could* be my cousin. I just didn't know. It all happened so long ago. But I felt I had to find out.'

'Why pick on me to sell the car?'

'I got a list of old-car dealers. You were the first – in alphabetical order. If you hadn't been interested, I'd have rung the next.'

We drove in silence for a while.

'Who was the bus driver?'

'I don't know his name,' she said. 'But he's an East German. When he knocked you out, I thought he was just a thug. Then he produced a photo of Toni. He wanted to know what the hell I was doing there. He thought you were following him – that you were an agent of some sort.'

'I am,' I said. 'I'm a water agent.'

Sara didn't even smile, and I must say I didn't expect her to.

'He told me that if I wanted to see Toni again, I'd better get back to England, and they'd contact me. He didn't trust me. He obviously thought I was going to twist him, but how, God only knows. So I took your SS and started off for Biarritz.'

'What made you come back?'

'The fact that I didn't trust *him*. After all, I'd only the word of that man I'd met in London who said he could help Toni. I'd no means of checking what he said, either about Toni or himself. The farther I was away from whatever was happening, the less chance I would have of influencing anything. So I turned round and came back.'

'Why did you choose the Monterrey?'

'There are five main hotels in Salamanca. I got their names from the tourist office. You weren't booked in any of the other four. You were the only lead I had, so I chose your hotel. That's why I even waited in your room, because then you couldn't leave without seeing me.'

'Who's the fellow without a face?' I asked her.

'No idea. He didn't say a word when we were in the bus.'

'I see,' I said, but did I?

I only saw part of the picture. I knew the fascination that the mystery of Hitler's death held for East Germany and Russia. Hitler's body had officially never been found, and the Communists desperately wanted to find it – or to know for sure what had happened to him.

A lot of evidence pointed to the fact that he had shot himself in the head, but this evidence was still largely circumstantial, like the theory that he had poisoned himself. Members of his staff had seen Eva Braun's body in his room in the bunker in Berlin and recognized her. They had also seen a man they took to be Hitler – because he was in Hitler's uniform – but they could not recognize the Fuehrer, because the front of this man's face had been shot away.

In years of attempting to prove or disprove whether Hitler had actually died like this, the Russians had painfully brought back to Berlin all the staff and orderlies they had captured in Hitler's bunker, and had ordered them to repeat their actions of the last few days of the war.

They had dug up hundreds of yards of earth around the Chancellery, they had examined dozens of charred corpses, but had they ever discovered either Hitler's body or the body of Eva Braun?

Were they buried elsewhere – *or had they died at all*?

I glanced uneasily behind me in the driving mirror. Nothing but darkness – as complete as my own mystification.

I looked across at Sara; she lay back against the seat, her face pale in the faint green glow of the dashlights. I think she was asleep, and I wished I were, too. I seemed to have lost count of days and nights.

I glanced again in the mirror. A faint phosphorescent glow brushed the rim of hill behind me, and then was gone. Some lorry, probably travelling north, I thought, stacked high with olives or frozen meat or drums of wine, or whatever else they carried at night in Spain.

I glanced again a few seconds later. The light was brighter. Surely no lorry could travel at that speed? I checked all my gauges: we had twelve gallons of petrol in the tank, the oil pressure stood steady at forty, and even with the headlamps on main beam, we were charging at five amps, but somehow none of these facts gave me any real reassurance. The light grew stronger behind me, and so did my unease – quite irrationally, I kept telling myself, for if it wasn't a lorry, it could easily be someone like me, making for Biarritz and an early flight to England.

There was no reason at all why this unknown should be

chasing me, but having been knocked out, kidnapped, beaten up and threatened with a gun, all within the last few hours, my nerves weren't what they used to be. The fact is, I felt so jittery that if someone had leapt out of the bushes and offered me a Phantom III with a torpedo body, owned by a peer all its life, kept in a heated garage, etc, I wouldn't even have stopped to take a look.

That's the difference between fact and fiction. In fiction no one on the side of the angels is ever hurt or frightened or tired for very long. In life, an awful lot of people are one or more or all these things nearly all the time, and, speaking for myself, I'd been all three for far too long. What I wanted now was to be on the first plane out to Lydd, then put my money in the bank, and forget that any of this had ever really happened. But if whoever was behind me was hostile, would I achieve any of these modest aims?

I dropped down to third and wound up the engine, and then slipped back into top, and we batted along for a bit at a steady ninety. Now and then, I would catch a blaze of headlamps in my mirror as he took a hairpin bend, and each time the lights grew bigger and brighter. It could only be minutes before he saw my silhouette, if he hadn't already, and at that speed, if he were after me, I didn't give much for my chances. I had to pull off the road somewhere and hide up and let him go by. Or if he didn't want to go, to have it out with him. But – where?

I turned off my own lights, and closed my eyes for a second to accustom them to moonlight. Two miles up the road, through a sharp bend and over a narrow bridge, the olives gave place to little feathery groves of trees by the side of a river. I throttled back to twenty-five, turned off the road behind a clump of trees, so that they would screen the car from the approaching headlights, and switched off the engine.

The night lay silent as a fallen shroud. Somewhere, an owl began to call, probably in protest at having its hunting spoiled, and behind us an unseen river gurgled over rocks. I put my hand down in the right-hand door pocket. The bus driver's automatic was still there. I woke Sara up, and handed the gun to her. Then I broke the revolver I had taken from Ackermann's guard, checked that it still held four rounds. I didn't want to use guns, but if I had to, I would.

'What's happening?' asked Sara sleepily, stretching luxuriously.

'I think we're being followed.'

I took her hand and we ran across the tufted grass, silver under the moon, towards the river. A small bank dipped down about three feet to a beach of soft shingle and the river. We crouched down together behind this bank, watching the line of the road. Personally, I'd rather look at a girl in a tight dress and watch for the line of the pants.

'What?' Sara began, but I hadn't time for talk. I pushed off the safety catch on the bus driver's gun for her.

'Don't fire unless I say,' I told her. 'And if I do say, fire low down, because bullets rise.'

Some midges were whining about, maybe because we'd broken up a beautiful thing between them. One settled on my neck and bit me. I cursed it under my breath. I had enough trouble.

The lights were now growing stronger to our right. I heard the rise and fall of an engine, as an expert worked his way up and down the cogs. Then the car came through the last bend like a dose of salts through a man with dysentery, over the bridge, and past us.

The huge headlamps bored out long bright tunnels of light, in which trees stood briefly and unbelievably green and then died in darkness as the car was gone. The engine backfired with a boom like a gun as the driver changed down for the bridge, and I felt Sara stiffen beside me. I put out my own hand on the safety catch in case she fired by accident, but she didn't.

The driver hadn't seen us. I suppose he had enough on his mind trying to coax upwards of two tons of heavy metal through the bend at that speed. Anyway, he was gone with a great bellow of open exhaust, and, silhouetted against the backward blaze of his lights, I recognized the familiar round tail and the raked V windscreen of the white Mercedes. Its exhaust echoed and re-echoed like gunfire going up through the valley, until distance dimmed it, and then there was nothing but the owl hooting and the whine of the gnats in my ears. They'd had quite a night for interrupttions; maybe they could make up for it by sleeping late.

We waited for another five minutes before we stood up rather sheepishly, and brushed damp earth off our clothes. Whoever was driving the Mercedes was also going north. All that lay in the north of this road was the frontier – and Biarritz. Was he planning to fly the car back to England?

I put my gun back in the door pocket and checked with the AA map; we had at least another forty miles to go before we reached San Sebastian and the frontier. I started the engine. My stomach still felt like a stone, for if we could hide off the road so easily, so could he. I could imagine an ambush, a few rocks across a Z-bend, or the branch of a tree thrown over the road to make us slow down, and then the spray of bullets from the darkness. The memory of the bus driver's shattered hand, the unexpected red rawness of pulped flesh, returned with uncomfortable clarity.

I found a bar of chocolate in the side pocket, broke it in two and gave Sara half. We munched this as we drove, more slowly now, because I wanted to give myself some chance if there was an ambush. But there wasn't.

I kept imagining I saw the white Merc, cold and menacing, in every pool of moonlight, for now my nerves were like frayed cuffs. I remembered David Scott-Moncrieff's story of the ghostly white Mercedes that had haunted the Great North Road in the nineteen twenties. All kinds of people swore they had seen this car, driven by a skeleton with another by its side. They had indeed seen the car – but David had been its driver with a fellow under-graduate as his passenger, both wearing black tracksuits, on which they'd painted luminous skeletons and skulls.

I suddenly realized how tired I was. I hadn't slept since God knows when. I hadn't eaten much for hours, except for this chocolate. It was madness to drive farther without a rest.

I glanced at Sara; she was asleep, still holding the automatic. I took it out of her hand and put it in the door pocket, and then drove the SS off the road on to a track that led I didn't know where, and didn't greatly care. I turned the car so that we were facing the road in case I had to make a quick getaway. Then I loosened my shoes, undid my collar, and leaned back on the hard bucket seat.

I must have slept instantly, for the next thing I remember was feeling sunshine warm on my face, and seeing three old shepherds wearing what appeared to be the cast-off clothes of some scarecrow, surrounded by a flock of sheep, come down the track.

I climbed out of the car and stretched myself. My joints had rusted together with cold and weariness. I nodded to the shepherds and they nodded back. I suppose they envied me. I certainly envied them the comfortable night I assumed they had spent, even shacked up with their sheep. Certainly, I thought, I must be the only character I'd heard of who'd had two chances with two girls in two days – and done neither and done nothing. It was all in my mind, I thought, and went off to have a pee and a quick wash in a trickling mountain stream.

When I got back to the car, Sara had awoken and apparently done the same, because she looked fresher. There wasn't much to say, so we didn't say it, but drove off up the road.

At Biarritz we could buy a meal, and maybe I would be able to plug in my electric razor in some washroom, but in any case I should be back in England within hours. We crossed the frontier at Irun and reached Biarritz about nine. The railway people weren't expecting us, for we hadn't booked, and so all they could offer us was the chance of a cancellation. But two other cars were already ahead of us, which meant that there wouldn't be very much chance. I figured I could drive north to Calais, but there was no guarantee we could get the car on a plane.

'If we can't get on a train, what are we going to do?' Sara asked me.

I hadn't thought of this, but the idea of hanging about indefinitely held no attractions whatsoever, for there was no certainty that we would even have a place next day. I feel like that fellow who ferried endlessly between Hong Kong and the mainland because neither side would let him ashore. I didn't like the feeling.

'What do *you* suggest?' I asked Sara, throwing the question back at her.

She said nothing, so I asked the booking-office clerk what he thought of our chances for a place on the train the following morning. He didn't think highly of them.

'This is the beginning of the holiday season,' he explained. 'It is a matter of any cancellation.'

So there it was. We left it there because we had nowhere else to leave it.

Half a dozen English cars stood in the station yard with luggage on roof racks, and children's toys on the back shelves. I supposed they had come off the train, and the families were having a meal before starting their holiday.

I parked behind a blue Cortina with go-faster tape along its side, buttoned down the tonneau, and then Sara and I went into the restaurant and ordered an English breakfast. After several cups of black coffee and a plate of bacon and eggs, I began to thaw out into a more human being, and gradually came back into the second half of the twentieth century.

A young couple with a small child were sitting next to me. The man wore a high-necked sweater with a polka-dot scarf, and he kept looking at me as though he wanted to say something. The wife I didn't go on, so she didn't register with me at all. Finally, this character cleared his throat and leaned towards me.

'Excuse me,' he said in a Midlands accent, 'but do you own that SS out there?'

'Yes,' I said, because I did, although anyone else could have it for a price. My price.

'You're parked next to my Cortina,' he said.

I didn't deny it. But what the hell was he getting at?

'Funny thing,' he went on, 'my brother-in-law had one of those cars years ago. Must be worth a lot now.'

I didn't disagree with this, either, although whether it was a funny thing depended on your sense of humour – or your sense of values.

'Of course, they don't make them like that any more,' the man continued. 'Haven't seen one for years, either. At least not in that condition. But maybe they go in pairs, or something. Yours is the second old car I've seen out there since I started breakfast.'

'What was the first?' asked Sara.

'A Mercedes. Long as a bus and only just room for two people. Fantastic thing. White.'

'See who was driving it?' I asked him, trying to keep interest out of my voice.

'Fellow in dark glasses. Middle-aged.'

'Did you speak to him?'

'Didn't have a chance. I was getting my car off the truck. I think he was trying to book on the train, but there wasn't any room. Two cars were waiting already for cancellations, ahead of him, so he pushed off. Last I saw, he was filling up with petrol. Must take a lot of juice, but perhaps he hasn't got currency problems to worry about.'

I supposed that would be the least of his worries, whoever he was. With the dollars in my bag it wasn't worrying me too much, either.

Just then, a loudspeaker crackled into a spiel of French. The train was about to leave. People began to walk towards the door. I paid the bill and followed them.

'What do you think?' I asked Sara.

She didn't ask me what about, and I didn't expect her to. We both realized we were thinking the same thoughts. I hate to leave loose ends, and I wanted to know who was driving the Mercedes and where he was going, and why he was going there. I guessed Sara did, too. I climbed into the SS, and drove over to the petrol station, and told the attendant to fill the tank. He was a talkative chap. Petrol-pump attendants, like barbers, usually are. I started him off by saying I'd heard he'd had another old car through that morning.

He nodded.

'A fantastic car, monsieur,' he agreed enthusiastically. 'Haven't seen one of those since I was a boy.'

'I think it's a friend of mine driving,' I told him, bending the truth a bit. 'I've just missed him here.'

At least the latter part of the sentence was entirely true.

'Did you see which road he took?'

'No, but I sold him three route maps. Special offer for everyone who buys more than thirty litres of petrol. He wanted the quickest route to Switzerland. Geneva.'

He snapped shut the petrol-tank filler. I paid him and climbed back into the car.

'He's off to Geneva,' I said to Sara.

'I heard,' she replied.

I sat there for a minute while the man wiped my windscreen with a chamois – not the animal, but the leather – and I dredged over in my mind what he and the young fellow in the restaurant had told me.

I already knew that Ackermann was on his way to Geneva, as fast as may be, in his own plane, because I'd been with him when he'd decided to go. He wasn't going there for the snow or to take the waters, or just to sit by the lake and watch the girls go by. He was going because of something he had read on that tatty, tattered bit of paper he had prised out from behind the door upholstery in the Mercedes.

He wasn't one of my closest friends, but even so I guessed he was rich enough not to move his jack in a hurry – unless he considered it mightily important for him to do so. And what could be that important to a rich man? It might be more money, because as some old millionaire, to whom I once sold a Bugatti Royale, told me, there are only two states in a man's financial life: you either have no money at all, or you don't have enough. Ever.

So, if it was more money that Ackermann was after, Geneva was well set up with banks and all the delicate precision machinery of numbered accounts and financial secrecy that the Swiss manage so well. The gnomes of Zürich. The tellers of Geneva. Money, as well as time, is the art of the Swiss.

On the other hand, it just might not be money. It could be some threat of exposure from the past, but this I rather doubted. Ackermann hadn't looked worried, and I'd seen rich men look worried when some little girl had come along with the proposal that she would publish some photographs or some letters he had forgotten all about, if he didn't come across with an open-ended charge account at Harrods or Kutchinsky's.

So, if I allowed that Ackermann was after more money – what the hell was the other fellow after? He certainly faced a hard drive in the heavy metal of the Mercedes, so it must be important to him, too. I wasn't a close friend of his, either, but reasoned that if he knew what the car had concealed, he would not have needed to become involved with Ackermann at all. Ergo, as my old Latin master used to say, when he wasn't saying sarcastic things about my Latin, he was after human flesh – presumably Ackermann's.

So what the hell was I after, except a bit of the other, which I didn't seem likely to get in this world or the next? Basically – and I'm a pretty basic person – I was after what Ackermann was after. Money. Dough. Specie. Geld. The folding stuff. The little green men on the kitchen table.

Ackermann might be out of my league financially, and probably sexually, too, but there are crumbs to be picked from the rich man's table, and my crumb could be that Mercedes. I didn't feel that whoever had stolen the car was a collector. It had cost him nothing, anyhow, and he might take a quick small price to be rid of it. So here was a chance to do a deal of which all dealers dream – to sell the same car twice over. And with a good paint job, and new upholstery and a bit of rechroming and a set of tyres with the name picked out in gold, I could shift this heap for five thousand quid of any rich nutter's money. I might even sell it back to Mercedes themselves for publicity purposes. In that case, it could be worth eight. This wouldn't be strictly ethical, of course, but what of that. We're not in Ethics, we're in Suthex, as one old Brighton queen told another. And I was in business to make money, not to horse about with academic considerations.

My mind was revolving as fast as the flywheel on a Honda 800. There might be risks, but then there are risks in crossing the road and going to bed, even alone. And with the number of people who die in bed, it makes you think you should sleep standing up like a horse.

I didn't fear Ackermann or the other man in a crowded city, because that's my background. It is only in the lonely country places that they might be dangerous, and even there I'd manage to keep afloat.

'What's wrong?' asked Sara, and the man with the chamois in his hand was staring at me as though I wasn't going to tip him or maybe was about to change sex. I did the former. The latter could wait, for my money, or for anyone else's.

'I'm thinking,' I told Sara, and believe me, I was.

I took out my *Autocar* diary and looked at the map in the back. I could drive north to Cherbourg, and even if I couldn't book on a Channel plane with the car, I could almost certainly cross by the sea ferry.

The distance, according to the scale, which was probably fairly accurate, was about five hundred miles from Biarritz to Cherbourg. From Biarritz to Geneva was only about seventy miles more.

I shut the diary and put it back in my pocket. I am not the sort of person to turn up the chance of a deal for the matter of a couple of gallons of petrol, so I made up my mind. Have a go, Joe, I thought. Your mother won't know. It didn't much matter even if she did, because she's seventy-eight, and alive and well and living in Ashton-under-Lyne.

'What's the matter?' asked Sara again, more anxiously this time.

'I've stopped thinking,' I said. 'I'm going to Geneva.'

'I thought you might,' she said. not really surprised.

'The question is – if anyone's asking questions, and I'm asking one right now – are you coming, or staying, or what the hell are you doing?'

'Am I still financing you?' she asked me.

She should go far, this girl, I thought; she sounds like a married woman already.

'I've enough money to cover the cost of the trip,' I told her.

'What do you expect to find in Geneva? Isn't enough, enough?'

'Enough of what?' I asked, thinking of one thing. 'I don't know what I'm going to find. But neither did Columbus when he set sail, or Edison when he joined the wires together.'

'Are you all right?' asked Sara.

'As right as I've ever been. I'm not sure what Ackermann's after in Geneva, but I'm damned sure the other fellow's after Ackermann. I don't care whether they get each other, have each other, or serve each other's nuts as shish kebab à la Geneva. Maybe they'll be so concerned with each other or what they're after – which isn't what I'm after – that they'll forget about the car. I think we can make enough to finance a number of trips if I can pick that up again.'

'I don't like it,' said Sara.

'You're not getting it,' I said, and started the engine.

It was as simple as that.

She already had the AA Continental handbook open at the road map as we set off. Curiosity might have killed the cat, but it wasn't going to kill us.

CHAPTER SEVEN

I don't want to bore you with details about driving up across the spine of France; of filling up with petrol twice, of eating meals in roadside cafés, changing a wheel in Albi, and having to hammer back a cylinder core plug outside Grenoble, when the water boiled and the overflow blocked on one of the hairpins.

Suffice it to say, as the Victorian novelists used to write when they couldn't be bothered to beat out twenty-eight chapters of descriptive crappo, we reached Geneva by eleven o'clock that night.

Our journey hadn't set up any records, but at least we were there. The first hotel I stopped at was full. The second had a desk clerk with a Viva Zapata moustache, and he stroked this and said, yes he *thought* he could help us, and if I would just care to drive my car into their garage, while madam waited, it would all be arranged.

I handed him my passport, and drove the car down into the basement garage. When I came back into the hotel, Sara had gone. The clerk handed me a card with a room number written on it. I took it and then something in his face made me turn back.

'Where's this room, then?' I asked him.

'Twelfth floor,' he purred. 'A single.'

'A *single*?'

The calendar on his desk told me it had been Sunday all day. It certainly wasn't my day. Six days shalt thou labour and do all thou hast to do. At this rate, I wasn't going to do anyone.

The man bowed, as well he might.

'The whole hotel is full, sir, except for these two single rooms. They are usually for couriers. I'm sorry, but it is all we have.'

'On the same floor?'

'I regret not, sir. Madam is on the third floor.'

I regretted that, too, a lot more than he did, but what the hell? What did the Moslems say? Prayer is better than sleep. Not always, though, I thought, as I followed the page into the lift; it depends on who you're praying to, and who you're sleeping with.

Fact is, after a bath, I was so damn tired that, as the writers of the schoolboy adventures popular in my youth used to say, I was asleep as soon as my head touched the pillow. I stayed that way, too, until half past nine the next morning, so maybe it was as well I was on my own.

I rang down to room service for a couple of fried eggs and four rashers, a pot of black coffee and some hot rolls and honey – to hell with the Continental breakfast. Then I rang Sara. When she answered, I heard water running in the background, and she said I'd got her out of the bath. I thought I'd rather get her in it, so I said all right then, and gave her my room number.

I felt like one of the three nuns: can't find none, ain't got none, can't get one. I was getting nothing out of all this, not even a kiss, that application at headquarters for a job at base. I wondered what George would say if he knew. But then he would never know. No one must ever know.

The breakfast arrived and so did Sara, and then I rang the airport.

As I expected, no one named Ackermann had flown in from anywhere, but a Mr Hans Burgdorff had arrived from Salamanca in a private Comanche.

'I've an urgent message for the owner of this plane from Salamanca,' I told the man at the other end of the line. 'I must have confused the name. It's a matter of life and death' – it certainly was that, if nothing else. 'Could you please tell me where he is staying?'

'The Bristol,' he said, after checking with someone else.

I thanked him. So now I knew something. I knew how George would rhyme Bristol. Bristol City – titty. I rang the

Bristol and was told that Mr Burgdorff was not in his suite, but that a message could be taken. I thanked the operator, and rang off. Any message for Mr Burgdorff I meant to deliver myself.

Sara and I left the SS100 in its garage, for it was far too distinctive, and after my drive on its hard springs and big wheels, I hankered after something a little softer on my backside, so I booked a self-drive Volkswagen – which was about as anonymous a car as I could find – from Hertz on the Diner's Club.

Funny thing about civilization, I thought, as I signed the form; if you produce a little plastic card with your name on it, people will immediately sell you all kinds of things all round the world without further question – but if you try to pay cash, you run into every sort of trouble. I always use the Diner's Club – and each time I sign it, I hope to die before the bill comes in. One day this wish will be granted. Was this what Omar Khayyám had in mind when he said, take the cash and let the credit go?

We didn't drive right up to the Bristol, but parked in a spare space about fifty yards along the street, where I could watch the main entrance. It was only as I sat there that I realized I had left both my guns in the SS. I told you, I would never make a cop; I do all the wrong things.

I hoped that no one in the garage gave the car a going over and found them, because the Swiss wisely don't like firearms being brought into their country undeclared. I also hoped I wouldn't need to use a gun, but it certainly gives you a feeling of security when it's there; you only miss it when it's gone, as the eunuch told the sultan. This thought led to another, and after last night, my mind was freewheeling over what a eunuch did for fun, when I suddenly saw Ackermann going into the hotel.

I just had time to recognize his face, and then he was gone. We sat about for another twenty minutes, and he came out again. I don't know what I expected him to do, or where I expected him to go, but we were out of the car and across the road before he was round the next corner.

It's a hell of a lot harder to follow someone along a crowded street than it looks in a film, because people get between you, and others stop right in front of you to look in shop windows, and you bump into them. Also, the person you're following may stop himself, and, unless you're lively, you can even bump into him, too.

Suddenly, Sara gripped my arm. I was just going to say, lower and slower, when I saw why. Kellner was also walking in the same direction, but on the opposite side of the road. He wore a light raincoat and a tweed hat. His face I didn't see, and it wouldn't have meant anything to me if I had, for he must have had a mask on, because no one was giving him a second glance. Only the set of his broad shoulders, the look of his head from the rear, gave him away. So, he must have been driving the Mercedes, he was the man who was following Ackermann. Fragments of what the barman in the Monterrey had told me about Kellner's conversation as he came round from the anaesthetic filtered back to me. A lot of things began to make a little more sense.

At an intersection, Ackermann waited for the lights to change, and we crossed within fifty yards of each other. Just at that moment, I saw a girl driving an open amber 1929 Packard with one of the very rare Waterhouse bodies, carrying two spare wheels on the tail, and I was split in two like a schizophrenic, half of me wanting to wave to her and make an offer, and the other half intent on following Ackermann. The other half won, but by a short head only. With infinite sadness I watched this amber beast glide away, and out of my life.

Ackermann turned into the marble entrance of one of those new anodized metal-and-glass buildings that are robbing the world's cities of all their ancient individuality. There was some phony metal sculpture outside, and, underneath, a bronze plaque: Banque-Suisse-Simplon.

'I'll walk on, and see what happens to Kellner,' I told Sara. 'You go in and see if you can find where Ackermann's going. He doesn't know you, so he can't recognize you.'

I walked to the end of the bank, which stretched for a

block, hoping the Packard driver would stop, but she didn't. So I did, and lit a cigarette, looking in at a window, through the horizontal plastic slats of the venetian blinds, at all the pretty, sexless antiseptic girls sitting in rows working adding machines, and the men in their Dacron suits, cropped hair and horn-rimmed glasses, rising executives, or whatever, threading their way among them importantly, carrying files.

These were only husks in the basement, I thought without envy; the worker bees. The real business would be done upstairs, by other men wearing hundred-guinea suits and hand-made crocodile shoes, with dead eyes looking out at each other from grey, massaged, centrally heated faces.

Looking through the window, I not only saw these birds with their little titties jumping up and down inside their blouses, which wasn't a bad way of spending five minutes, but, more importantly, I could see Kellner's reflection in the glass.

He was glancing through a magazine he had bought from a stand in the street, but he was also watching the bank. I don't think he was any more of a pro than I was. I had a wild desire to cross the road and say, 'Hello, and how are things going, then?' but at that moment Sara came out.

'He's taken the lift to the eighteenth floor,' she said.

'What's up there?' I asked.

'Special Deposits. There's a board in the hall to show where all the offices are.'

Special Deposits meant nothing to me. They could refer to anything from pigeon droppings to minerals in the earth, but I suppose the term had some banking significance. I thought briefly of my own overdraft, and then the traffic lights changed and Kellner was crossing the road, his magazine folded neatly under his right arm. He was walking away from us, and then he paused as though he had just remembered something – or maybe he was just pretending he had just remembered something – and he turned round and went up the steps of the bank.

Had he recognized us, or didn't that matter either way

now? And, what could he do in any case? Things like this seem so easy when you see them on the box, because they are predetermined and the pieces slide perfectly into place like a jigsaw puzzle, but in life very little is predetermined, and for all I knew, both these men could be walking through the bank, and out into a different street, and I'd lost them for ever.

I took Sara's arm and we went into the hall. It smelled slightly metallic with the air-conditioning, and people were milling around trying to look important, and maybe they were, for at least they knew where they were going and what their business was, which was more than we could say about ourselves.

There were three sets of lifts in the back of the hall, each serving six floors. Kellner went through the third door, and I watched the signs light up as the lift soared past the thirteenth, fourteenth, fifteenth, sixteenth, seventeenth floors and stopped at the eighteenth. Special Deposits again.

It came down without any intermediate stops, and we were the only passengers to go up in it. Piped music was playing *South of the Border*, which all took me back a long way, and I wished I was staying back a long way because I couldn't think what the hell I was going to say when I reached the eighteenth floor, or who I was going to say it to.

The doors puffed open by compressed air, and we were out in a long corridor with walls covered in brown hessian between impersonal, anodized metal doors. To the right of the lift, on thick-pile carpet, was a curved black desk with three telephones and an intercom. A girl with her hair piled high on her head, because she'd nowhere else to pile it, was typing a letter at a side table. She swung round in her swivel chair, but the front of the desk was covered in, so I couldn't see her legs.

'Can I help you?' she asked, with a receptionist's professional brightness.

'Friend of mine just came up,' I said. 'I didn't even know he was in Geneva. Name of Burgdorff.'

She looked at me a bit sharply then, as though she might say something more, but all she said was: 'He's in with the manager. Room 1802. Will you wait?'

She made a gesture towards two black settees with those big round buttons on the leather, like they used to have in the upholstery of Edwardian cars.

We sat down, and now that I was right on the edge of action, my mouth felt dry, and my knees were trembling a bit, and I was glad of the seat, which shows I'm growing old.

'You are English?' asked the receptionist.

'Yes,' I said. I suppose I must have looked shabby or something. I certainly felt it.

'Are you all together, then?'

'How many of us do you mean?' I asked.

'The other gentleman.'

'What other gentleman?' I asked, as though I didn't already know.

'He came up just in front of you. He is also waiting for Mr' – she glanced briefly at a note she had made – 'Burgdorff.'

'Where is he waiting?' I asked.

She nodded slightly up the corridor to the left.

'In the men's room.'

Well, whatever he was doing there shouldn't take him all that long, and apart from my own bank manager, Kellner was about the last person I wanted to meet. I tried to keep my feelings out of my face, so I stood up to take my face away.

'I'll have a look at these abstract paintings while we're waiting,' I told the girl. 'The other fellow you mentioned isn't actually a friend of mine. In fact, we're rather in competition, so I'll move down the corridor just in case we meet.'

I smiled weakly at her, as I suppose a commercial traveller would if someone has just beat him to an important appointment.

Sara and I walked down the polished black rubber floor, stopping opposite the ludicrous messes of paint and bent raw metal that had been framed and hung on the walls, no doubt at enormous cost to the bank shareholders. Nature I love, I thought, and next to nature, art. In fact, when you can sell pictures that have been painted with a donkey's tail, it's nigh on time for people like me to be moving into the artistic field.

The lift stopped again, and the doors hissed pneumatically. A man in a white Continental raincoat, with straps at the cuffs, came out, bowed towards the girl, showed her a card. She pointed to the manager's door, and pressed a buzzer.

The man crossed the corridor, glanced briefly at us, tapped on the door, and went inside. He didn't look like a bank clerk to me. There was something about his purposeful tread, his broad shoulders, and his dark bristley hair, so short it looked as though it had been sprayed on his skull, that all spelled cop to me. The washroom door still stayed shut, and I didn't feel inclined to open it.

I turned back with Sara.

'Look at this magnificent creation,' I told her, and pointed to six coils of copper wire and a lot of red ochre on a mirror hanging on the wall. The mirror was useful because I could see when the washroom door opened.

I stood looking, trying hard to hear what was going on inside the manager's room, but although I could hear voices I couldn't understand what they said. Also, they could have been talking in French or German, which didn't help me any. The whole thing seemed a waste of time. We might as well go down eighteen floors to the street, have a coffee, and say we'd tried. But what had we tried? Nothing, as the eunuch told the sultan.

Dr Johnson once declared that we dig our graves with our tongues, our teeth, or our tails, but I seemed to be digging mine standing up, looking at a picture I didn't like, trying to overhear a conversation I couldn't understand.

No one seemed to be doing much business in the corridor, whatever they were doing in the offices – even the receptionist had disappeared. Suddenly the manager's door opened so quickly that I just had time to turn my back towards it so that whoever came out wouldn't see my face. I heard someone click the lock button in the centre of the door handle and then they jumped for the lift. I half turned to look in the picture mirror. Ackermann was standing, face creased with concern and impatience, watching the flickering light above the lift door as it lit up the figures: sixteen, seventeen, eighteen. The doors hissed open.

'Stop,' a voice ordered him. 'Stay exactly where you are.'

Ackermann turned slowly towards the voice, and so did I. The washroom door was open. Kellner stood framed in the doorway, one foot jammed against the door so that it couldn't shut. In his right hand he held a gun as though he knew how to use it. The corridor was still as a tomb, and now just about as healthy.

'Who the hell are you?' asked Ackermann. It was a good question.

Behind him, the lift glowed clinically clean and bright and inviting under the fluorescent lights. The tune had changed; it was *Begin the Beguine*. The doors began to close. He pushed one foot between them, and they opened again.

'You don't recognize me, do you?' said Kellner, as though this was the most obvious thing to say, and from his point of view I suppose it was. 'But you will. You tried to kill me once, years ago. In a house in Berlin. There was a Mercedes that we stole when our truck broke down. The box we took from the bunker. Remember now?'

'My God,' said Ackermann. He was obviously remembering, and he seemed to shrink, as though someone had let the air out of a big balloon. It wasn't the beguine that was beginning, I thought; it was the end.

'Now you know what it's like to see the other end of the gun,' said Kellner. Then he fired twice.

At that range, the bullets lifted Ackermann up against the portal of the lift, and then he fell, half in and half out, and the doors closed against his body, and then opened and closed again, the electronic locking device puzzled by the unexplained obstruction. The receptionist had come back to her desk and she was screaming and fists were pounding on the inside of the manager's door. I pressed the button to release the lock. The door ripped open and two men leapt out as though they were on fire.

The first was the cop; the second, a rather older man with rimless glasses and receding silvery hair. I guessed he was the manager. For a second they seemed to stand like figures in a frieze, and then the policeman was kneeling by Ackermann's side. Kellner had gone; so quickly that I didn't even see where, but the receptionist had. She was pointing at another door.

'Where does that lead to?' I asked her.

'The roof. The fire escape.'

I pushed open the door, and the policeman was running with me, and the manager a little way behind, repeating 'Mon Dieu', but whether in hope or prayer I didn't know, though the words added a touch of French to our pounding feet on the aluminium stairs.

'How many floors?' I asked him.

'Two.'

The cop slid his hand under his left shoulder, and when he took it out again a gun had grown from the palm.

'Who are you?'

'Just passing through,' I told him. 'From London. I deal in old cars. Want my card?'

'Later,' he said.

We were on the top of the stairs now, and the door in front of us was plain wood, painted matt brown on a two-way hinge. He kicked it open and I ran in behind him. After all, he was being paid for this. No one would pay me a pension for being a disabled car dealer.

We were out on a flat roof with a tubular rail all around it. The lake glittered bluely in the distance, and on every side the roofs of smaller concrete buildings, edged with anodized metal, stretched up towards us. The view was fantastic, but somehow I didn't feel in the mood for it.

Kellner was climbing over the rail. He paused when he

saw us, pulled his gun and fired. A shower of concrete dust blew out from the wall just above my head. I dropped on my hands and knees. The policeman stayed standing. He fired once, twice. Kellner's armament fell out of his hand and he didn't pick it up. He couldn't, for one of the bullets had broken his wrist. He hung half over the rail, facing us, his body bent and rigid with pain. His hat had come off, and the hair of his wig fluttered in the wind.

We ran towards him, and then he seemed to slip backwards, and lost his balance and fell. I turned away. I hate the sight of blood, even if it's not my own, and there seemed to be a lot of Kellner's blood on the roof. Sara was framed in the doorway, leaning against the wall, trying not to be sick. Only the policeman seemed unperturbed.

'I'll get an ambulance,' he said in English.

'What's the use?' I asked. 'We're twenty floors up. He'll need an undertaker.'

'Not at all,' he replied, putting his pistol back in its shoulder holster. 'He's only fallen one floor.'

'One floor?'

I looked over the railings. It was quite true. Kellner lay on his back, arms and legs out as though on some kind of invisible cross, on another flat roof. His eyes were closed and his face was the colour of this paper.

'Don't you see?' asked the policeman irritably. 'He hoped to jump down to that floor, climb in through a window, catch the lift there, and he'd have been away.'

It all seemed very open and shut to him, but then everything usually does, in one's own business. Maybe the sight of a 1921 Airedale that I've a client looking for would have puzzled him, but not for me, for I don't mean the dog but the car.

'I didn't know,' I said, and I didn't really want to know. The manager was now looking fearfully over the edge at Kellner.

'What a terrrible thing,' he said, not specifying which particular thing he thought terrible: Kellner shooting Ackermann or jumping off the top of the building.

'Yes,' I agreed. 'It's bad for the bank. You don't want this sort of thing in the papers.'

'*Not* in the papers,' he said in anguish. 'It must never appear there. You're not a reporter?'

'No,' I said. 'Just a student of life.'

'Please?' he asked.

'Nothing,' I said. I also seemed to be studying death a bit too closely; first, Mrs Meredith, then Diaz and now Acker-mann.

The manager held open the door. We went down the stairs into the corridor. The policeman was already speaking on the receptionist's telephone, cupping his hand around the instrument so I couldn't hear what he was saying.

'Of course,' said the manager to no one in particular, but principally to me, because I was nearest, 'Mr Burgdorff was marked as soon as he gave the account number. I had to keep him talking until I could fetch our friend here, the superintendent of the Fraud Commission. I hope I did the right thing.'

He looked uneasily at me.

'You were just wonderful,' I told him. After all, why not! I might want to borrow money from the bank one day.

We were in his office by now, and I noticed that already the methodical Swiss had put a sheet over Ackermann's body. By the time we came out it would be moved and the floor cleaned and there would be no trace of anything as disfiguring as death.

'It was an extraordinary feeling when he gave me that number,' the manager went on; he had a touch of the verbal squitters, this character, I thought.

'What number?' I asked him.

'The account number, of course. What else?' He seemed irritated at such financial ignorance and naïvety.

'What account number?' asked Sara. 'And whose account?'

The manager didn't answer. The policeman came into the room.

'You knew this gentleman?' he asked me.

'Which one?' I parried.

'Either. The one who was shot or the one who did the shooting?'

'I've met them,' I said.

'Perhaps you would come with me to the Commission?' he said, making it a request rather than a suggestion.

I agreed. This wasn't the time or the place to start arguing the odds, and anyhow I'd nothing better to do except to try and unravel the mystery. He had a car and a driver outside a side door. The three of us sat in the back. I noticed that the handles had been removed from inside the rear doors. Just in case a reluctant passenger had a sudden wish to get away, I supposed.

In his office, there was the usual business of producing passports, then saying why we had been where we were, and then we were given some quite drinkable coffee, which we drank. Finally, after a lot of telephoning, speaking in tongues I didn't understand, with other men coming in and out carrying files, which they showed him, holding them open for him to read and looking at me anxiously in case I could read upside down, which I can, but not in French, the policeman said: 'You're quite free to go'.

'Perhaps you can give me a lift back to my car? There are probably about twenty-eight parking tickets on it by now.'

'Of course,' he said, pressing a buzzer, 'and I would like to see you at the Bristol, after lunch. If you are free?'

'I'll be free if you don't jail me,' I said.

I guessed that the place was being watched and that my room had been searched. Policemen aren't such idiots as they are sometimes made out to be.

His driver took us back to where we had left our Volkswagen, and then we drove to the Bristol. I looked at my watch. We had hardly been out an hour, and in that time one very rich man had passed over the last frontier to join the only real democracy – death. And another man, who for some reason had hated him and followed him across Europe to kill him, wasn't, in my own unmedical view, so far from making the crossing himself.

I suddenly felt my age, and I would rather have felt something more pleasant, like a really fine charlie, say a thirty-eight, young and round and firm.

Sara and I had had lunch sent up to my room. We had hardly finished when the telephone rang. The inspector was downstairs and on his way up. I had the old Whyte & Mackay ready, and opened the door to him. He was off-duty and he looked less formal, and I could tell from his attitude that we were in the clear, because if we hadn't been, he would have been accompanied by another half-dozen cops with their hands in their jacket pockets. I poured him a whisky, which he drank, and so I poured him another, and he treated that the same way.

'So, what was it all about?' I asked him, because I had to say something.

'Interesting case,' he said academically, in the way a surgeon speaks of some poor devil who has had his nuts off under the knife and yet still perversely manages to perform. It's interesting and unusual, but it doesn't affect him personally either way; it's only a job, and if he weren't doing this, he'd be doing something else.

'For the last year of the war – this man Kellner – who, of course, we're charging with murder – was Hitler's double. After the July plot to assassinate Hitler, the Fuehrer was frightened of appearing overmuch in public, so Kellner would take the salute at any parades and so forth which the Fuehrer felt it prudent to miss.

'During the last days, in April 1945, some of the top Nazis were fleeing while they could, and others announced that they intended to die with Hitler in his underground bunker in Berlin.

'The Gestapo, however, had evolved a plan for Hitler to escape to South America. This would mean killing Kellner, and then burning Kellner's body, wrapped in a blanket, so that it would appear that Hitler had, in fact, killed himself rather than surrender. In the meantime, Hitler would have escaped in disguise.

'They couldn't kill Kellner in the bunker – there simply

wasn't room. Also, the risk of discovery was too great, for the place was so crowded and such a shambles that someone would be bound to hear the shot. So they had to kill him outside. The Gestapo accordingly worked out an ingenious scheme for this.

'They gave Kellner a box, which they told him contained secret papers, and a sealed envelope, which he was to deliver by truck to a certain house in Berlin.

'Ackermann – he was called Horstmann then – travelled with him. As soon as the box was unloaded, his job was to shoot Kellner in the face to make certain that his teeth were destroyed, because teeth provide the only positive way of identifying a burned body.

'Another Gestapo officer travelled with them, disguised as the truck driver. These two were to bring back Kellner's body, wrapped in a blanket, and then they'd burn it in the Chancellery gardens, before witnesses, who would believe it was Hitler's body.'

The inspector paused. I filled his glass again with neat whisky. He didn't complain.

'On the way, the truck had a puncture, so Horstmann – or Ackermann as you know him – commandeered a Mercedes, the only car he could find. They transferred the box to this and drove to the house. Then he shot Kellner in the face.

'He thought he'd have a look in the box just to see what it contained, before he did anything else. He'd also been told it was Foreign Office papers, but he just wanted to make sure. In that box he found one million United States dollars in ten-dollar bills.

'He also opened the letter, but he couldn't understand it because it was in code. Even so, a million dollars was enough to be going on with. To hell with carrying Kellner back to the bunker. They'd never have a chance like this again – so he and the driver took off with the cash.

'Twenty kilometres out of Berlin, someone at the roadside warned them that American troops were ahead. They just had time to throw the box of money into a lake, and Horst-

mann pushed the envelope down behind the door upholstery of the car before they surrendered.

'They served a few months for minor war crimes, then
came back to the lake, ostensibly as skin-diving instructors
at a leave camp the American Army had set up there. They
dived until they found the money. They divided it between
them.

'The driver used his share to finance a motor business in
Hanover – he'd been in the motor trade before the war.
Horstmann changed his name to Ackermann – his mother's
name – and went to Spain, where he made another fortune
by buying land and developing it along the coast.'

Hanover. The only car firm I knew there was Tobler
Autos, which had tried for so long to buy every 540K Mercedes roadster they could find. Now I began to understand
why. Well, they wouldn't be in the market any longer, at
least for that particular model.

'Both men believed that this money must have been originally meant to be picked up, either by Hitler or by other
Nazis who needed to finance their escape route. They
calculated that if a million dollars had been set aside
for this, then what could the message in the letter be
worth?

'Wasn't it just possible that this could lead to even more?
But to find the letter, they had first to find the car where
they'd hidden it, so they both bought every Mercedes of
that model they could find – except the one they really
wanted.

'That's where you came in, Miss Greatheart. For some
others also wanted to find what had been carried in this car,
and why it had made this sudden, unexpected last journey –
the East German authorities. There's a great deal of rivalry
between Communist countries, as you may know. Especially
about this question of Hitler's death. When he died – and
how. And the East Germans wanted to succeed where
Russia had failed.

'They traced the car – and you. Then they approached
you, and explained that they wanted the car offered to

Ackermann, so they could see what he did then, and why it was so valuable to him.

'In all this, everyone seemed to have forgotten Kellner. Ackermann and the driver had written him off completely in 1945, because they thought they'd killed him. But in the confusion and their own haste to get away, they didn't stop to make sure.

'In fact, Kellner lived, but with a virtual loss of memory. He did odd jobs for a while, then he was taken up as a lover boy by a rich German widow. She died and left him her money, and a house in Cyprus.

'He was staying in the house when there was some kind of explosion. A building firm was blowing up part of the cliff to put in a road for a new development. The sudden noise turned a key in his mind, and unlocked the recollection of another explosion – obviously when he was shot in the face – and he recalled a car with a three-pointed star on it, a box of secret papers, a drive to an empty house.

'He began to have grotesque nightmares and headaches, and finally he came to London to see a psychiatrist. One day, on his way back to his hotel, from Harley Street, his taxi was stuck next to a bus in a traffic jam. On the bus, he saw a man whose face turned another key to the past. Diaz, the man who had driven the truck and then that car so long ago.

'Kellner followed him to his hotel. There was an argument. Diaz insisted he'd never been to Berlin in his life. He was a Brazilian. Probably both of them got pretty het up. Maybe they fought, or maybe Diaz just tried to escape and Kellner tried to stop him. Anyhow, according to Kellner, Diaz fell and cracked his skull on the floor and died.

'He went through Diaz's papers, and found that Diaz was in London trying to buy a Mercedes – of exactly the same type that he'd been driven in twenty-five years before! Surely it must be the same car?

'He went down to see the owner – some old woman in Kent, to try and persuade her to sell it to him instead, for he was convinced it held some clue to what had happened so long ago. According to Kellner, the old woman was dead when he reached her. Maybe she'd had a heart attack, maybe he killed her, *I* don't know. We're only charging him with one murder.

'Anyhow, he got away with the car, and since he knew from Diaz's papers that Diaz was going to deliver it to Ackermann's house in Spain, he decided to deliver it himself.

'But, then *you* came in' – he looked at me accusingly, and I looked back at him just as accusingly – 'There was that business in the bus. Kellner struck his head on the roof. When he came to, his memory had returned completely.

'Now he knew the real reason he wanted to see Ackermann. He thought he'd know him when he saw him. He'd waited years for this. He wanted revenge, but he didn't want any trouble for himself. He was rich, you see, and the rich are always careful. Maybe that's why they *are* rich.'

Maybe it was, I thought, but it didn't affect me. I wasn't rich.

'Anyway, Kellner hired a car, drove to Ackermann's house and then he saw the guard dogs. He wanted to know what was happening inside, but how, without being caught? He couldn't get inside himself, but worked out an ingenious scheme for overhearing what was being said.

'He drove back to Salamanca and bought two Japanese midget walkie-talkie transistor sets, and a bow and some arrows from a sports shop. He tied one of these sets to an arrow – it was the size of a large fountain pen – and fired this into some creeper outside the house. Then he simply listened in to what was happening to you.'

I remembered that house, cold under the moon; the rustle of the dry ivy, the arrow with the black cylinder hanging by its barb.

'Unfortunately for him while he was doing this, somebody tampered with his car.'

The policeman looked at me. I looked back at him blandly. He went on: 'He was faced with almost certain discovery, unless he could get away quickly. So he stole the

Mercedes, for that was his only means of escape. He knew Ackermann was going to Geneva, because he'd overheard him say so. When he couldn't get on a plane there, he decided to drive – as you both did.'

'How do you know all this?' I asked him.

'Kellner has told us a lot. He realizes he's in no position to do anything else. He's got a broken back, and he'll be in hospital for many months. He gave us most of the leads. We took things from there.

'When Ackermann decoded the message he found in the car, he flew here and contacted the bank, and said he wanted to remove the contents of a secret safe-deposit box with a certain number. He made an appointment with the manager. When he gave the manager the number of the deposit account, it was checked, and the manager found himself in rather an odd position.'

'How odd?' I asked, thinking of sex and the forty-nine positions of the Kama Sutra. Or is it sixty-nine? Happy soixante-neuf!

'Odd in the banking sense,' said the policeman, pouring himself more whisky. 'You see, under Swiss law, while the identity of people holding numbered bank accounts is never disclosed, if these secret accounts are not claimed within twenty years, then they revert automatically to the bank.

'The numbered safe-deposit account Ackermann was now claiming had been deposited nearly twenty-five years ago. So the bank had already claimed its contents. When Ackermann phoned, the manager looked up his books and saw that the deposit box contained ten million American dollars in one-hundred-dollar notes. This was interesting enough, but what was serious from the bank's point of view was the fact that *all these notes were forged*.

'They were part of millions printed in Germany during the war to drop over Allied countries to disrupt their currencies. Most of these forgeries were dumped in Lake Toplitz when they weren't used, but, clearly, ten million were put to a better purpose by some clever character.

'Whoever he was, he kept the good dollar bills and put

the forgeries into the bank. Much the same thing happened when the spy Cicero sold the D-Day secrets to the Nazis. He was also paid a fortune – in forged notes.

'As the deposit manager said, when Ackermann gave him the account number, he was marked.'

I wondered who this unknown financial juggler had been, this man who had made ten million so cleverly and so easily. Had he been a high Nazi, or an unknown civil servant? Or perhaps he was an embassy official, or maybe even a humble messenger with sharp ears, who had overheard a conversation and acted upon what he had heard? What gigantic financial deals in property and mineral rights had been backed by this money?

The inspector was speaking again; like judges and wives, policemen like the sound of their own voices.

'As soon as the manager realized Burgdorff was claiming this money, he called me in. I must say that Burgdorff or Ackermann, or Horstmann or whatever his real name was, played things very cleverly when he told him the money had been forged. He was obviously shocked – as who wouldn't be? But he recovered quickly and said he'd some papers about the original deposit back in his hotel.

'We had nothing on him, but even so I didn't want him to go alone – just in case. He asked the manager to ring his hotel – the Palace – to ask his secretary to get the papers ready.'

'But he was staying at the Bristol,' I interrupted.

'Exactly, but we didn't know that then. While the manager was on the phone he said he'd call the lift. I was putting on my coat when the door shut. I thought the wind had blown it to because a window was open in the office. But he'd locked it from the outside.

'He could have escaped easily enough, because it would take the manager a minute or two to get the janitor to release us from the office, and even when we were out we'd have concentrated on the Palace. The only man he'd forgotten – for the second time – was Kellner.

'We searched Ackermann's room at the Bristol and found

where he'd come from and then we phoned the Spanish police. They were very cooperative, and went to his house and found an East German national badly wounded, being kept a prisoner. He also helped us with a statement.'

'Who told him anything?' asked Sara.

'Diaz,' I said. 'He must have been the Gestapo driver.'

'Right,' said the inspector approvingly.

'Odd thing about Diaz,' he went on. 'Our East German friends found him in London just before Kellner got on to him. They leaned on him first. They told him that Ackermann had been talking, and as a result life could be hard for him in both the East and the West – but they assured him they wanted nothing out of him except a few facts.

'Diaz believed he was in no position to argue, so he talked. He'd just got back to his hotel when Kellner came banging on the door. He was terrified. He couldn't believe Kellner's story about seeing him in the street. He thought the East Germans must have tipped him off, and that Kellner had come to kill him.'

'Who was the East German who drove the bus?' I asked him.

'Someone quite unimportant. When Kellner decided to get the Mercedes, he asked his hotel to give him the names of some dealers in this type of car. They put him on to some other man who had a bus which could transport the car, someone called Ruper.

'This man suggested that the car was repainted for safety's sake. It was done very quickly, down at a country garage, but the following morning, when they set off, the bus had a new driver. He explained that the other driver had been taken ill in the night.

'Kellner didn't care, but he should have done, for this new driver was an East German agent.'

'I see,' I said. But I didn't see very much, or very far.

'My cousin?' said Sara. 'What about him?'

'It's not for me to say,' replied the inspector carefully. 'But no doubt the East German authorities will honour their deal. There's no reason why they shouldn't. You've done your part, after all. Only time will tell.'

I stood, only half listening to him now, looking out over the city, watching the cascade of lights, the glitter of the lake, and the long spine of mountains behind. There were questions still to be answered, and maybe, like the man said, time would tell some of them, but not all. Time knows too many secrets ever to tell them all.

Then I looked at Sara and saw the lights of the city reflected in her eyes; or maybe they were stars, or maybe something different altogether.

'I'm sorry you've had all this trouble,' she said to me gently, as though she meant it.

'I'm not worrying,' I told her, and actually, I wasn't, for I hadn't done too badly.

This was better than the double-headed deal I had imagined in Biarritz. This was the original, actual, physical, three-sided profit-making of which all traders dream, as the old Greek sailors dreamed of the happy isles. My motto had always been: 'If you can't make money, make love', but here I had the chance of making both.

First, there was Sara and the prospect of a lot of mileage together. Next, I'd shown one profit on the Mercedes, and as soon as this inspector cleared off, I was going to show another damn quickly, for I'd every intention of hooking that car out from wherever Kellner had parked it. I'd give it a quick go-over, then sell it again, the second time around. Wouldn't you, if you were in my place?

After all, they don't make them like that any more. And, believe me, they never will again.

THE GOD-FATHER
MARIO PUZO

'A sensational success . . . its heroes are
villains of the most evil kind'
—**SUNDAY EXPRESS**

'A big, blunt, battering-ram of a book,
one to shock and stun'
—**SATURDAY REVIEW**

'Plenty of scenes of tough love-making
and brutal slaughter'
—**SUNDAY TELEGRAPH**

'Big, turbulent, highly entertaining novel
that moves at breakneck speed'
—**NEWSWEEK (45p)**

A SELECTION OF
POPULAR READING IN PAN

FICTION

ROYAL FLASH	George MacDonald Fraser	30p
THE FAME GAME	Rona Jaffe	40p
A TASTE FOR DEATH	Peter O'Donnell	30p
TRAMP IN ARMOUR	Colin Forbes	30p
SHOTGUN	Ed McBain	25p
SIEGE	Edwin Corley	30p
THE LINK	Robin Maugham	35p
AIRPORT	Arthur Hailey	37½p
HEIR TO FALCONHURST	Lance Horner	40p
REQUIEM FOR A WREN	Nevil Shute	30p
MADAME SERPENT	Jean Plaidy	30p
MURDER MOST ROYAL	Jean Plaidy	35p
CATHERINE	Juliette Benzoni	35p

NON-FICTION

THE COUNTRYMAN WILD LIFE BOOK (illus.)	edited by Bruce Campbell	30p
OLD YORKSHIRE DALES (illus.)	Arthur Raistrick	40p
THE REALITY OF MONARCHY	Andrew Duncan	40p
THE SMALL GARDEN	C. E. Lucas-Phillips	40p
HOW TO WIN CUSTOMERS	Heinz M. Goldmann	45p
THE NINE BAD SHOTS OF GOLF (illus.)	Jim Dante & Leo Diegel	35p
SILENCE ON MONTE SOLE	Jack Olsen	35p

These and other advertised PAN Books are obtainable from all booksellers and newsagents. If you have any difficulty please send purchase price plus 5p postage to P.O. Box 11, Falmouth, Cornwall. While every effort is made to keep prices low it is sometimes necessary to increase prices at short notice. PAN Books reserve the right to show new retail prices on covers which may differ from those advertised in the text or elsewhere.